ALSO BY VICTOR CANNING

PANTHER'S MOON
THE CHASM
THE GOLDEN SALAMANDER
A FOREST OF EYES
THE HOUSE OF THE SEVEN FLIES
BIRD OF PREY
THE MAN FROM THE "TURKISH SLAVE"
A HANDFUL OF SILVER
TWIST OF THE KNIFE
BURDEN OF PROOF
THE MANASCO ROAD
THE DRAGON TREE
OASIS NINE (and other stories)
THE BURNING EYE
A DELIVERY OF FURIES
BLACK FLAMINGO
THE LIMBO LINE
THE SCORPIO LETTERS
THE WHIP HAND
DOUBLED IN DIAMONDS
THE PYTHON PROJECT
THE MELTING MAN
QUEEN'S PAWN
THE GREAT AFFAIR
THE RUNAWAYS
FIRECREST
THE RAINBIRD PATTERN
FLIGHT OF THE GREY GOOSE
THE FINGER OF SATURN
THE PAINTED TENT
THE MASK OF MEMORY
THE KINGSFORD MARK
THE DOOMSDAY CARRIER
THE CRIMSON CHALICE
BIRDCAGE
THE SATAN SAMPLER

Fall from Grace

VICTOR CANNING

WILLIAM MORROW AND COMPANY, INC.
New York *1981*

Originally published in Great Britain in 1980 by William Heinemann Limited

Library of Congress Catalog Card Number 80-83325
ISBN 0-688-00195-5

Printed in the United States of America

First U. S. Edition

1 2 3 4 5 6 7 8 9 10

For Eileen M. Cond

Semper Fidelis

Fall from Grace

CHAPTER ONE

WHEN MRS HINES came into the cottage sitting room she knew he would be there for his shabby old motor car was parked on the concrete outside her garage alongside the orchard. She had walked, as she did every Friday, two miles down to the village and back to take lunch with an old friend and he had arrived while she was out. He knew where the key was hidden and had let himself in. Nearly six months since she had last seen him . . . and God knows what he had been up to in that time. There was no despair in the thought. People on the whole liked him and he usually fell on his feet. He was, Lilian Hines thought, an over-optimist who occasionally fell into a little wickedness. Nothing serious—at least, not the things he told her about. He was as unlike his father, her long dead brother, as he could be. To tell the truth he was in nature more like her own, also long-dead husband who had acted as father to him for many years—tomorrow was going to be a golden day, something good would turn up. It usually did, too, but often the glitter was not from gold. His father had been drowned in a sailing accident, and his mother had died in giving birth to him. She and Bill had taken him under their wing. Which was nice for her for she knew by then that she would never bear children. This one—little Johnny Corbin then, blue-eyed, fair-haired and with the spirit of an imp—was now well into his thirties with the imp in him grown to an engaging devil who was firm in the belief that the world owed him a living. There had been a time when she had hoped, even sometimes prayed, that he would change and settle down, but that hope had long worn thin, though in the process she had lost none of her affection and love for him.

He lay back in an armchair, his feet up on the window seat, and now and again he snored gently. The tray on the table held an omelette-stained plate, left-over toast and a bottle of Guinness. Drink at least, she thought, was never one of his weaknesses. Money, yes: though when he made it he seldom kept it for long. Women, too—though there again he never kept one for long or—for he was disarmingly frank with her sometimes—they were not his to keep. But God had given him green fingers and good hands. Plants grew for him, cuttings struck for him, dogs and horses acknowledged his touch and handling. God had given him many gifts which he treated lightly. She sighed, turned away, picked up the tray and went into the kitchen.

The sound of the running water in the sink must have wakened him for after a little while he came in to her, put his arms around her from behind, and kissed her cheek.

"Auntie Lil, my lovely one. I made the mess. I'll clear it. You sit down and tell me all about things."

He took her place at the sink and cocking his head round to her said, "You've got a new dress and your hair's done differently. And both suit you."

She smiled. "And you haven't changed a bit. Four months and two postcards."

"And a phone call."

"Only when you wanted me to send on your letters. Where are you from now?"

"Well . . . I was in Hampshire for a while, working on a trout farm. Then I went up to Wales to stay with friends."

"Don't tell me you've got friends."

He laughed. "Dozens of 'em. I may go back to look after their house for a month while they go on holiday. But now I'm here."

"Which means you're broke."

"Which means I just got homesick."

"And how long are you going to stay homesick?"

"Until something turns up or you kick me out. You've let the garden go a bit, I see. I'll start on that for you tomorrow. This place up in Wales. My God, you should have seen the garden. Marvellous once. Still is in a way. But overgrown to hell."

"Sometimes I think you like plants and trees more than people, Johnny."

"I'm sure I do." He turned and gave her a grin. " '*Oh, Adam was a gardener, and God who made him sees——*' "

She laughed, for this was an old game dating from his boyhood, and then said, " '*That half a proper gardener's work is done upon his knees.*' "

"Nobody had been doing that up there for a long time. I brought a few plants down for you. They're in the car."

"Thank you."

He paused in the drying of his omelette plate and said, all bantering gone from his voice, "God, that's what I'd like. A place like theirs and the money to keep it up."

"You could have it, or something near it if you put your mind to it."

"I know. That's the bloody snag, isn't it? Putting your mind to something."

"If you put your mind to it, you could do it. I never understood why you didn't go on with your writing?"

"Oh, that. God no. That was just a way of filling in the time it took a broken leg to come good. No, what I want is to marry a rich girl and spend her money for her."

"If you think I'm going to say you don't mean that—then I'm not. That's what you do want and you'll never get it. Thank God."

"Am I going to get a lecture?"

"Not from me. I gave that up years ago." She stood up. "I've got to go and feed the hens. There's some mail for you in your bedroom. Then I've got dinner to think about."

"No you haven't. I'm taking you out. I phoned and booked when I got in. And it's all right—I shan't be borrowing a tenner from you to pay for it."

Up in his room he sat in the sun on the window seat. The room had been his since a boy; school groups on the walls, prep school, then public and then Oxford just for eighteen months when he had left from his own choosing, bored with the place and anxious to get out into the world. On the dressing table was a photograph of his mother whom he had never known and another of his father of whom he retained few positive memories. On the wall above the bed were three Redouté prints of roses—*Rosa inermis*, a *damascena aurora* and last an *indica fragrans*. Roses were far from his favourite flowers, but Auntie Lil had given them to him for a long-distant birthday and so they held pride of place. Just as she held pride of place in his heart. Most women below the age of thirty odd were tiresome though they had their uses, and nearly all of them—no matter their age—gullible one way or the other.

He picked up the letters waiting for him. For a moment, his eye was caught by the sight of Auntie Lil, a working apron over her new dress, feeding the hens in their enclosure while one of the old donkeys, Samuel, waited with his long, prehistoric grey muzzle over the orchard fence for the titbit which would certainly be waiting in her apron pocket for him. Aged donkeys, stray cats and dogs, birds with broken wings . . . Come unto me, all ye that are weary. In some ways that included him.

That there were only a few letters waiting for him gave him no surprise. He wrote few himself. There was a bank statement which, while not pleasing, did not depress him, since he had fairly recently been able to pay off a large part of his overdraft. For the moment he had enough cash in his pocket to face a limited future. Beyond its moment of exhaustion he could not bring himself to look. Something would turn up. There followed three bills, two of which he tore up with the bank statement and dropped into the waste-paper basket. The third he kept, smiling, and touched by the handwritten note at the bottom from his tailor—*A little on account would restore our slightly flagging good-will.* Dear old Sims. A most understanding man. One of the old school who knew exactly the touch to keep his account from going into the discard.

The last letter was in a very good quality envelope and the date stamp—which he always looked at before opening a letter—was less than a week old. He opened it and read:—

Dear Mr. Corbin,

I have recently had the very great pleasure of reading your book Green Pleasures *which I found of great charm and distinction. I could write more which would be pleasing to you, but do not because I am hoping that you will give me the satisfaction of saying it in person. And here, too, I should make a confession of self-interest for I would very much like to put to you a proposition which you might consider to be not without advantages and pleasure to you, and one which would for me hopefully lead to the satisfaction of a long-held and so far neglected duty.*

I shall be in London for two weeks staying at the above address, and would consider it a kindness if you could find the time to come and have a talk with me. My signature, I am sure, will convey to you that I am of good standing and not some tiresome old gentleman with a bee in his bonnet—a fact which could be confirmed too by your publisher who so kindly furnished me with your address.

Yours sincerely,
Michael Testerburgh

Corbin dropped the letter on the window seat and wondered who the hell was Michael Testerburgh, staying now in London at an address in Park Lane. Nice letter though, he thought, feeling the fine touch of pleasure from an appreciation of a book —his one and only—which he had written some years ago, a book whose reviews had been good but whose sales had been minimal. Well, it was nice to get, but he could not waste time going to London to have a cosy chat with some old buffer who probably collected authors or—more boring—wanted to be one himself.

The next and last letter changed his mind. It was from his publisher and in part read—

. . . *I was at a party recently and met someone who had just read* Green Pleasures *and had been tremendously impressed by it and wanted to get in touch with you. In view of his standing I broke a rule and gave him, not only your London club address—as we normally do— but also your home address so that he could write to both and have a fair chance of catching you soon. I gather, too, that he might have something to offer you which you could find profitable and enjoyable. So, if you get a letter from the Bishop of Testerburgh, think before you chuck it in the waste-paper basket in your usual fashion.*

John Corbin screwed up his publisher's letter and dropped it into the waste-paper basket. With the Bishop's letter in hand he went downstairs and rummaged along the bookshelves in the dining room, found a rather out-dated copy of *Who's Who* and carried it back to his bedroom.

The entry for the Bishop revealed that he was the Right Reverend Michael Boyd Darvell. He was an Oxford Master of Arts and a Doctor of Divinity, having been born in 1924 and educated at Winchester College and Exeter College, Oxford. He had held various appointments as a curate and as a chaplain and also various lectureships in Theology and Medieval History in colleges. He had several publications to his name—none of which stirred Corbin by their titles . . . *Some Papal Decretals of the Diocese of York, An Outline of Canon Law in the Church of England*—and was a contributor to the *English Historical Review* and the *Journal of Ecclesiastical History*. He had married a Dorothy May Latham in 1950 and had one son. His address was The Old Palace, Testerburgh.

John Corbin sat for a while considering all this as he watched Aunt Lily through the window. She had fed Samuel and was now giving him a dry shampoo with her hand about his neck and head. A skylark was singing somewhere unseen. Summer was drowsy over the land. The thick pads of aubretia in the small rockery were beset with bees and from the top of the lilac hedge a garden warbler complained in a sweet, broken voice. Was this, he wondered, one of those days when something happened unexpectedly and left one with a nay or yea freely to choose and some deep instinct counselled one to pick the nay . . .? That was the feeling in him at the moment. No logical feeling, nothing that could be rationalized. Just uncanny feeling. There was no sense in him which urged either response overwhelmingly, but there was—as he had at times in the past known—the whisper of a voice somewhere telling him to resist discarding from the cards he held to draw a couple of new ones from the pack in the hope of improving his hand. He had not told Aunt Lily yet, but he had been offered a job by a friend in a tourist agency as a courier and the prospect had pleased and excited him. He spoke French and Italian, and the prospect of summer beaches and holiday adventures appealed to him. Girls in their summer frocks were fair and easy game, but willing widows and wine-touched matrons, though often less fair, were more lastingly profitable. What could a bishop offer? He had an idea. When his publisher spoke of 'something profitable and enjoyable' his choice of adjectives carried a meaning quite different from the sense he himself attached to the coupling of those words.

He stood up and read the Bishop's letter again and was on the point of screwing it up and dropping it into the waste-paper basket when he found himself putting it into his pocket and walking from the room. Oh, God, he thought, I've been here before.

Going from the house he met Aunt Lily and said, "Just going to stretch my legs for a while. Be back soon."

"All right, dear. Isn't it a marvellous day? God's in His heaven."

"Then I walk without fear."

At the garden gate he was joined by Angus, the ancient red setter. The two walked into the nearby village where Corbin went into a call box. For a moment or two he debated with himself about reversing the charges and then decided against it. Whatever it was that the Bishop might require of him there was no point in risking a first bad impression. He was a man of God, and God was a powerful ally and all-seeing. He could keep things from Aunt Lily by not using her phone but not from God. The eye of Heaven all places visits . . . dear, dear what was that an echo of? Whistling gently to himself he began to dial the London number from the Bishop's letter. Outside the red setter lay in the dust snapping at the flies which troubled his muzzle.

When Corbin came out of the booth it was with an appointment to meet the Bishop on the following Tuesday.

* * * *

Fifty yards after turning off the dusty country road into his driveway Harry Barwick drew up on the small, stone-balustraded bridge which crossed one of the side streams of the main river. A trout was rising steadily under the overhang of a weeping willow. Swallows flew low over the water as they hawked the hatching flies. Beyond the bridge the drive turned sharply into an avenue of poplar trees which he had planted ten years ago, but grown tall now so that they hid all but the roof of the far Regency house. He lit the cigarette which he allowed himself here—the first since leaving his London flat to drive down to Hampshire.

After his father's death he had taken over the small family building business and within ten years had turned it into an international concern. Normally he liked to pause on the bridge and allow himself the satisfaction and pride he felt in his own success and. the ownership of this place . . . a private and treasured moment or two of self-congratulation. But today neither ritual nor habit held any importance. Now, before he drove on and entered the house and went up to their bedroom where his wife, Sue, would be bathing and changing for the evening, he knew that he had to make the decision either to keep his mouth shut, to lock away forever what he knew, or to bring it all out into the open. She had got into scrapes before. She was a sentimental, gullible, romantic woman, occasionally unfaithful to him as he was to her, but there was that between them which they called love and which easily survived her stupidities and his frequent cavalier attitude to her. But this time it was money—and that to him was important, its misuse abhorrent to his Yorkshire nature, its importance supreme because he had had to make what he had in the hard way. What riled him most was that if she had wanted money she needed only to come to him. Why should she want money, and want it without his knowing it? Not that it was a big sum so far as he was concerned. Two thousand pounds. In God's name for what? He gave her a handsome allowance and paid all her bills. Oh, forget it, he told himself. But it was not easy to forget. Mysteries were not his style. Unsolved they were always an itch in the mind. Still . . . it had to be wiser to keep the thing to himself. Probably in the end she would come out with it of her own accord. Just as she always did when she had one of her not so rare romantic flings. He had been jealous about those at first but in the end—because she was his wife, the mother of his two boys, and just what he wanted socially and as mistress of his house—he had accepted this flaw in her love for him, just—as he had no doubt—she accepted that he had a mistress in London and had never mentioned the fact to him. And God knew, too, that whatever their individual failings they still went on enjoying a full and passionate relationship. Forget it, Barwick, he told himself. Money it might be, but he could spend that and more for a week-end in Monte Carlo for two without turning a hair. Nobody has complete happiness.

Common sense said just look after what you've got. He would say nothing. In a few days the itch would go from his mind.

He threw his cigarette into the river and drove on. At the end of the poplar avenue he slowed for the passage of one of Sue's mandarin ducks and her brood to cross the gravel and file over the lawns down to the river. The stone urns on the terrace were heraldic with blue agapanthus which Gusman, the gardener, had brought on in the greenhouse. The beds below the terrace were immaculately regimented with a parade of scarlet geraniums. He smiled to himself as he heard Sue saying, 'That bloody Gusman, he never lets anything grow naturally.'

He got out of his car, carrying his brief-case, and went up the wide steps to the front entrance. He was a stocky, vigorous man in his middle forties with a pleasantly moulded, heavy face, his dark, curly hair greying a little; a happily married man with two boys, twins, very soon to start public school—an advantage never granted to him. And at this moment, too, he was a man who knew himself to be far too wise to risk even the remotest chance of upsetting the apple cart of his happily married life by fussing over a piddling sum of two thousand pounds.

He dropped his light coat on the hall chest and went upstairs smiling, looking forward to the warm and loving ritual of returning home. In their bedroom the door to the bathroom was slightly open and a radio was playing softly, but even as he crossed the room the radio was switched off and her voice called, "Harry!"

"Yes, love."

"Lovely man. Early home. Be with you in a moment."

"No rush."

He went into his dressing room, dropped his brief-case on to a chair and then took off his jacket and tie. From the tray Sue had set out on the window table he fixed himself a malt whisky with a flick of water and then went back into the bedroom. He dropped into an armchair, sipped his drink, sighed with pleasure, and let his eyes rest on a Dutch eighteenth-century flower painting that hung over the head of their great double bed. No Gusman regimentation there, he told himself. Just a riot of mixed blooms and the brilliance of a solitary Red Admiral butterfly on one of the glossy leaves of a spray of pink magnolia. Christ, that had cost far more than a thousand and he had bought it for her without an eye blink in the days when he could ill afford it. The whisky warming him, he saw her as he had first seen her standing behind the jewellery counter at Harrods . . . golden-haired, blue-eyed, pure Botticelli then . . . now, he grinned to himself, rather more Juno than Aphrodite. She had turned aside all his advances for two weeks before accepting an invitation to dinner. He had wanted to go to bed with her, but she had refused and gone on refusing. Marriage was then far from his mind. He still had his way to make, still had a lot of the ladder left to climb. Then, when she had finally and unexpectedly said 'Yes' to their becoming lovers, he had found himself shaking his head and saying, 'No, not for us. Marriage first.' And never a moment's regret. Whatever their faults, whatever they did, they had held together.

The bathroom door opened and she came in and stood poised in the first moments of the ritual of reunion, smiling, a great blue bath robe draped about her, the light from the lowering sun catching her fair hair through wide mullioned windows. With the panache of a matador handling his cloak she swung the robe to one side and for a moment or two the full mature glory of her body was his and her beauty suddenly strung tight the sinews of his neck with the sharp anguish of love and desire. She was all he wanted for wife. Whatever secrets she had she could keep.

As she closed her robe he got up and went over, held and kissed her, and said, "You're a bloody marvellous woman."

She smiled. "And you're my Harry. Friday. No staff, no guests—so we dine alone. No, not yet——" She moved his hands from her. "Get me a drink first."

"Fair enough. There's no hurry."

He went into the dressing room and got her a whisky. When he returned she was sitting on the side of the bed, her face turned to the window. Outside there was the quarrelling of sparrows on the roof and the sudden scream of a passing swift and then, without her turning, she said, "Harry . . ."

"Yes, love?"

She stood up and came to him, took her drink and briefly sipped at it, and then said, "Harry . . . I've got something important to tell you. It's serious."

He saw at once the change in her face and in his moment of confusion the word 'woebegone' came into his mind. Misery marked her and the sight darkened his well-being like a cloud covering the sun.

"For God's sake, Sue. What's the matter with you?"

"Everything . . . disgust with myself most."

He put his whisky glass down on the table and with a sudden premonition of the impending truth said sharply, "I don't want to hear anything."

"No, Harry—you've got to hear me. And don't try to fool me because I know that you must know something already. The last thing I want at this moment is for you to be decent and shut your eyes to what you know because . . . well, because that isn't the half of it and I've got to get something straight between us."

"No, I don't want to hear anything. Just let whatever it is die. We both step out of line sometimes—so what? Nothing can really touch us."

"No, no . . . I've got to go on. I had a phone call from Peterson today. This morning. He told me that you had taken my London jewellery in to be revalued for insurance some days ago because of inflation . . . and that professionally he had to be honest about it. He told me that he'd been trying to get in touch with me for some days, but you know I've been away staying with the Kitsons until today."

"Sue!" As he silenced her he reached out and took her hand. "You don't have to tell me anything. I know it all and I don't care a bugger about it. All right—let's get it into the open and forget it. Somehow you got into a jam for money and like an idiot, instead of coming to me, you take your pearls along to Peterson, sell them, and he makes up a replica set of artificials. Naturally when I asked him to revalue your stuff he was professionally bound to tell the truth." He squeezed her hand affectionately. "So what? So what? You needed some money for your bookmaker or one of your hard-up family. Fine. I don't mind."

With tears in her eyes and her face flushed and shining without make-up, she said, "You're a darling, Harry, and I love you. But the money had nothing to do with a bookmaker or my family. I paid the money to a man . . . had to pay it, and you can guess for what."

"No—since there's no stopping you—you tell me." He got up and walked to the window.

"Well . . . I was stupid enough to write him two or three affectionate letters."

"Two or three?"

"Three. And more than affectionate. I got carried away. He said he'd send them to you if I didn't pay."

His back to her, he said sharply, "You should have told the bastard to do it. It wouldn't have made any difference to me. We both go a bit astray at times."

"That's not all he said. He said he'd send the letters to you and also copies to some of our friends. I couldn't face that. Not after all that we've both built up socially down here."

Turning his face from her because for the moment he had reached the limit of trust in himself he looked out at the close-cut lawns and the red gold of the setting sun on the river and slowly began to curb the anger in him, not anger because another man had known her, but because this sod whoever he was had sent in a bill for his services. He smiled bitterly. A little while ago he had sat in his car and decided to keep silent, to wash all thought of the pearls from his mind. The gods must have been laughing their heads off. They had already marked him for one of their dark revels. What a damned simpleton Sue had been not to call the man's bluff. No one but a damned fool would have sent the letters round with his own name on them . . . For a moment or two a picture of Sue in bed with another man came into his mind. He pushed it easily away. But the thought of this bastard making her pay for the privilege, reading her mind and knowing that she would never call his bluff . . . By God, she'd been damned right to tell him. It was all over to him now. If the gods were laughing, let them. He was going to have his satisfaction, too. He was Harry Barwick, a Yorkshire tyke, and a tyke with a sharp bite.

He turned away from the window and went back to Sue. He smiled down at her and said lightly, "Well, you really let yourself be taken in, didn't you?" He rubbed the back of his hand against her cheek affectionately.

"Oh, Harry—you should give me a hiding and kick me out."
He grinned. "I can think of a better thing to do than that."
She stood up and put her arms around him and he held her under her bath robe, loving her body, loving her, as she said, "Oh, Harry, you're so damned good to me . . ."
"And what the hell do you think you are to me? You're my Sue. Just Harry and Sue—and not a single worry now in your mind. Over dinner we'll have a cosy chat and get the whole thing sorted out. You may not have understood, but I happen, for all my faults, to love you. What we've got is the solid eighteen-carat thing, not just some gold-plated imitation."

* * * *

The man, Harry Barwick thought, would have been hard to place for what he was professionally. He sat in the chair across the desk from him, a little out of the sunlight from the window, listening politely and saying nothing yet, not even giving a nod or a face movement to indicate sympathy or understanding. In fact he gave the impression of being wooden and slow-thinking. His name was James Helder; a big, bulkily built man wearing a heavy pepper-and-salt tweed suit with a waistcoat, but his pale, unmoving face showed no sign of the heat of the hot summer day. His white shirt was immaculate, his knitted black tie precisely adjusted, his black brogues highly polished, and his white breast-pocket handkerchief showed the tips of two precise pyramids. He had come highly recommended by a source which Barwick respected. He had refused the offer of a glass of sherry and a cigarette and sat now with an unopened notebook on his knee. For a while, after he had begun to outline his problem, Barwick had felt himself becoming a little irritated by his manner. The card on his desk read simply *James Helder* followed by a London telephone number. The friend who had recommended him had said, 'He lives somewhere in North London, but all you ever get is his telephone number which is unlisted. He's dead straight and efficient. But if he decides he doesn't want the job or doesn't like you—then wild horses won't move him. He'll sit with a closed notebook on his knee. He'll let you talk and when you've finished if he doesn't open it to make notes as he questions you—then he's turning you down and there's no appeal.'

That warning was in Barwick's mind now as he explained things. He said eventually, "That's the rough outline. This man played about with my wife and then—under threat of telling me about it—blackmailed her. I can give you his last address, but he's long left that. I'd like to know where he is now. I'd like you to know, too, that so far as my wife and I are concerned . . . well, it's made no difference of any consequence to our lives. So there you are, Mr Helder. I hope you will be willing to try and help me."

As Barwick finished speaking, Helder pursed his thick lips and his dark hazel eyes regarded some spot on the wall behind the wide walnut desk and his fingers tapped tentatively on the cover of his closed notebook as though some doubt rested with him of the wisdom of opening it. Doubt there was for he had just heard a very old story, and old stories were boring and above all things Helder hated being bored. It happened all the time . . . an attractive, long-married woman falling for an adventurous young man of few principles, a great deal of charm, an engaging manner, but with a lack of money—and this last a personal affront to him every time that he met someone who had never known such want. When he did—and not necessarily only with women, he would guess—then he instinctively began to indulge a predatory instinct stimulated probably more by envy than real hard want. Inside Helder was a shy philosopher and humanist whose thoughts and compassionate nature were seldom revealed in his habits of speech which tended to be banal and stilted unless he made the deliberate decision for them to be otherwise. At the moment he felt that he did not want any part of this common marital drama except—and this was producing his hesitation over opening his notebook—that Barwick had said as he explained the situation, "I assure you that if you trace him I don't want violent revenge or any such nonsense. I'm a Yorkshireman. I want my money back. I also want him to see me and know that if I wanted to I could destroy him. But there would be no point because he's well set to destroy himself without any help from outside. True punishment comes from God. No man can escape it."

It was, of course, a statement which the humanist in Helder could well have chosen to challenge from a pragmatic base. He guessed that this John Corbin—for that was the name of the seducer—was blissfully beyond redemption and cynical of Divine retribution. Oh yes, the world was full of John Corbins. God had abandoned them long ago. But not the Devil. Very often, though, he turned on his chosen, much to their dismay, and it was well within his powers, when Barwick came face to face with Corbin, to present him with a picture of the man in bed with his wife, and so find violence rising in him and take manly, if not godly, action, thus giving the Devil another score to mark up against his old adversary. So, less for Barwick's sake than from his own long-running interest in the strife between the powers of light and darkness, Helder—already betting on a win for the Devil—decided to take the case and, with decent propriety but no deep feeling, hoped that he would lose his bet.

Taking a short length of Cumberland lead pencil from his pocket Helder opened his notebook and said, "I'll do what I can for you, Mr Barwick. Would you give me the address Corbin was staying at when all this happened?"

"Yes, of course. He lived in a rented, furnished cottage about five miles from us. Blackthorn Cottage. It's just outside a village called Forton. The owner is a Miss Simpson who, when the cottage is let, lives with her sister in Forton. My wife tells me that she heard indirectly that he went off owing a month's rent."

"Naturally. It's a well-known form of economy for his kind. Did he have a car?"

"Yes. But I don't know what kind. By the way, I would like to stress that I want all this to be just between us. I don't want the police brought into it in any way."

"Naturally." Helder closed his notebook and stood up, saying, "I'll be in touch with you from time to time, Mr Barwick."

A little surprised Barwick said, "Is that all you want from me?"

"Why, yes, sir. All I need is a starting point and then I either go backwards or forwards. I'll let you know when I've found him, but I don't expect it to be soon. The Corbins of this world may be short on virtues, but they have a very highly developed sense of self-protection. The chameleon only changes its colour. That's rudimentary compared to the Corbins—they can vanish into thin air right in front of your eyes."

Helder took his leave and Barwick was left alone finding himself puzzled, impressed and slightly irritated because he felt as though he had just been consoled by a not very sincere parish priest rather than almost over-pompously taken on to the books of a private detective.

Helder went home to a ground-floor flat in a large mid-Victorian terraced house close to Hampstead Heath where he lived with a widowed sister, somewhat older than himself, called Constance, who kept house and looked after him but gave priority to her hobby of collecting grasses, foliage and flowers to dry and then set into picture frames which she gave away mostly to her many friends and occasionally sold to a local arts and crafts shop. She was a small, active, dark-haired woman, frank in her manner and speech, wise in the ways of the world, and usually outspoken about them. She enjoyed her brother's complete confidence and considered that he was abusing his talents by employing them in an unworthy and sordid profession.

He said, "How would you like to drive me down to Hampshire tomorrow?"

"That I would love, James. I'll take my pressing books with me."

"Good."

"And what is it this time?"

When he had told her briefly of Barwick's troubles, she said, "Really, James, why do you interest yourself in such squalid and common affairs?"

"Ah, yes, why? Because of people, I suppose."

"You should have told him to give his wife a good beating and tell her not to do it again. There's always a chance that, if she has any sense, she would follow his precept."

"And how much would he have paid me for that?"

"Little. But you have enough already. I do wish you could rid yourself of this unwholesome interest in other people's troubles and be like the rest of the world—content to read about them in the newspaper and then quickly forget them. We have the police and the priests. Leave it to them."

Helder chuckled. "The thing is too big for them. The Devil is winning handsomely at the moment. They need all the help they can find."

"You don't mean a word of it. You just can't resist the excitement you get from meddling in other people's affairs. I think the real truth is that you get an unwholesome pleasure in putting yourself in the place of all these people and imagining what it would be like to be as they are, to think like them and to act like them. You know, James, there is something rather unnatural about you, but I will say you conceal it very well in public."

"Thank you, my dear Constance."

CHAPTER TWO

ON THE SAME day as Harry Barwick engaged the services of James Helder, John Corbin was also in London. Before going to see the Bishop of Testerburgh Corbin lunched with his publisher. In the course of his varied occupations and adventures he had long learned the value of briefing himself as fully as possible about the character and personality of new employers or potential victims before coming face to face with them. Experience, too, had taught him that there was often a wide discrepancy between other people's assessments and the actual truths later revealed to him.

The Bishop, he had learned, was always ready, indeed sometimes over-ready, to preach or to speak out publicly against the evils of the times. In particular he was uncompromisingly outspoken about the suppression of Christian and human rights in the Soviet States and their satellites. He was a man of courage and compassion—his publisher had said—with a sharp tongue in the defence of Christian virtues, and he had often succeeded in embarrassing the Church of England hierarchy in his younger days by preferring denunciation to diplomacy. Yet it was acknowledged that he was a man who never sought publicity for his own sake or to further his ambitions. It was, too, a generally held opinion that he might well with the mellowing of a few more years stand a better than outside chance of eventually becoming the Archbishop of York and possibly of moving on to become the Archbishop of Canterbury, Primate of all England.

His father, long dead, had wanted him to go into the old family business of merchant shipping and ship-building which was now a public company that had considerably and profitably diversified its interests over the years. But at Oxford Michael Boyd Darvell had decided that his true vocation lay with the

Church. Although he seldom lived there, he owned the family house and estates—Illaton Manor—in the West Country. He had one child, a son, now married, who farmed in Australia.

Listening now to the Bishop as he expressed the enjoyment he had taken in reading *Green Pleasures* he could imagine how impressive he would be in the pulpit. His voice even in conversation carried a touch of the pulpit manner, the cadences skilfully controlled, the richness, which pleased Corbin, marking a clear and loving respect for the language itself. He was a big man, his dark hair a little touched with grey, his face strong and slightly hawkish, a face forceful in repose but often as he spoke touched with an almost impish smile. Now and again he steepled his hands, just lightly rested his big square chin on them, and paused in his speech as though he wished to mark fully the reaction in his listener to his words, a pause which Corbin found faintly embarrassing since it gave him the impression that in some way this man could read and follow his listener's thoughts. He came to such a pause now and after a moment or two, broke it by saying, "Am I embarrassing you, perhaps, with so much praise for your work, Mr Corbin?"

Corbin shook his head. "No, my lord. Since it made little money for me I am only too ready to take all the praise which anyone will give it. I know that I made a good job of it. It's nice to hear others confirm my opinion."

"Well, you did make a good job of it. May I ask how you came to write it?"

"Of course . . ." Corbin hesitated for a moment, tempted to tell the truth—which was that he had been forced to drop from a bedroom window to escape the unexpected home-coming of a husband and had gashed a leg badly on a stout garden stake. The wound had turned septic so that he had had to retire to Aunt Lily's cottage to recuperate and had used his idleness to write the book, the idea for which had long been in his mind. He went on, "I was left a little money, not much, but enough to give me time to write. I've always been interested in botany and plant collecting and particularly in the men who'd risked their lives in the past to bring to Europe rare plants. And also in men who had made and loved great gardens. I just selected three men and got to work."

"And how did you pick them?"

"I made a list—and then used a pin, trusting in God to guide my hand."

The Bishop leaned back in his chair, laughed, and said, "Then He served you well. Bishop Albertus Magnus—the first plant-hunter known to history. Then William Turner, Dean of Wells Cathedral, the first most considerable English botanist. And the last, Henry Compton, Bishop of London, who had all the gardens of the Fulham Palace at his command. Yes, surely God's hand was predominant."

"To me the choice lay on the prick of a pin, but if you tell me it was God's hand I am in no position to doubt you. But of more importance to me at the moment, and I mean no disrespect to the Divinity, is why you should have wished to see me personally to tell me how much you liked the book. Most people write a nice letter, some ask for an autograph, and a few optimistically for a loan, thinking me no doubt to be a wealthy dilettante whose purse opens at the touch of flattery . . ."

Corbin was enjoying himself—recognizing the instinctive shift of mood and speech he could deploy to meet and charm parlour-maid or parson, bar-side scrounger or boozy baronet—and at the same time being flattered to sense that the Bishop liked him. It was good to be liked and a sound basis for self-advancement and easy rewards.

The Bishop leaned back in his chair now and laughed. Then he said, "I like your frankness, Mr Corbin. Very well, just one more question—which do you prefer, plants or people?"

"Oh, that's easy, my lord. For pleasure plants. For profit people."

"Then—if you were willing—I could supply you with both. The plants thriving, but the people dead." He paused and smiled broadly, his dark hazel eyes glinting, and said, "I shall assume, I'm sure correctly, that you have not come here without making some enquiries about me and my background. Is that not so?"

"I confess that I have picked my publisher's brains."

"And very correctly too. Never venture into the unknown without first prayer and then due provisioning. When I mention Illaton Manor and its gardens you will be with me. Yes?"

"Yes, my lord."

"The grounds were laid out by my great-grandfather and then further developed by my grandfather and father. All were shrewd business men but lovers of plants and gardens. All of them kept very full diaries, not only of their day-to-day life, but of the additions and alterations they made to the gardens. At one time it was my ambition to edit these diaries and have them printed privately just as a family record. Alas, this has become impossible. The time is denied me. But when I read your book I realized that rather than just edit the diaries, I would prefer to have a general book written about them in the style of your *Green Pleasures*. I would pay you for the time it took. You could have free quarters and board at Illaton, and when the book was finished—if a publisher considered it of interest to the general public—it would be your property. May I say, too, that I do not just want a book about the gardens. The men who made them were colourful characters. I want a full rounded account——" he smiled, "——pleasure and profit, plants and people. Does this interest you?"

Corbin was silent, thinking. The Devil, he thought, more often than people imagined looked after his own. Apart from the work involved—which he guessed he would enjoy—he would be quartered free and paid no doubt handsomely. Not pressed to go from one droll adventure to another, not be under any obligation to seek occasional profit in misshapen passions, not live like a gypsy from boarding house to rented cottage and more often than not finding himself leaving them with rent or score unpaid. Perhaps for once, the fanciful thought occurred to him, this was not the Devil's work, but the hand of God pressing gently on his shoulder to steer him back to the paths of righteousness. In a rare access of contrition, he felt momentarily disgusted with himself and his life. But, as so often in the past, he felt the moment pass. There was no God and there was no Devil. The world was a wasting asset charging idiotically in orbit, mankind on its back like fleas on a dog.

He looked deliberately and squarely at the Bishop, holding his eyes and, although he knew that he wanted to go to Illaton and would go, he decided for his own pride not to leap or bark in desire at the bone being offered him. His own *amour propre* demanded that he maintain at least the façade of the man he knew he could never be. There was no going back to be remodelled. He knew himself, occasionally regretted what he was, but realized that there was no changing his nature.

He said, "It is a very attractive offer, my lord. And a very generous one. Also a very unexpected one. But since I have already half committed myself to another project, nothing like as attractive, I may say, I would prefer to sleep on it for a night."

"Of course. I wouldn't expect you to decide right away. You must think about it. But quite unashamedly I hope you accept for I am sure you are the right man for it. I shall be in London for the next two days. All you have to do is give me a ring. And now—in no way to tempt you, but as a practical matter—I've written down the financial arrangements I propose." He pulled a sealed envelope from his pocket and handed it to Corbin. "Read it when you've left here, and then let me know. I must warn you, of course—" a broad smile softened the powerful face, "—that I shall pray for the answer I want."

Corbin grinned. "Since God must be clearly on your side what hope have I got, my lord?"

The Bishop shook his head. "No man can know God's ways. That is why we often find suffering when we look forward to celebration."

Sitting in the bar of his club in Brook Street some time later, a large whisky in front of him and at its side the Bishop's envelope, unopened as yet because he knew the terms would be generous and that anyway he was going to Illaton, Corbin found himself wishing that he could believe that God was a little on his side, that if he could not change his character . . . all those sordid ploys with women and cheating others over money . . . then at least he could learn to live with himself comfortably, that God would give him just that touch of charity for he was tired of going nowhere and pretending that he was enjoying himself, a prowling fox without the brute virtues of the true animal itself. It was a rare feeling and after his second whisky he knew that it would be gone—thank God for that, or was he looking in the wrong direction? He grinned to himself and then opened the letter.

It was written in a neat Renaissance script, and the terms

were more generous than he had expected. He was offered a handsome monthly salary, the use of a cottage—furnished—on the estate or quarters in the Manor itself. He could take his meals at the Manor whenever he wished and was also offered a subsistence allowance for providing for his wants at the cottage plus domestic help from the main household. All expenses directly concerned with his work, such as the hire of a typist, typewriter and dictating machine should he need them, and the cost of any necessary travelling would be met. Over and above this he would be regarded as one of the family and free to invite any friends down to stay with him. The library at the Manor—where the diaries and other records were stored—would be his for the duration as a work room for himself. The Bishop had finished—*I would not want you in any way to regard yourself as an employee but as a friend who is doing me a service. The Manor is run by my sister-in-law Miss Margaret Latham. She is a charming, forthright lady with a heart of gold and—when circumstances require—a sharp but honest tongue. Since you both love flowers and plants I can foresee no reason why you should not get on well together.*

Corbin had dinner at his club and then caught a late train home to Kent. When he arrived Aunt Lily was in the kitchen, making herself a cup of cocoa before going to bed.

When she asked him if he had had a good day in London he said without hesitation, "Yes, love. I went up to meet a friend I'm going to caretake for in Wales. It's all fixed up and I'm driving over there tomorrow to take charge of the place because he and his wife are going off sooner than they expected. Do you know what I saw walking up from the station just now? Glow-worms. Remember how, as a boy, I used to collect them and . . ."

As he went on talking she smiled to herself knowing from the past that the sharp change of subject meant that he had no wish to discuss his Welsh job, knowing too—though not without a familiar sense of unease—that the last thing she could do would be to ask him for his coming address. *He walked by himself and all places were alike to him . . . waving his wild tail, and walking by his wild lone. But he never told anybody.* Aye, and she had long guessed, a true Tom Cat. Women, she knew, made fools of themselves over him. God knew why. She was a fool about him

. . . but she loved him. There was goodness in him, but he neglected it, treated it brusquely, almost as though he regarded it as a weakness.

As she turned to go, a *good-night* on her lips, he said, "I had a bit of extra luck today so I bought my best girl a present."

He handed her a little paper-wrapped parcel.

"Oh, Johnny—you shouldn't have——"

"Yes, I should. Take it upstairs with you." He leaned forward and kissed her forehead.

She went up to her bedroom and opened the packet. Inside was a gold brooch on which had been mounted in delicate running scrolls a Victorian golden guinea. She sat on the side of her bed, cocoa in one hand, the brooch in the other and found herself full of feelings for which she could find no adequate words. He was beyond her comprehension. She knew only that, sure as she was of his care-free, conscienceless life—so many little signs and her own instinct had long convinced her of that—he was nearer to her than a true son and she loved him.

Downstairs Corbin sat happily in the small sitting room drinking a nightcap. He would call the Bishop tomorrow morning from the telephone booth down the road and tell him he would be happy to accept his offer and proposed to go down to Illaton Manor right away. He could drive there in a day, but he decided to spend a night on the way to discharge an obligation which it had occurred to him would be a little act of propitiation towards the gods who might then be prepared to bless his new venture.

* * * *

The day after Corbin had gone to London to see the Bishop of Testerburgh, James Helder and his sister went down to Hampshire to see Miss Simpson at Blackthorn Cottage. With Helder driving they travelled in his well-cared-for but almost twenty-year-old Rover car. On the way back his sister knew that she would be required to drive, for Helder, at the end of a day's enquiries, liked to sit alone in the back with his thoughts and speculations.

They had an early picnic lunch in a field by a river and afterwards Helder left his sister to go about her collecting of wild flowers and grasses for pressing. Forton was a small village on the upper part of the river Test and Blackthorn Cottage, a little way out of the village, stood by itself with a small strip of garden running down to the river. It was reed thatched and not very well maintained and the garden, too, was neglected but had an overgrown, untidy charm. To one side of the cottage was a wooden garage with the paint flaking from it. Helder guessed that Miss Simpson had little spare money and probably less physical vigour to keep the property in order. Just the type, he thought, to fall for the confident talk of one of the world's many Corbins and so—for he liked nothing better than to anticipate such revelations—find herself cheated out of his last month's rent. Compared to Mrs Barwick who had found herself having to pay for her amorous pleasures she was small fry, but that would not, he felt, have mattered to Corbin for he was, he guessed, no respecter of size limits when he went fishing.

The woman who answered the door to him was in her early sixties, her iron-grey hair cut short and untidy, her face small and lined, the cheeks highly coloured and her blue eyes a little misty as though she were perpetually on the point of tears. She wore a green smock with large pockets, from one of which protruded the handles of a pair of secateurs. Her legs were bare and on her feet were shapeless leather sandals. She was a very small woman and she looked up at him now as though she expected either to be assaulted or to be given bad news. Timidity and uncertainty, Helder guessed, had been her companions all her life. He felt immediately protective towards her and acknowledged an immediate compassion for her.

"Miss Simpson?"

"Yes . . ." The single syllable was a tiny sigh.

"My name is Helder. I wonder if you could spare me a little time? I work for a firm of debt collectors and I'm trying to trace a man called John Corbin who, I understand, once rented your cottage."

"Oh, dear . . ."

"Perhaps you'd like to see my card?" He made a move to reach for his wallet in which rested four or five assorted cards to cover his various aliases.

"Oh, no, no . . . that's all right. Do please come in."

The door opened straight into a large, pleasant, but untidy sitting room with an open fireplace which was filled with an arrangement of flowers in an old brass coal scuttle.

Miss Simpson removed a pile of magazines from an old chintz-covered armchair, asked Helder to sit down and then went herself to a wooden settle by the fireplace and perched there holding the magazines to her chest as though they were of some comfort to her. Then with an unexpected abruptness she said, "Did he owe much money?"

"A certain amount—to his tailor. My firm have taken it over from them. That's our business. A sordid one. One sees too much of the wrong side of human nature. Did you like him?"

"Oh, yes. Very much." She smiled suddenly, as though pleasant memories had revived in her. "He was charming. And so helpful around the garden. He used to work for hours on it. But I'm afraid it's gone back dreadfully since he left. I can't cope properly with it. And even if I could afford help there's none to be had. Did you say Helder?"

"That's right. So he liked gardening?"

"Oh, yes. Not only liked it. He knew about it. He was such a nice young man. Of course, while he was here I went to live with my sister in Forton. But I used to come over often. He was a good cook, too, and gave me some splendid lunches."

"Did he leave a forwarding address?"

"Oh, no. He just went . . ." There was a quick tremble of her lips. ". . . unexpectedly. Just left a note. But the place was all in apple-pie order."

Helder nodded and smiled gently. "But, perhaps, he forgot to settle up his rent with you?"

"How could you know?" There was genuine surprise in her voice. She let the magazines drop flat on her lap and spread her long thin hands over them.

"Because the world is full of John Corbins and I've dealt with quite a few of them. Shall we say there's no true wickedness in them? They're just careless about other people's feelings and property."

"Well, he didn't exactly not pay it. He left a note saying he would send it on. But he must have forgotten it, mustn't he?"

Because she so clearly hoped so Helder had no desire to disillusion her. He said, "Perhaps. How did he pay you in the start? With cash or cheques?"

"Oh, always in cash—and usually I got some little present as well. A pot plant or *marrons glacés*. He knew they were my favourite."

He would, of course, thought Helder. The nice, generous but small touch which inspired confidence. And no payment by cheque—that closed that avenue . . . though probably it had never been open for Miss Simpson would never have remembered the name of the bank or its branch and probably, too, never had her cancelled cheques sent back to her.

"That was nice of him. Did you ever come to know what work he did?"

"He said he worked for a London antique dealer, and he was in this area for a while to attend sales. But he never said what firm."

Helder looked at an oak, gate-legged table by the window with twist-turned barley-sugar legs which he guessed was a genuine late seventeenth-century piece, and asked, "Did he ever make you an offer for your table over there?"

"Oh, yes, he did. But I couldn't part with that. It's been in the family for ages. But I sold him a Georgian tea-caddy, and he paid me handsomely."

Handsome is as handsome does, thought Helder. Corbin had probably made a quick and nice profit on it. An eye for good things, and a snapper-up of anything which would show a ready profit. No forwarding address, no cheques . . . he had a feeling in his bones that Corbin was going to be hard to find. Well, that was how he liked things to be. What was the point of work unless it was beset with frustration and difficulty? Even before he asked the next question he knew almost certainly what the answer would be. Nevertheless he asked it because he believed in being thorough.

"Do you have a telephone here, Miss Simpson?"

"Oh, no. I used to but I had to give it up. Anyway there's a call box just down the road."

On the small, oak, gate-legged table close to a brass jug with a solitary peacock's feather pluming from it was a small and well-worn box camera. He said, "I see you've got a camera. Did you ever take a photograph of him?"

Miss Simpson gave a little laugh. She was more at ease now and relishing a little company, especially of an unexpected kind. Her sister, Helder knew, would hear all about his visit.

"It's funny you should ask that. I did once. You see he'd done so much for the garden that one day I said I'd like to take a photo of him in it. But he said no."

"Why?"

"Oh, he was laughing and talking some nonsense about if you had your photo taken you lost a little bit of your soul. 'Course I didn't believe a word he said. And then a few days later I did take his photograph. He was in the garden dead-heading the Peace roses with his back to me, and I called out to him . . ." She gave a little and surprisingly girlish giggle. "When he turned I took him and, before he could say anything, I said, 'Now I've got a tiny bit of your soul, and I want it to remind me of the man who's done so much for my dear garden'. Mind you, he'd asked me to lunch that day and we'd had sherry before and wine with—otherwise I'd never have done it."

"And what did he say?"

She shook her head with pleasure and said, "He was charming about it. He gave me a little bow—he had perfect manners, you know—and said, 'I let you have it willingly. In what safer and kindlier hands could it be?' Wasn't that nice? I'll get it for you."

She got up and went to a little wall cupboard beside the fireplace and rummaged in it for a while and then came back and handed the photograph to Helder. It was a reasonably good picture showing a fair-haired man in his early thirties, Helder guessed, wearing an open-necked shirt and corduroy trousers. There was a look of half-surprise and half-amusement on his face, and the face was good-looking, rather squarish in features, the kind of face which, given the good manner that clearly went with it, probably made him instantly likeable. But of much more interest to him was that the photograph, taken clearly from the cottage front door, showed in the background a car on the hard standing outside the small garage. It was an old Humber Sceptre and the registration plate at the front was clearly visible.

Helder said, "Well, he looks a nice enough chap." He handed the photograph back to her.

"Oh, he was, Mr Helder. And you know, though it's probably soft of me, I'm sure that one day he'll turn up and pay me. We were such good friends. He was just temporarily hard-up, I'm sure, and didn't like to say anything to me to my face."

"I don't think that could apply to his tailor, do you?"

"Well . . . I don't know anything about that. Anyway, tailors are used to waiting a long time, aren't they?"

Helder stood up, smiling, and said, "I suppose they are." Then, as he reached for his notebook and pencil, he went on, "Did Mr Corbin have any girl friends or visitors here, or talk to you about any of his acquaintances in the district?"

"Not that I know of. But then I wasn't here that often. But I'm sure he must have had friends. I can't imagine a lovely man like that without. I brought my sister over once and she met him. She went really quite soppy about him. I know she's ten years younger than me but it was quite ridiculous. All the way back she talked hardly of anything else. But then she is a little bit . . . well, not with her feet quite on the earth. She's been married twice and when she put her last husband away he left her quite well off and she keeps saying that she isn't going to settle down for the rest of her life with nothing in it except a cat and a garden. She's over fifty and she goes on these holiday cruises every year. Hunting, she calls it. Still, she's very kind to me."

Helder chuckled and said, "Well, you know the old saying—hope springs eternal. And now I must thank you for your kindness in seeing me." He handed her a page of his notebook on which he had written his London telephone number. "I wonder if by any chance Mr Corbin does turn up to pay you whether you would be kind enough to ring me at this number and let me know about it? Reverse the charges, of course. But, if I may say so, I think it would be as well if you said nothing to him about my visit. I don't want you to be at all embarrassed. After all young men may be careless about their tailors' bills and pressed sometimes to little extremities of conduct even with those for whom they have affection—so it would be wise for you to keep your counsel."

"Oh, I certainly wouldn't mention it to him. I wouldn't know how to." She glanced at the photograph in her hand. "Such a nice young man. And such green fingers. I used to say to him sometimes that I was sure that if he stuck a walking stick in the ground it would take and sprout leaves."

Walking back to rejoin his sister Helder thought that John Corbin might have green fingers but they were also sticky fingers . . . great charm and an easy manner. How many such had passed through his books? And if he did turn up at Blackthorn Cottage Miss Simpson would probably be unable to hold back from telling him all about the visit of Mr Helder. Not that it mattered. John Corbin must have been chased before and—at a guess—never been caught. Well, well, how nice it would be to upset that pattern. He could see the corners of Miss Simpson's mouth trembling and near tears misting her eyes. He worked now for Mr Barwick. But he was tough and resilient. If he ever found Corbin for him the man would have little chance of getting his money back, but might settle for giving Corbin a good hiding. But Miss Simpson now . . . she really was helpless, one of those gentle, trusting people who suffered because they were the little, stray, destiny-marked victims of the world's Corbins. Easy game. Well, the truth was that if Barwick was paying him—and he would serve him well—he was, in fact, going to be working more for the Miss Simpsons of this world than the Barwicks.

His sister drove him back to London. He sat in the back flanked on one side by her large basket full of flowers and foliage and water plants. Plants . . . good at gardening . . . John Corbin in the photograph, secateurs in hand. There were so many sides to human character. And how often, he thought, when one went a-hunting did one find that the traces of villainy petered out but the little acts of virtue persisted in people's memories to be used as far more certain guides.

That evening in his small study at Hampstead Helder called a not always over-willing friend at New Scotland Yard. The preliminaries done, he said, "I'm interested in a man called John Corbin. He drives a Humber Sceptre with the registration number KLM 500 N. Can you check with the car tax authorities for his address?"

"You know I can't and won't. It's strictly unethical."

"On the contrary, this is a matter of ethics, that branch of philosophy which is concerned with human conduct and character. Particularly of one, John Corbin, who bilks landladies and in the transports of illicit love finds himself assessing the blackmail price for not revealing all to some devoted husband."

"You're breaking my heart. The world is full of them."

"Sadly, yes. But it's also full of a lot of nice things like friendship and one good turn deserving another. You might even have a file on him."

"Now, don't ask me to check that."

"Good Lord, no. That would be unethical. Like you sometimes asking me to help you."

There was silence for a while and then the voice at the other end of the line said, "All right. I'll see what I can do."

"That's very kind of you."

The following morning Helder received a telephone call. The address of John Corbin was care of Orchard House, Beacon Lane, Crowborough, Sussex.

That morning, too, at half-past ten John Corbin called at Blackthorn Cottage. He gave a brief knock and walked into the sitting room where Miss Simpson was sitting in her armchair reading the *Daily Telegraph* obituary column. She stared at him for a moment, her face loose with surprise and then, with a sudden smile, said, "Oh, my . . . where did you come from?"

He grinned. "Out of the blue. Return of the prodigal—bearing gifts. No need to kill the fatted calf. My love, how well you look."

He went over to her, bent down and kissed her and, as he stepped back, he dropped a parcel and an envelope into her lap. He stood smiling down at her, waiting for her to recover and thinking how much he liked her. She was another Aunt Lily—though softer and infinitely less capable of looking after herself, and she was also one of the very few people who had stirred his conscience.

Her hands fiddling absently with the parcel and envelope in her lap, she said, "Oh, Johnny . . . how marvellous."

He sat down on the fireside settle and said, "Now—first of all my apologies. I had to leave hurriedly . . . there was trouble in the firm in London, and they hadn't sent my monthly commission cheque . . . and the whole thing was a real mess-up. Oh, I won't go into all the details but I've left them. Anyway, I'm all right now and have got another job—and in the envelope there is the money I owe you. And the parcel . . . well that's a box of *marron's glacés.*"

"Oh, my favourites."

"And am I forgiven? I've really had a worrying time and I didn't like to write to you because I wanted to come in person to be forgiven."

"Oh, Johnnie—of course I forgive you. I never believed for a moment that you had just gone for good."

He smiled. "I've put a little extra in the envelope. Conscience money . . ." At that moment he really was glad that he had come back and made things good with her. His affection for her was real. So real that now he wondered why he had ever been tempted to cheat her. The paradox had worried him for a while. She was so small and helpless . . . like a child, trusting. You're a bastard, Corbin, he thought. But at least a little less of one now. He went on, "I'll do a little work for you in the garden, and then I'll take you out to lunch. After that I must be off. I've got a new job up in Wales and have to get there some time tonight. And now tell me how you've been. And your sister? And all the local gossip."

"Oh, nothing new happens down here. Everything is just the same. I want to hear about you. Tell me about your new job."

"Oh, that. It's nothing new really. I'm just going to act as a sort of caretaker for a couple of months at a house in Wales which belongs to two friends of mine. They're going abroad. I'll do a little antique buying from there on my own account. They've got a nice garden, too. That should keep me out of mischief . . ."

As he ran on chatting to her Miss Simpson was remembering Mr Helder and was wondering if she should tell him about this visit. But almost at once she knew that she could not do that. It might upset Johnny to know that she knew he owed his tailor money. And, anyway, for all she knew he might well have paid the bill by now . . . walking into the shop out of the blue as he had walked in here. She might give Mr Helder a ring after he had gone, might . . . she wasn't even sure of that. And anyway she could not ask him point blank what his address would be in Wales. In his early days here she had learnt that he always avoided answering any direct personal question. Funny, he was so friendly and approachable, but never let you know anything about his real self. Still, people had their own private affairs and were entitled to keep them private . . . though personally she always found it a great comfort to talk her troubles over with someone, even with her sister who just pretended to listen and the moment you stopped went straight on with a catalogue of her own troubles and silly romantic hopes.

Corbin stood up and said, "Well, that's enough about me. I'll cut the front lawn for you and run a hoe through the herbaceous border. Then we'll go and have some lunch."

While he was cutting the lawn he found himself wondering why he had come back and paid her. Perhaps, he thought, because she had something of Aunt Lily about her—though Aunt Lily was far less defenceless than Miss Simpson. Maybe there was something in his nature that made him turn to middle-aged women. Some Freudian touch? Looking for the thing he had never known—a mother? Could be. What did it matter, anyway? He was content to feel good at coming back. The gods might be obliging enough to chalk it up in his favour.

When he had done the lawn he went round to the back to fetch a hoe and stopped to go into the little lean-to greenhouse where Miss Simpson grew tomatoes. She had neglected to pinch out their side shoots, but had been clearly over-watering for a lot of them were ring-split. The herbaceous border was thick with weeds and he set to methodically and without hurry to clear it. *Gardens are not made by singing—'Oh, how beautiful!' and sitting in the shade.* That was what he would like to do . . . to have three or four lives to put end to end and then make a garden from scratch and care for it through to its maturity. He would gladly make a compact with the Devil for that favour and go contentedly to Hell at the end. Probably would go to Hell anyway but it would be nice to leave a paradise behind where there had once been wilderness. Gardens and women; long- and short-term pleasures. An old and not always welcome query floated into his mind. *Why was he the way he was?* God's work or the Devil's or a simple, undesigned, random conjunction of chromosomes? No answer. Idle question. He took out his knife and cut some suckers from the base of a polyanthus rose. Prune out the unwanted. One day the old rattling skeleton would take him with his scythe, and not a thing would mean a button thereafter. Not that the Bishop of Testerburgh would have agreed with him.

He took Miss Simpson out to lunch, gave her Chablis to drink with her grilled sole and bought a bottle of gin for her to have in the cottage.

She said, "You shouldn't."

"Why not? People can let you down. As I nearly did. But a quiet glass of an evening . . . or maybe two or three . . . puts the world to rights."

"You shouldn't say that. About nearly letting me down. You would never have let me down."

But as he drove away he knew that he would have done. Had he really been going to Wales he would never have made the long detour to see her. Only the accident of driving westwards to Illaton Manor with Blackthorn Cottage on his route had taken him to her. Conscience he might have in small degree, but only coincidence running in harness with it could prompt him now and again to small acts of contrition.

After Corbin had gone Miss Simpson sat for some time in a happy mood going over in detail the memory of his visit and also wondering if she should take the trouble to telephone the nice Mr Helder who had visited her, leaving his number and telling her that she could reverse the charges. In the end she decided that there would be little point in so doing. All she could tell him was that Johnny had gone to Wales and Wales was a big place, and anyway—she gave a little giggle born out of her Chablis—she was sure that Johnny would eventually pay his tailor. It might take a little time but tailors were used to that. As she sat there she held in her lap a last present which Johnny had handed her as he sat in his car before driving off, saying, "Just keep it behind your back until I'm gone. It's something I did quite a while ago. It'll go well with your gin in the evenings."

It was an autographed copy of his book *Green Pleasures*.

* * * *

Helder knew at once that this time he was dealing with no Miss Simpson. After leaving his sister to go off for a walk across the nearby golf course to collect ferns he had gone into the local post office and asked them if he could be directed to Orchard House to be met with the immediate response, 'Oh, Mrs Hines' place?'

'No, the name I've got is Corbin. Mr John Corbin.'

'Yes, that's right. Mrs Hines is his aunt.'

And here was Mrs Hines, standing at her doorway, fair hair long greyed, wren-bright eyes alert, the sleeves of her jumper rolled up, her well-worn corduroy trousers baggy and stained.

He said, "I hope I haven't caught you at an awkward moment? But I'm looking for a John Corbin. I was given this address."

"By whom?"

"At the local post office."

"But before that?"

"You would like the truth, of course."

"Naturally." There was no quaver or touch of concern in her voice.

"Well, I happen to know the make and number of his car and—quite unethically perhaps—I got a friend in London to trace his address through the licensing authorities at Swansea."

"You have very useful friends, Mr . . .?"

"I'm sorry. Helder. James Helder."

"And your business?" The question was flat and firm. Mrs Hines, he thought, might be full of some concern but she had too much pride—and perhaps experience—to show it. Other men on similar errands might well have stood here before him.

He gave her a small smile, and said, "What if I told you I am a debt collector?" He fancied he caught the swift passage of a tremor on her lips.

"What debt?"

"Say his tailor?"

"I wouldn't believe you. He's one of the few he does pay. Do you know his name?"

"Do you?"

"Yes, I posted a letter with a cheque—on account—to him yesterday. My nephew left it with me."

"I see. Then would you prefer that I told you the truth?"

"Isn't that the right and honest thing to do?"

"Not necessarily. I don't like upsetting people with unpleasant truths if I can avoid it."

"Mr Helder, I'm beyond being upset. I think you had better come in." She led him through a lounge where a hoover stood on the carpet and a pile of cushions from chairs littered the window seat, and said, "I was just having a turn out here. We can sit in the dining room."

The dining-room windows looked out over the yard to the donkey paddock and a wired-in hen run at its side overhung by a lilac tree in full bloom. She motioned him to a chair at the head of a well-polished refectory table and took a seat herself at the other end of the table as though she wanted space between them. Space and time, he thought, in which to deliberate and weigh his words. He could guess her kind and her feelings as a preliminary debate went on within him as to how much truth would be kindness or whether the full truth alone were not by itself unvarnished and frank the real charity he had at his disposal.

Aunt Lily said, "Would you like a glass of home-made wine?"

"No, thank you, Mrs Hines."

"I think you're wise. Our last batch was really well below standard. I have no sherry to offer you. His mother and father died young. My husband and I brought him up. He's a delightful person and talented, but he's always been in trouble. I never know what kind because he never confides in me. But I love him and pray for him. So you must not expect me to be over-helpful to you. Is your matter serious?"

"Not really. Dishonourable and marginally criminal. I must tell you that I'm a private . . . well, investigator . . ." It was a declaration he always loathed making and usually avoided. There was no choice here. This woman wanted the truth. That was the real kindness he could do her, and anyway the truth would only confirm what she clearly must have guessed for herself.

Aunt Lily stood up suddenly. "Oh, Lord, forgive me—I've

left the chicken scrap mash on the stove boiling . . ." She went out quickly and through the open door to the kitchen came the sour smell of potato rinds and scraps cooking. When she came back she carried two wine glasses between the spread fingers of one hand and a half bottle of wine in the other.

She set them down on the table and said, "I'd forgotten. He bought some Chablis the day before he went. There's a little left." Without waiting for any reply from him, she began to pour the wine and, as she did so, said, "I just want the absolute truth from you, Mr Helder. That's something I never had from John. Just the truth. It's easier to bear than suspicions . . . not that he ever told me a lie. Just evaded the truth."

Taking his glass Helder said, "Human nature in my experience, Mrs Hines, is not to be changed. When the drunkard becomes a rabid teetotaller he simply substitutes one mania for another. The transition from saint to sinner or sinner to saint is the easiest one in the world. But with your nephew we are not dealing with either of these extremes. From my limited knowledge—all second-hand I'll admit—his is a problem of frustration. He is really looking for himself, his true self. If he found it he might, of course, find it to be a bad self. At the moment I think he fluctuates from one to the other. Do you agree?"

"Possibly. But I'd much rather you told me the facts. But, Mr Helder, don't expect me to do anything that would harm him. My marriage was barren. He was and is my child." For a moment the glint of tears touched her eyes.

"Well, the facts are these, Mrs Hines."

Aunt Lily sat and listened to him, her glass of wine untouched and forgotten. There was no surprise in her at what she heard. He gave her no names or addresses. And as she listened she could not find it in her to have more than a marginal sympathy with the woman John had seduced and then made pay for the pleasure. She was far more concerned with the cheating of the woman who had rented her cottage to John and, breaking in on Helder's talk, asked for her name and address.

He said, "I'm not sure that I should give it to you."

Stubbornly, she said, "You *will* give it to me. I shall write and send her a cheque for the money which is owing. I promise that is all I shall do. There is no question of my visiting her and probing further."

"Very well." Helder wrote the name and address on a page of his notebook and handed it to her, and then asked her, "Did he give you any indication of where he was going from here?"

"Oh, yes. He always does that. But always so vaguely that I never believe it. He said that he was going to look after the house of some friends in Wales while they were on holiday. But I am sure that wherever he is it is not in Wales."

"If you ever did have his real address—would you let me know? I've written my telephone number on the piece of paper with Miss Simpson's address."

Aunt Lily shook her head. "You are too intelligent, Mr Helder, not to know the answer to that already."

"You wouldn't?"

"No." Aunt Lily sipped her Chablis, gave a small, weary sigh, and went on, "But if ever I know it or should he come back here I shall make it clear that I know all about his shameful behaviour, and that there can never be any place for him here until he has sent the two thousand pounds back to this stupid woman he seduced."

"But you say he has no money. So how could he do that?"

"Quite easily, Mr Helder. I should explain that before my husband died he put four thousand pounds in trust for John. The income only was to go to him until he was forty when he would be free to touch the capital."

Remembering the photograph he had seen, Helder said, "But he's a long way off forty, isn't he?"

"True. But there is a clause in the trust deeds which allows me to draw on the capital before he reaches the age of forty at my discretion and on his behalf. I am given entire discretion as to the interpretation of what 'on his behalf' might constitute."

"He knows this?"

"Oh, yes."

"Has he ever asked you to do this—draw money for him?"

Aunt Lily gave a faint smile. "In the past, yes. But he gave up trying to persuade me years ago."

"So you could do it right away?"

"Not without his knowledge."

"And you will do this?"

"Most certainly as soon as I know where he is. And now, Mr Helder, I think I should like you to go." There was the soft shine of tears in her eyes as she finished speaking.

"Yes, of course." Helder rose. Mrs Barwick, Miss Simpson and Mrs Hines . . . and John Corbin working on their emotions, their love and affection with the instinctive and mechanical expertise of a juggler keeping his spinning plates in the air . . . He went on, "I'm sorry I had to come and see you. If you ever want me you have my telephone number."

When he had gone Aunt Lily poured the last of the Chablis into her glass. She finished her wine and went out to the paddock where the two donkeys came to greet her, butting their muzzles against the palms of her hands. It was only then that the tears came. That same day she wrote a letter to Miss Simpson, enclosing a cheque, and explaining why she was sending it.

CHAPTER THREE

JOHN CORBIN TOOK two days to motor down to Illaton Manor. The first night he spent with a girl friend in Exeter, Sarah Barnes, whom he had known from his Oxford days and who was now teaching botany at a local grammar school. They had carried on a long and irregularly spaced intimacy. Sarah had early learned never to take anything he said as gospel. Her emotions, however, being as vagrant as his own, she always enjoyed their meetings.

As they lay in bed that night Sarah sighed with content and said, "East, west, north or south?"

"From here—north. Up into Wales. You've put on a little weight. It suits you."

"Liar to the first. Thank you for the second. What is it with you, Johnny? Do you think if you ever tell some little truth about yourself you'll lose part of your soul?"

"Have I got one?"

"Nobody can escape that spiritual endowment. You can't lock it up in some old attic."

"I don't see why not. That's where you put useless old lumber."

"One day it will escape. You'll be in a proper fix then because you won't know how to handle it. Why did you ever shut it up there in the first place?"

"Because I don't like to carry excess baggage."

"You've never loved anyone, have you? Not even yourself?"

He laughed. "Every time I find myself in this situation with you, Sarah, love, we have the same conversation. Why do people always fuss over other people's hang-ups or problems? It's all so intruding. I was born the way I am and I don't want to change it metaphysically. Though I wouldn't object to it financially."

"You're a waster, but a nice one. And don't tell me you wouldn't like to be different. Everyone would in some way. And I don't mean cash. One day you're going to find yourself falling in love—though not with me, I hope—and then you'll be in a corner."

"If so, I'll handle it somehow."

"Or maybe, it won't be love. Some other emotion or some grand temptation. The Devil keeps his eye on people like you. You must know that. He's in no hurry. He just waits for the right opportunity to come along."

"Your mother must have been a gypsy fortune-teller."

"I never knew who she was. I was adopted. They never told me until it was years too late to rouse any curiosity in me. Just as I have no curiosity about your coming down to Exeter from Sussex to go to Wales. Most people would stick to the M4 and go across the Severn Bridge—or if it were North Wales go up to Gloucester and over the river there. I was just a free bed and fun for the night on your way west. Admit it."

He laughed. "My dear love, you misunderstand the power of friendship. I had time on my hands and I came to see you."

"My dear John, it's nice to hear that you class me as *vaut le détour*. Well, I'm going to sleep. I shall be up and away before you in the morning. Just shove the key back through the letter box, and keep your hands off the family silver."

"It's a promise."

She went to sleep quickly, and he lay awake untouched by anything she had said. The moment you got close to anyone and they began to read you a little they always wanted to start taking you over. Except when it was done in bed after love-making it was all so bloody boring, and even after love-making mildly irritating. He was what he was. So what? If God and the Devil chose to tussle over his immortal soul it was no business of his. He put out his hand and caressed her naked flank and she gave a little grumble of pleasure in her sleep. She was gone when he woke in the morning late. He stopped at a florist's on the way out of Exeter and sent her flowers and a note which read—*I would go out of my way any time to find joy with you.* But as he wrote it he was thinking that no time was ever wasted in spasmodically renewing a friendship. Friends were there to be used and so entitled to an occasional courtesy call. By the time he was out of the town and rising to the slopes of Dartmoor he had forgotten her.

He stopped at Tavistock for lunch and also to buy himself a guide book which contained a chapter on Illaton Manor which he read over his beer and sandwiches. The original house had been a farmhouse with nearly a hundred acres of land overlooking the river Tamar from the Cornish side at the head of a steep valley which ran down to the river which was here still tidal. The farmhouse had burnt down in 1835 and the Bishop's great-grandfather had bought the place in 1840. On the site he had built the present Illaton Manor, using the local granite stone, and had begun to turn the hilly wood and farm land into a garden and estate. Although he was a busy and prosperous business man he was also a keen botanist and naturalist, as were all his heirs. The Bishop's grandfather, Alfred Boyd Darvell, had inherited Illaton in 1891 and had made additions and alterations to the estate, and these had continued when the Bishop's father, John Boyd Darvell, had inherited the place in 1911. He had died in 1950 when the Bishop, Michael Boyd Darvell, born in 1924, had come into the property.

Chewing on his ham sandwich John Corbin was touched with envy at the thought of the successive generations of Darvells who had had the time and the money to create over the years the gardens and landscapes of Illaton, who had the vision to plant, not just for their life-time but for the future, trees and shrubs whose glory they would never see in full maturity. To take an old farm and rough hill pasture and scrub woodland overlooking the Tamar and turn it into a paradise—there was true love and devotion. He could find it in his heart to condemn the Bishop who clearly—though proud of his home and estate—had turned his love and devotion to a different worship. He kept the place going, of course, but Corbin wondered how often he grubbed now with his own hands, pruned and—more important—laid out further plantings for the generations to come.

He lit a cigarette and remembered suddenly the first time the true miracle of growth and propagation, the elemental power of

Nature to persist, had overpowered him when Aunt Lily had shown him how to take a cutting from a Busy Lizzie which she had as a house plant. He had put it in a jam jar with water and marked each day the small growth of the fragile white roots emerge. From that moment he had been trapped . . . maybe, perhaps, he grinned to himself, because he had discovered that Nature if you treated her right would give you something for nothing. From the first miracle with *Impatiens sultanii* he had gone on to know others, the joys of first growths, first flowerings and final fruitings. And, a contradiction he could never explain to himself, he had found that whereas he had no true love of sustained work or application either in his studies or his friendships both these came naturally to him where plants and gardening were concerned. He loved to hoe and weed, unhurried and methodically, to feed and water, to prune and spray . . . all those, for some, tedious labours which made a garden, flower beds and shrubberies no more than Sisyphean toiling, but not for him. He grinned now as he thought that of old Adam there was much in him, but the attribute he valued most was an almost lust for delving, and no envy that from an acorn he might plant he would never live to see a great oak grow. Man had lost the Garden of Eden millenniums since but the hope of creating another lived in every true gardener's breast.

An hour later, after losing himself once or twice in the maze of small lanes to the west of the Tamar, he drove up to the granite-pillared, wrought-iron gates of Illaton Manor and then down the drive to where the house stood, over two hundred feet above the river, a drive that passed under Monterey pines and copper beeches and through massed shrubberies, marking with delight the great leaves of a Chinese rhododendron and the large, fragrant white flowers of *Rhododendron auriculatum* just coming into full bloom . . . his eyes caught by and marking, some in bloom, and some long bloomed, camellias, mimosa, magnolias and cornels, hydrangeas and eucryphias. Finally, under the shade of a giant Deodar cedar, he parked on the open gravel space before the Manor and sat for a moment or two looking at the house.

A wide fan-shaped run of steps ran up to the balustraded terrace which spanned its front. It was a severe, though not unpleasing building, with two floors above the ground floor, the windows tall and flanked with green shutters to close against the winter storms that swept up the river valley and down from distant Dartmoor, but the severity was softened along its front by growths of magnolia, clematis and climbing roses.

A few minutes later he was sitting in a large drawing room that faced south with a distant view of the river, talking to Miss Margaret Latham, the sister of the Bishop's wife and, so he had gathered, for all practical purposes the mistress of the house. On the telephone, when he had spoken to her from a call box in Exeter before going to Sarah's flat for the night, to tell her he would be arriving this day, she had sounded a little cold and mannered, even brusque, but he soon realized that this was merely the result of the deceit which the telephone could work. Later he was to learn that she hated the contraption, as she called it.

In her mid-fifties she looked older, her hair grey but with just the hint of a blue rinse in it, her face weather-touched, almost an autumn pippin apple, her eyes a warm faded blue which made him guess that her hair might once have been blond. She wore khaki drill gardening trousers and a pale-blue cashmere sweater with the handles of a pruning secateur poking from one pocket. Neither trousers nor sweater were immaculate. She reminded him of Aunt Lily. Though, whereas he had often known Aunt Lily's face to tremble on the point of dissolution at hurt or sadness, he could not imagine Miss Latham easily allowing any weak emotion to be shown to the world. She was brisk as a terrier, bright as a bird, and straight to the point because time was precious and there was always too much to do. But when she smiled, which she did often and without evident reason as though some private whimsy had occurred to her, the imagination caught fleetingly the picture of her as a young and pretty corn-haired, blue-eyed young woman delighted with the prospect the world must have had to offer her. Somewhere along the line, he thought, as they chatted over China tea and oval Marie biscuits, the world must have disappointed her.

"Dear Michael sent me a copy of your book to read. I enjoyed it very much. First-class job. As a matter of fact I read it in bed during an attack of sciatica." She smiled. "I have a leg which is surer than any barometer if there's rain coming. Your book was better than any medicine—took me right out of myself. Oh, dear, I do apologize for speaking about my infirmities—but they do become old friends after a while, don't they?"

"Well, certainly more dependable perhaps."

She gave a hearty laugh, and then went on, "Now, Mr Corbin—would you like to live in the house or have the guest cottage?"

"Which would you suggest, Miss Latham?"

"Well, if I were a young man I would choose to be on my own with the freedom of coming up here when I become bored with my own company."

"Then I'll take the guest cottage."

"Are you always so easily persuaded?"

Corbin grinned. Already he was beginning to assess her measure, knew that he was going to like her, and wanted to please her and stand in well with her. He said, "No, I'm not, Miss Latham. In fact I had already decided that I would like to be on my own in the cottage."

She pursed her lips, bright eyes on him and said, "I can see I shall have to watch you. Do you go regularly to church?"

"Not so much now that it is turning its back on the language which Shakespeare was happy with."

"How true. And by the way, you can get all your milk and eggs from the home farm and if you leave an order with the cook or with me we'll see that you get anything else you want. And what do you know about honey fungus?"

"You've got it? On a cherry, yes?"

"We have. It's attacked one of our *Prunus serrulata*—a Tai-Haku."

"Then dig it up and burn it."

She nodded approvingly and then eyed him in silence for a moment or two before saying, "A no-messing-about answer—and quite right. Harrison wanted to try all sorts of damn-fool remedies. Now you can back me up." She stood up. "All right—now you can drive me down to the cottage and I'll show you around and how everything works, or should work. The fire smokes in a strong northerly, but you won't be needing fires yet. And sometimes the automatic electric pump that supplies the cottage with well water packs up. I'll show you the trick of priming it. We have the mains up here, but the dear Bishop can't be persuaded to have it laid on down there." She laughed as she led him from the room. "There's a certain unhealthy streak of uncalled-for husbandry about him at times. But don't tell the dear man I said so. And, by the way, don't let Harrison bully you. You must stand up for yourself. Remember you're a guest, not an employee . . ."

He said, "Who's Harrison? The head gardener?"

"Yes. Very opinionated. But a jewel beyond price."

The guest cottage was a converted timber-framed barn which stood in a small hollow about half a mile from the Manor. One large room downstairs served as a sitting room and dining room and the kitchen, though small, was well equipped. Upstairs were two bedrooms and a bathroom and a small study or working room which looked westwards to the Cornish moors marked here and there by the tall grey stacks of long-abandoned tin mines. Miss Latham showed him round at what was almost a brisk canter and then took him outside to a pump room which was a lean-to shed at the back of the cottage and explained to him how to prime the pump.

"About once a month it just pumps away like a mad thing and nothing comes up. It's operated by an automatic switch controlled by a float in the main tank in the roof. Harrison says it needs a new foot valve at the pipe bottom in the well. I just think it has a mind of its own and goes on strike now and then to call attention to itself. Machines get bored you know."

"Of course. And bad-tempered." He smiled. "I'll come and talk to it occasionally to keep it in good humour."

"Oh, and there's a dog. He's called Cassidy. Whenever anyone stays he takes up his quarters here. You'll have to feed him. When the place is empty he lives at the Manor. I think some visitor on one of our open days must have abandoned or overlooked him. Anyway, he belongs. You like dogs, Mr Corbin?"

"Not particularly, Miss Latham."

"Neither do I. But he doesn't mind."

"Well, then neither of us have to beware of giving our hearts to a dog to tear."

Her blue eyes fixed him and then she smiled and said, " 'There is sorrow enough in the natural way—From men and women to fill our day.' Not one of my favourite poets. I find him rather coarse."

"We could quarrel about that."

She laughed and he could imagine her young and very pretty, and he wondered why she had never married.

As he drove her back to the Manor, she said, "Now, one other thing. Whenever you leave the cottage—do lock the doors and shut the windows. On visiting days we get an irritating proportion of people who are no respecters of other people's property. There's only one key—so don't lose it. I must get some others cut. Come up tomorrow and I'll show you the library and all the letters and diaries of the Darvells—thick with dust, I may add, and in no way catalogued or in order."

"I look forward to it." Which he did. He was, some instinct told him, going to be well set here and going to enjoy himself There could be at least a year's work, and no need for him to make any provision for himself by deceit or shabby stratagems. Perhaps this was a turning point . . .

When he got back to the cottage the dog was waiting for him. It was a yellow, rangy dog with a ridiculous twist of tail and brown eyes. It followed him into the cottage and sat by the empty open fireplace while he helped himself to an early whisky from the well-stocked sideboard. When he went to bed that night it settled down on the small landing outside the bedroom. It was, he thought, as he listened to an owl calling in the nearby woods, a dog that lacked the prevalent fulsomeness and ready assumption of friendship that characterized most of its kind. That suited him.

The owl stopped calling and then the silence was broken by the mating grunts and calls of the frogs which inhabited a small lily pool at the back of the cottage which he had seen as he took a stroll around after eating the supper he had cooked for himself. He sighed contentedly. He was lodged well and with interesting work ahead, work to which no time limit had been set and without doubt, when work was done, he would be able to find some satisfactory diversions to stop Jack from becoming a dull boy.

The next morning, just as he was finishing his breakfast, he heard a car stop outside the cottage. A few moments later there was a knock on the door. He went and opened it with Cassidy following at a distance. Standing outside was a young woman, some few years younger than himself he guessed, dressed in light drill trousers, a hacking jacket open over a blue shirt and with a man's flat cap tipped forward over her black hair which was pulled into a neat bun at the back of her head. Her eyes were dark, very dark, and her complexion sun-browned. Out of habit he quickly stripped her in his imagination and approved of the result, thinking too that if she belonged around here the possibilities of diversion were not too remote.

"Mr Corbin?"

"That's right. John Corbin."

"I'm Rachel Harrison. I expect Miss Latham mentioned me."

"Oh, yes." He smiled. "But just as Harrison. I thought she was talking about a man. I'm delighted to be corrected."

She held out a newspaper to him. "Welcome to Illaton. I brought you a *Daily Telegraph*—is that all right?"

"Perfectly. Miss Latham didn't mention that you did a newspaper round."

"I live down at Illaton Quay. I sometimes bring the newspapers up in the morning and other odds and ends. I see that Cassidy has taken up residence."

"Oh, yes. But he's no conversationalist. Won't you come in and have some coffee?"

"Well, why not? Thank you. And after—if you wish—I'll take you up to the Manor and show you round the gardens and so on. Would you care for that, Mr Corbin? Before you start delving into the family papers?"

"Yes, very much."

She came in and was at once at ease while he fixed coffee for her. He liked that. And he liked her. She was sure of herself because, he guessed, she knew her own mind and was going to make her own assessments. There was arrogance in supposing that because you sensed someone liked you that they would be prepared to do anything about it. In a way, he hoped that the game would not prove easy to take. The kill was nothing, the chase brought true fulfilment. Even as he thought this—unable to quell his own natural instincts—he thought, Oh, hell, here we go again and this time there was nothing truly to be gained. She was no Sue Barwick to pluck or little Miss Simpson to bilk. Just one simple sensual emotion. A divertissement when he surfaced from work on the Darvell papers. Perhaps, just for once, he should take a firm hold on himself and resist temptation. But even as his thoughts ran counter to the talk between them, she sitting with her coffee and a cigarette, he had to acknowledge to himself that the thing looked as though it were going to be too easy . . . so easy, that he wished he could have the will-power to resist for once. What a hopeless thought . . . somewhere a button had been pressed and he had to respond. She was telling him now how much she had enjoyed *Green Pleasures*. What a damned bore that was. Just because you'd written a book people thought you were something special.

To stop her talking about the book, after a decent interval, he said, "Tell me about Miss Latham. I took to her very much."

"Oh, she's marvellous. Everyone likes her. She's a classical case, too."

"What do you mean?"

"Well, she's in love with the Bishop. Was long before he married her sister. Don't ever say a word against the Bishop or she'll write you straight out of her book."

"Thanks for the warning. Is there any word to be said against him?"

"Not really, I suppose. Except that deep down he's ambitious. He'd like eventually to make Archbishop . . . York or Canterbury."

"Does he have any chance?"

"Miss Latham thinks so."

"And his wife?"

"I'm sure she'd like it. But I don't think anyone knows what she thinks or dreams about. She just follows him like a shadow. Does all the right things."

"You don't like her?"

"Let's say she doesn't come in Miss Latham's category."

"I see. And what about you, if I may ask? What brought you into horticulture?"

"Just chance I think. I went to a posh girls' school—Benenden, but I didn't want to go on to University. I liked gardening and gardens from a child. Then out of the blue, I don't know . . . I suddenly decided to make it a business as well as a pleasure. I went to horticultural college for three years and then I did three years working in a big nursery—Hillier's in Hampshire. Then this place was advertised and I got it. But in the end I want to buy a small nursery of my own. Nice dream, don't you think?"

"Why not?"

She smiled and lay back in her chair so that for a moment or two he had the familiar agony of seeing her without clothes, full breasted and sun-tanned and felt the blood tingle in his cheeks.

"Money."

"Ah, that." He laughed. "Well, you never know."

She shook her head and, putting down her cup, said, "I think we'd better be on our way. You sure you want to look round today?"

"Absolutely—so long as you are my guide."

He reached out a hand and helped her up from the chair. It was their first moment of physical contact and he made no effort to prolong it, the ritual moves, he sensed, would come naturally without planning. He knew it and she knew it, he was sure. For a moment or two the prospect was entirely without appeal for him. He was here to work, perhaps to find himself at last, to go on from *Green Pleasures* to do something worthwhile with his life. That was what he wanted—but in his heart and out of his self-knowledge he knew that Eros was not to be denied.

They took two hours walking around and he quickly realized that she was more knowledgeable than he was, but she laid no personal stress on this as some people might have done. There was no arrogance in her. When they met any of the gardeners working under her she stopped and introduced him and her manner was friendly and it was clear that the men liked her. The garden was laid out formally on the plateau around the Manor house, but its real beauty and charm for him lay in the plantings which had been made from the beginning of the nineteenth century in the hanging valleys and combes which ran down to the river. In one of these was a small lake overhung by Deodar and Blue Atlas mountain cedars and a magnificent swamp cypress with here and there a few Chusan palms to give a brief tropical effect. Beyond the lake, on a shoulder of the riverside cliffs was a large maze of laurel hedges which ran out to a Grecian-style temple of marble which overlooked a steep drop to the river below. Ferns grew everywhere and the well-kept paths twisted and turned through banks of rhododendrons, under overhanging magnolias whose names she chanted almost like a litany . . . *soulangiana* . . . *mollicomata* . . . so that after a while, knowing the indigestion of surfeit, he hardly listened intelligently as he thought of the years and years of hard work and love which generations of the Darvells had put into the place. And knew envy, too, for a family that could have been so endowed and able to create all this. Also at the back of his mind was the balancing thought that love was not to be measured by size. In their own way Aunt Lily and Miss Simpson knew the same joy and passion for their own small gardens.

He escaped—he smiled to himself as the word came unbidden into his mind—eventually to the Manor, knowing that the quality of his love of plants and shrubs and trees was looser yet perhaps more spontaneous than hers. For him they were individuals who responded to cherishing and care. For her they were always on parade to make a show. When he and Aunt Lily gardened they were humble but caring servitors. For Rachel Harrison they were subjects who had to behave. Basically, he felt—though this in no way militated against the erotic sympathy which he sensed between them—for her they were all part of a changing pageantry and parade to draw the admiration and wonder of visitors and thus enhance her reputation. At that moment he felt himself wondering over the wisdom of getting into bed with her. How much more than sexual pleasure might not be expected of him? She might well want to marry him and put him on parade too.

At the Manor Miss Latham met him. She was dressed in a light grey coat and skirt, a cameo brooch at the throat of a white blouse and a straw hat held in place by two jet-tipped hat pins over her grey hair. She told him that she was going out to lunch, but a tray would be sent up to the library for him and, as she took him to the library, said, "I see you've met Harrison."

"Oh, yes."

"That sounds a little guarded."

"Not at all. I liked her."

"Naturally. The male eye is at once captivated."

He laughed. "Well . . . let's say if I were a *Clerodendron trichotomum* and come September time weren't on parade all in white I'd get a sergeant major's rollicking."

Her laughter joined his, and she said, "Ah, but she's a dear girl. It's not for herself she wants the parade, you know. It's for the people who come to see it. Anyway, I will now make you privy to all the old account books and diaries and letters of the Darvells. And since the dust will be thick in your throat by lunchtime I've told them to send up a carafe of white wine for you. You're luckier than I am. I'm going to lunch with the Vicar. He's a home-made-wine fanatic. I fear today it could well be dandelion."

The library, which was on the first floor, was at the south end of the house and looked out over part of the gardens and the crests of a wood which covered the fall to the river. A single large window took up almost the whole of one wall. The other walls were furnished with glass-fronted bookcases and oil paintings of various Darvells, while in a corner close to the fireplace stood an old-fashioned Chubb safe of which Miss Latham gave him the key, saying, "All the stuff you will want is in there. The dear Bishop did start once to sort and catalogue it, but he never got far. So I fear you must start from scratch. Oh, dear—it does seem rather dreary work for a young man like you to be doing."

"I expect I shall survive."

"I'm sure you will . . ." She paused for a moment and her faded blue eyes were bright with spirit. ". . . I get the feeling that you are a natural survivor . . . or shall we say the cat that walks by itself?"

"You could say nothing to which I could take exception, my dear Miss Latham."

"Ah, now you flirt a little with me. How nice. I shall face the dandelion wine happily."

As she stood smiling at him in the pause before she went he saw her suddenly as a young girl . . . saw her in love with the

Bishop and losing him to her sister . . . saw her now, loving still, but happily resigned.

When she was gone, he went to the safe and opened it. A pile of files and some deed boxes, loosely stacked, fell out at his feet. So much, he thought, for the Bishop putting the family papers in order. He picked up the files and boxes and carried them to the long refectory table that ran down the middle of the room.

* * * *

Two days later Aunt Lily received a letter from Miss Simpson of Blackthorn Cottage. It read:

Dear Mrs. Hines,

*This is to thank you for sending me your cheque in settlement of your nephew's account with me. It really was a most kind gesture on your part, and a very touching one. However, I am returning the cheque because I am happy to tell you that Johnny—I refer to him so because we had become very friendly—called in here some time ago now on his way to Wales and settled up his account with me—as in my heart I always knew he would. He is a very nice young man, but like so many these days a little bit careless in his relationships. However, I'm sure that you know him and understand him far better than I do. He also presented me with a copy of his book—*Green Pleasures*—autographed personally to me. A great compliment! I have read it with immense pleasure . . . such distinction, wit and humour, and, of course, full of his love for growing things. I really do think he has a gift for writing which he should settle to seriously. But with a practical gift as well. My garden languishes with neglect under my poor and less vigorous care!*

I am enclosing, too, a silk handkerchief of his which he left behind. And, once again, thank you for your very kind gesture.

Yours sincerely,
Ada Simpson.

The handkerchief was freshly laundered and ironed. In one corner, picked out in black silk, were Johnny's initials. It was one of a set of six which she had hand-embroidered for a now distant birthday.

Liking the tone of Miss Simpson's letter, Aunt Lily sat down and wrote a letter of thanks to her and found herself being more spontaneous and confiding than she could ever have been in the first letter.

... I am sure you will have guessed by now that Johnny always causes me anxiety when he goes off into the blue without ever leaving me a forwarding address. It is a quirk which he has had since a very young man—so, please, dear Miss Simpson, if he should ever get in touch with you I would be glad to hear about it. How often the young can be unnecessarily cruel simply for the want of a little thought about others. However, I will spare you the moanings of one who should know better than to expect too much from the young and carefree. But if you ever hear from him or he calls on you, do please let me know about it.

I miss him, too, in the garden. Sometimes I have fancied that plants mean more to him than people. In addition to the garden I have two donkeys, nearly a dozen hens, and a nice old setter bitch. All company and comfort to me. So I suppose if one lacks the comfort and presence of one's own kind one at least should be grateful for the dependence on us of God's humbler creatures.

That evening, too, Aunt Lily telephoned Helder in London—principally to be able to say something in Johnny's favour—and told him that her nephew had repaid Miss Simpson on his way to Wales.

Helder said that he was very glad to hear it, but after she had rung off he sat unimpressed. John Corbin's character pattern was only too familiar to him. In the midst of their completely ruthless and amoral lives the John Corbins of this world felt compelled to make the occasional oblations to the gods of chance. A little not-too-expensive kindness here, a rare good deed to assuage self-disgust, even at times an isolated self-sacrifice to bring them close to the shriving of some sin. Conscience in some degree inhabited them and now and again it demanded recognition if only of a minimal kind.

The next morning, at his own request made some time before he had heard from Mrs Hines, he went to see Mr Barwick in his office. He was mildly blunt with him.

He said, "Mr Barwick—how long are you prepared to wait

until I turn up this John Corbin? So far, as I've already told you, I've come to a dead end. He's just taken off and the compass bearing he's given is, I'm sure, a wrong one. Of course, if you're prepared to make it a police matter—which you could, then without doubt they would find him."

"The last thing I want is to have the police know anything about this."

"Your wife knows you are trying to have him found?"

"No, she doesn't. But she would if I called in the police. I just want you to find him and then let me handle him. Do you think he's deliberately covering his traces?"

"Mr Barwick, that would be second nature to him. But if you told your wife what you were doing and I could have a discreet word with her—then something might turn up."

"I don't want her bothered at all. Surely you can get a line from this aunt of his or Miss Simpson?"

"From the first I can expect no help. And Miss Simpson has nothing more to give. On his way supposedly to Wales he paid off his debt to her."

"Are you telling me the whole thing is bloody hopeless unless you have a stroke of luck?"

"More or less."

"Then that's what we wait for. That's what I'll pay you for, and will go on paying you for. I can be patient. One, two, three years . . . some time I want to be face to face with him. Just that."

"Very well, Mr Barwick. Then we leave it like that."

"Exactly like that. And Mr Helder—don't tell me you haven't been in this situation before. At what looks like a dead end."

"Yes, many times."

"And what eventually happened?"

"In the main nothing. It's very easy to disappear in this world if you know you are wanted. The world is full of missing people living quite normal lives. The more the world documents its inhabitants the easier it becomes. Identity is a document, a piece of paper. The number of missing people is staggering. Three-quarters of them are living normal lives somewhere."

"Poppycock—this man doesn't know he's wanted."

"He doesn't have to. He was just born to travel light and change destinations at the smallest whim, Mr Barwick. Worse still, he has a gift for exciting affection and loyalty. The combination is an irritating and formidable one. If a man knows he's got to cover his traces he's open to mistakes. If he doesn't give it a thought then one has no grounds for deduction. However, if you're content with things as they are, then so am I. It's a pity though you won't let me talk to your wife."

"What the devil could she tell you that she hasn't already told me?"

"The things you would never think to ask her."

"Such as?" The question was put belligerently.

"Her answers to the questions a woman would ask and a man never think of."

"But you could?"

"Yes, I could. If I couldn't I wouldn't be doing this kind of work. That's why you're paying me, I hope—because I can do something that you can't."

Surprisingly Mr Barwick laughed and said, "My God, Helder, you're an odd, arrogant bugger."

"Yes, I believe I am in my quiet way."

"Well, I'll think about it."

"Thank you, Mr Barwick."

That evening while he and his wife were having a drink before dinner in their London flat Harry Barwick, who would never have considered himself an impulsive man, found himself saying, "Sue—there's something I want to ask you."

"Yes?" She turned from where she was standing, drink in hand, at the window looking out at the brown sweep of tide running up the river, the evening traffic moving across the Albert Bridge and the near greenery of the trees in Battersea Park, the sunlight crowning her fair hair with a faint halo.

"It's about this chap . . . Corbin. And——" he went on quickly, "——let me make it clear that you don't have to let me go any further than this if you'd rather not."

"If you want to ask me something why should I mind? You've a right."

"Well, I've never told you this, but I've hired a man to try and find him."

She smiled then. "I've never asked you, but I guessed you might have. But what would you do if you found him?"

"I don't know exactly. Punch the bastard on the nose? Probably not. Try and get the money back? I should think he's blued it all by now. No, I guess I wouldn't know what. Perhaps just have the satisfaction of catching up with him and then play it by ear from there."

She came over and sat on the arm of his chair and kissed him on the forehead. "Harry, I'm sorry . . ."

"No, I don't want any being sorry stuff. It's all over—as though it had never happened between us. But it's something quite different from that. I just feel that I don't want him to have the satisfaction of getting away with it. I just want to come face to face with him . . . and have him know that there are a lot of things I could do, might do. I don't know. I just have this feeling that I want to be face to face with the bugger."

"If you never did—would it make any difference to us?"

"You know it wouldn't. But the point is I just want to find him. Can you understand that?"

"Yes, I can. And I can understand, too, what you want to ask me."

"How do you mean?"

"Well . . . isn't it a bit like going to a doctor? He can ask questions and they're all impersonal so far as he's concerned. And you know he's never going to do or say anything unprofessional."

"You've got it a bit wrong. I don't want to ask you anything. But I did wonder whether you would have any objection to seeing my chap."

"What's he like? Shabby mackintosh?"

"God no! He's a sort of cross between a church warden and a rather stuffy old uncle. But he's got something that impresses me. I don't like him, but I respect him. What do you think? Would it upset you? I suppose he thinks that you might be able to give him some clue or something that would help him."

"This means a lot to you?"

"I suppose it does. I just want to come face to face with this Corbin. But I don't want you to have to do anything you don't fancy. You just say *no*—and we forget the whole thing."

She stood up and went back to the window and after a moment or two said, "Of course I'll see him. But not here—down in the country."

"You say that now, and I know why. But think it over for a day or so. Then let me know. You may want to change your mind."

She turned and shook her head. "Oh, no. If it's what you want, then I want it. We don't want any ghosts floating around, do we?"

He got up and went to her. With his arm around her he said, "You're more than I deserve . . ."

She shook her head. "Nonsense—it's the other way round." She turned and kissed him, feeling his arm firm about her.

CHAPTER FOUR

LIFE HAD BEGUN to take on a pleasant pattern and his days to be shaped into a comforting routine which he had not known for a long time. Some mornings Rachel called at his cottage with any supplies he had ordered and he would drive up to the Manor with her and walk back by himself when his day's work was done. Sometimes he drove up in his own car, would no more than glimpse her from the library window as she went about her work, but she would call at the cottage and have a drink with him before going down to Illaton Quay. There was nothing forced between them, no touch or caress, no admission of the compulsion towards each other that they shared.

Some mornings before he went into the library to work he would walk for an hour through the high summer splendour of the gardens with Cassidy at his heels and make now the acquaintance of some tree or shrub, some wide planting or landscaping that, apart from its beauty and splendour, would take him back to the littered refectory table in the library where in an old account book or the yearly work diary of Darvell grandfather or great-grandfather the simple genesis of present ripeness and maturity would be recorded . . . *Paid this day to R. Preston of Calstock, Mason, the final settlement of Twenty Pounds sterling for the building of the long wall in the new garden, bringing total cost of same to Eighty Pounds sterling*. Eighty pounds for the making of a walled garden where he had walked five minutes before, the wall rich with clematis and roses, *Tropaeolum speciosum* and jasmine, and the border below a riot of shrubs and flowering plants . . . *Kolkwitzia amabilis, hypericum* 'Rowallane', *pittosporums* and *cytisus*. Today he knew that no one could build such a wall for less than eight hundred pounds. He could imagine the old wilderness which the Darvells had turned into a paradise, and admire each generation's vision in setting hand to a creation they would never live to see in its maturity. Discounting the obvious sentimentality—though it was far from his nature to disavow sentiment—he had a tender and admiring regard for the men who had such a love for Illaton that they gladly set in motion so much work which they would never live to refresh their eyes on in its full ripeness. Though he would never have said it openly to anyone he was sure that in the order of human love gardens came close to God and perhaps next to human love.

The mass of stuff from the safe was in a chaotic muddle and for his first days he could do no more than sort it out slowly into different categories . . . diaries, letters, accounts, and plans for the various layouts for future plantings. Once this was done he would have to go methodically through each pile and begin making notes which eventually he would have to digest and order into a readable account of Illaton. Not some stilted guide book, nor meticulous record, but—as he had done in *Green Pleasures*—an entertaining, in its right sense, and a popular, in its best sense, work which would be a tribute to all the past Darvells and which would bring pleasure, too, to the Bishop and absolve him from his own fault of neglect.

Usually he had lunch on a tray in the library by himself, though there were some days when Miss Latham would join him, and others when she would entice him, almost to the point of mild bullying, down to the dining room to share some special dish which she announced could not be rightly enjoyed unless it were eaten in style and in company—such as a fresh-run salmon taken in the nets off Illaton Quay. He was not long in understanding that, although she had plenty of friends in the district, and entertained quite often, she was lonely, not from lack of company, but from a need for some close confidant, and he had a suspicion that, for some reason—perhaps that the Bishop had chosen him and therefore he was some kind of pale surrogate for the man she loved—he fed some small part of her closely bridled long-nursed anguish. How many people, he thought, who loved hopelessly, soothed their anguish by talking to someone about the object of their hopeless and forever homeless dreams. With a kindness which he always found ready in him for her sort . . . the sort, too, of all the Miss Simpsons and his Aunt Lily . . . he found it easy to maintain a delicate and comforting relationship. Not father confessor, or even *fidus Achates*, but an undemanding listener in whom discretion and sympathy had been discerned. When he felt it needed he would feed her weakness with some remark or question that gave her fresh impetus. She was wealthy, too, in her own right, so Rachel had told him. Well, that was always a nice thing to know. He lived in the Garden of Eden at the moment—but the Fates might at any hour call turn-out time, and if they did he knew that she could be prevailed upon not to let him go without some provision.

Lunching with her one day, he said, "Is it true, Miss Latham, that there's a possibility that the Bishop might one day . . . well, go on to much higher things?"

"You mean York or Canterbury?"

"Yes, I do."

"It's a possibility . . . not just for him, but for any Bishop."

"Is it something he would want?"

"Oh, dear, Johnny—what a question."

It was the first time that she had ever called him by his Christian name and he made no sign of the use.

He said, "I don't understand how that kind of thing works. But I suppose like a lot of high preferments in this world virtue sometimes is conditioned by expediency?"

"Yes, I think that's true. I sometimes wish that the dear man would pay a little more attention to . . . well, some moderation of his public remarks. Mind you, he has improved a lot. But, bless the dear man, there's a fire in his belly about some things. Quite rightly too. But sometimes——" she gave him a swift, almost mischievous grin, her blue eyes lively with spirit, "——I wish he would not rush into things . . . political things. You know . . . Amnesty and human rights, and religious freedom."

"Christ took a scourge to the money-lenders in the temple."

"And quite rightly—because it was possible and the result certain. But you can't whip the masters of the Kremlin into giving a genuine charter of religious freedom to their peoples . . . their slaves. One freedom begets another. This they know."

"But someone has to speak out—as the Bishop does."

She smiled. "Of course—but it is better for *that* someone not to be too highly placed and with the possibility of being even higher placed to do it. The Establishment is as sensitive as a jelly-fish. I deplore it, but it is the truth. It would be better if the Bishop—though I would not dare even hint this to him—moderated his public protests considerably. Let him wait and nourish his feelings privately until, if God so willed, he was in a high position and unassailable. But there it is, some men cannot see that the truth is often the enemy of ultimate immunity to serve God and Christianity. Does that sound cynical?"

"I don't think so, but a lot of people would. Nevertheless, you may be quite wrong. Perhaps this is the time to speak out as loud as one can. In fact, I think it is. Thunder from the pulpit. Diplomacy is an age-old expediency with little to do with Holy Writ. But religion has now come into the market place and must raise its voice unashamedly with the other hustlers and pedlars."

Miss Latham leaned back and laughed. "Oh, Johnny—that is the first time I've ever heard you talk in something of the manner in which you write. But you may be right. Perhaps one day, who knows, there will be a Crown Appointments Commission of the General Synod of the Church that will decide to move with the times and then the Bishop's name could be one of the two submitted to the Prime Minister, and maybe the one which in the end is nominated by the Crown on his advice. Now, delay no more over this delicious soufflé . . . and, yes, you can help me to a little more *chianti bianco* . . ."

Later that afternoon, working over his material, reading the garden diaries, the old ink faded to the colour of sere oak leaves, he found himself a little touched with pity that so much love in her could have turned to a protective worship which, though she might not recognize it, made her very vulnerable to his kind. How often, he wondered, did she fall for some plausible begging letter, how many acting lame dogs had she helped over stiles? In other circumstances than the present he could have abused her good nature and generosity himself. The Darvells had never suffered from such compassion as hers. Already in his random glances at the diaries he had noted entries detailing the dismissal of gardeners for being drunk or immoral practices, and one—*Mrs. Grange, the housekeeper, this day informed me that the under house-maid, Mary Gould, is four months gone with child by Anstey the groom.*

Summoned Anstey at once and gave him the choice to marry the girl forthwith or to leave my service at once without any character commendation from me. He said at once that he would marry Mary Gould, knowing full well that without a good word from me he would find no employ within fifty miles of Illaton. Told him he could have the Wood Cottage rent free but to be refurbished by his own labour and expense. Am glad he stays for I have met none to bring on a horse as he does and so unstinting of care with his charges. So all parties go their ways well satisfied. So had written the Bishop's great-grandfather in 1854 who in his last years had commissioned the little temple overlooking the river to be built, and whose portrait by Sir Martin Archer Shee hung over the fireplace in the dining room.

That evening Rachel called on him on her way home which she had done once or twice before. They chatted for a while over their drinks and then as he finished telling her the story of Anstey the groom, she stayed silent for quite a while, looking straight at him, her dark eyes fixed on him and he had the impression that she was deliberating some move on her part, some move that she might at any vagrant disruption suddenly decide not to make. He gave her time, watching her without embarrassment and then as he saw the slight shift of her eyes and the gathering of herself to rise, he said, "Why don't you say it?"

"Should I?"

"Of course. Because if you don't now you will some other time. You know that, don't you?"

"Yes, I do. What is it about you . . . about us?"

He shrugged his shoulders. "We'll know when it comes. I'm happy to leave it like that."

"You've had something like it before? You see—I haven't."

"Something like it, yes. But it fizzled . . . died away on the midnight air, or like a rainbow, boldly there, all beauty through the rain and then, the next moment, just rain. You like that kind of talk?"

"From you, yes." She laughed. "You're an odd sod, aren't you?"

"That's better than just being a plain run-of-the-mill sod. Just now though I'm beginning to think there's hope for me and I mustn't let it slip by. Somewhere there had been waiting this time-slip, this Illaton, this you which I could easily have missed.

Nearly did miss because I as near as a touch threw the Bishop's letter to me in the waste-paper basket. Then when I got here and saw you I told myself that it was meant. Is this helping you any?"

"Yes. It's nonsense, of course. But it helps."

"Nonsense is only the other side of logic. But you don't get to spin the coin so that you can fake its fall. The gods do that and don't bother to fake either. So spit it out, my dear Rachel."

"Astonish you?"

"Yes, of course. Do that."

"I must be mad."

"Then go along with it. You can't escape it. He said so."

"Who? What are you talking about?"

"The one who said, 'But do thy worst to steal thyself away, For term of life thou art assured mine . . .' "

"Who said that?"

"Shakespeare. Who else? But I have to confess that there are times when I prefer Kipling—that's the earthy sod in me. Now—spit it out."

"I'd like to take you out to lunch on Sunday."

"I accept."

"Oh, good!"

He went to her and took her right hand, feeling the dryness of skin from her gardening and imagining without lust the smoothness of the rest of her body. It was all happening and he had decided to go along with it. If it were not to be proved true, then it would be a diversion and always handy refreshment from work on the Darvell papers. He said, "Can Cassidy come too?"

"Of course."

He kissed her sun-browned knuckles and saw the shadow of honest soil beneath her finger nails and knew that even so had Eve's been, and knew as well that even if it proved that Eros was playing him false it would be a diversion and a glimpse of some paradise always to be denied him.

When she had driven off he stood in the evening and considered it a pity that the season for the singing of nightingales had passed, but then how often the gods were slipshod about small details. Swifts passed overhead screaming and high above and out of sight a Concorde aircraft devoured time noisily. Time with its something or other bears all our sins away. How true. At this moment he felt completely shrived.

* * * *

It was no surprise to Helder that Barwick had changed his mind about his seeing Mrs Barwick or that his wife had acquiesced. Whatever her personal feelings it was clear that they would be suborned to her desire to please him. The erring wife had no grounds for opposition. To please him, no matter how, had to be all her desire for it was in a way the final act of shriving. Nevertheless as he talked to her now in the large sitting room overlooking the terrace and the water garden, the windows open to let in the summer scent of flowers and new-mown hay from the meadow across the river, he sensed that the whole affair had become a matter of indifference to her, relegated to a commonplace occurrence which the passage of time might well find her repeating with someone else. Confession brought, after a self-denying interval, the licence to sin again. The fidelity of a true marriage, whether she understood it or not, would always escape her—and Barwick too. Too many marriages foundered on the rock of self-will despite all the navigational aids of goodwill.

He said, "If you think, now that I'm here, it is all going to be too embarrassing, Mrs Barwick—then say so, and I will go. I am sure that your husband will understand."

She shook her head. "I'm not embarrassed. And I'm sure that you won't say anything that will make me so, Mr Helder. Naturally, I would rather this wasn't happening, but—and I mean this—I love my husband and if this is what he wants . . . well, then it's all right."

"That's very good of you. But tell me, which would you prefer—that I caught up with John Corbin or not?"

"It's a matter of indifference to me, But my husband wants it . . . though I doubt whether he will really do anything positive even if you find him. Harry's no saint. What could he do when he comes face to face with himself? He keeps a woman in London. I don't mind. And I don't mind talking to you. Ask what you want Mr Helder. You won't embarrass me." As she spoke she got up and walked to him and took his almost full sherry glass and smiled at him. "You should have said you're a dry sherry man." She went to an English lacquer cabinet on a carved gilt stand which had been turned into a drinks cupboard and filled a fresh glass with dry sherry for him. Helder, taking the glass from her, asked, "Did Corbin ever talk much about himself?"

"Not a lot. And when he did I didn't necessarily believe him. I'd read him pretty well, and I knew what I was doing. But, of course, quite frankly he was worth it. He just knew how to treat a woman. Naturally a lot of men do, but his way was different. Even when he knew I was encouraging him, he didn't rush in. I used to think about it a lot before we . . . well, before it really started. He didn't push aside all the small things and charge straight for the bedroom pulling me along. Afterwards when we were able to talk freely, I asked him if this was the way he always was and he said something very nice. He said women were like gardens and good gardeners were always patient and could wait for the time of full flowering because there was joy, too, in marking the first budding, the first signs of leaf. The glory of the true flowering was a reward for all the love and care which had gone before. Sounds sloppy, doesn't it? Saying it to me at my age. But I shall never forget it. Harry never in his life could say anything like that, or even think it." She paused and smiled. "I suppose in your time you've had a lot to do with silly women like me?"

"I think you're far from silly. But you know now that he's a rogue, don't you?"

"You're damned right I do. But I don't really care much. It's all over. The money means nothing. I was bloody silly about that—but it came right. That's one thing to be said for Harry. I can't think why he's still fussing about it. But he is and there it is. So feel free to ask me what you want."

"Thank you. I presume that Corbin never mentioned the names of any friends—or where he came from, or what he really did in life?"

"No . . . well . . . He said he'd been abroad and was back on leave."

"Abroad where?"

"South America somewhere. Pretty vague, isn't it?

"It's been used before, yes. Did you make love in this house?" The abruptness of the question left her unmoved, which interested him.

"Oh, no. That I couldn't have done. We had a few week-ends in hotels, but I was never very comfortable. Harry and I have friends all over the place. We could easily have been unlucky and run into one of them. I had to say no in the end."

"So what did he do?"

"We used to go to Exeter. He had a friend there with a flat, but she was away and had said he could use the place. It's only a few hours drive from here and we would go down, sometimes for a night, sometimes for a long week-end." She paused for a moment and then said lightly, "My God—listen to me. I'm telling you things that Harry doesn't know because he's never asked me."

"Can you remember the address? The name of the woman who had the flat?"

"Yes, I can. On the flat door was one of these little brass holder things for a card. Her name was . . . now let me think . . . yes, Miss S. Barnes. Yes, that's it because I asked him who she was and he said an old girl friend from his university days. He was at Oxford, you know—or so he said."

"He was there. And the address of this flat?"

"Oh, yes. It's Yeo Mansions, Grove Road. Near the Cathedral." She looked at the open pad on Helder's knee. "Aren't you going to write it down?"

"There's no need. I shan't forget. Tell me, he had a key for this flat? He didn't pick it up at the porter's lodge or anything?"

"I wouldn't know. He was always there before me and I always left before him."

"And why did you ever come to write him letters which he later made you pay for?"

"Oh, dear . . . yes, that . . ." She went to the window and looked out. Helder waited patiently for her to go on. She was a tall, well-built woman, a robust animal, surrounded by every luxury a husband could give her, but every so often the emotionally starved animal demanded attentions which Harry Barwick never suspected—so she turned to someone else for them. In a way, he supposed, one could make a case for Corbin except that he should have obliged her without degrading her and ruining all memory of an idyllic passage in her life. She turned, shrugged her shoulders, and said, "I suppose because I was sloppy. Until I married, Harry was the only man in my life. Harry I'm sure has never written a love letter in his life. I mean a real love letter. John Corbin did—and I . . . well, I adored it. And I wrote back. Mind you I wasn't taken in by him. It was all fun and games. Make believe. There had been others before him. But he was rather different. He wrote me poetry too."

"Poetry?"

"Oh, yes. The first man who ever did. Can you imagine my husband doing that? Not in a million years. I've burned them all. But I remember some of them . . ." She turned from the window and quoted, " '*O, never say that I was false of heart. Though absence seem'd my flame to qualify. As easy might I from myself depart As from my soul, which in thy breast doth lie* . . .' Isn't that wonderful?"

"It is indeed, Mrs Barwick. Clearly a very talented man." Not for anything would he have disillusioned her by telling her that it had been written well over three hundred years before Corbin's time.

Mrs Barwick came back to him and for a few moments looked down at him before saying, "Now I know that I like you. You're a very kind man."

"Thank you. But I'm just doing a job in the best way I can."

"No, I don't mean that. I'm sure you are very good at your work. But you're very gentle too with people's feelings. You see, I've been mad about poetry all my life and I remember it. Just give me a line—and you know what I want."

Helder smiled and quoted, " '*From you I have been absent in the Spring* . . .'?"

" '*When proud-pied April, drest in all his trim, Hath put a spirit of youth in everything* . . .' I never let on that I knew the Sonnets probably better than he did. Why spoil the fun? And he did write some of his own and it wasn't bad. I used to work once in Harrods and when times were slack or my back ached to hell I'd just go off into the other world . . . calling back the poetry I knew. And more than that—I enjoyed every minute with John, though I would only say this to you. I love my husband—but sometimes a woman finds that love is not enough. Now I think you had better go before I become too indiscreet. Unless, of course, there's anything else you want to ask me?"

Helder stood up. "I don't think so, Mrs Barwick. You've been very kind and very helpful."

He drove back to the spot on the river where he had left his sister collecting plants and they had a picnic lunch together. On their way home they made a small detour for him to call on Miss Simpson at Blackthorn Cottage. When he rejoined his sister she asked, "Was she happy to see you?"

"Very."

"And why did you go to see her again?"

"Out of kindness. She leads a lonely life. And anyway, you never know, do you, what the gods will send?"

"From the smugness of your tone, James, I fancy they did send something."

"A little. When John Corbin called to settle up her account he also made her a present of a book. It's called *Green Pleasures* and written by him. Would you be good enough to get me a copy, my dear? It's published by Collard and Simms."

* * * *

With Cassidy in the back of his car he drove down to Illaton Quay on Sunday morning. The sky was cloudless and the tide was running in fast covering the mud flats. High above the wooded heights a pair of buzzards circled lazily on a rising air current. Rachel's place was a converted old stone warehouse standing apart from the other houses and cottages and the inn.

As he drew up she came out to him wearing tan-coloured slacks and a high-necked cashmere sweater, a carryall bag slung over her shoulder.

He kissed her briefly, almost formally, on the side of her cheek.

She said, "I've borrowed a small boat with an outboard engine. What about Cassidy? Do you want him to come?"

"He'll make up his own mind."

Cassidy took one look at the small dinghy as they went down the quayside steps and then turned away and flopped down in the sun by a stone bollard.

They went up slowly on the tide, a handful of young black-headed gulls keeping them company overhead, the great rock and tree-scarped rise of the Illaton bluff throwing back the echoes of their small motor. Rachel sat at the tiller and he squatted in the bows and watched her and wondered why he was taking it all so calmly and making no effort to analyse or question the certainty in him, not the obvious, soon to be realized part of it, but the overall inevitability. Nothing had ever been like this before and he was neither rejecting nor welcoming it. He could sit, it seemed, almost apart, a spectator watching himself and her without any will of his own. Just as nothing could untimely change the flow of the tide which carried them upriver so, he was sure, nothing could deflect or break the course of this day's foredeemed sequences. For a while, perhaps forever, he mused, this day would mark them. Coming to Illaton had been a gift, but he knew now only the first of many and there was no particle of cynicism in him. He was content to let the conjunctions—already determined—of time and chance and place frame for them both a true bliss.

He said suddenly, "Has anything like this ever happened to you before?"

She shook her head. "No. Something like it . . . but far from it."

"It could be bad. I'm not a very nice sort."

"It could be anything. Bad or good. But I don't have any choice. Don't want any choice."

"What would we do? I'm a gypsy. No money except a few thousand quid waiting in trust for me when I'm forty. I'm unreliable and have itchy feet."

"I'll butter them." She laughed. "Don't look so serious, Johnny. I'm a very practical person and good with money. I want a proper nursery of my own . . . our own, if you'd like that. No damn garden-centre place. Perhaps specialize . . . alpines or shrubs. I've got fifteen thousand pounds."

"You'd need a lot more."

"Borrow, beg, or steal?"

He laughed and then lit two cigarettes and handed her one. "I'm good at all three."

"What do you want?"

"Something much the same as you do. Or so it seems at the moment. Yes, I think that. And I want the other thing, of course—though I didn't know it until I came here."

"'And what's that?"

"'I'm sick of the hired woman. I'll kiss my girl on her lips!'"

She laughed. "And so you shall. But for now sit square on the thwart. You're giving the boat a list. Was that a quotation?"

"Yes."

"I practically never read anything but technical books and nurserymen's catalogues."

"Well, a little fiction creeps in even with them."

The river swung round a sharp bend and there before them was the long straight reach of the Tamar running up to the Calstock viaduct, its lofty piers and graceful arches spanning the river and the village houses, bright and colourful, almost Italianate, clinging to the right bank.

They went ashore and had a bar lunch at the inn on the quay and afterwards walked up the river beyond the tidal point. As though to greet them as they sat down in the meadow grass, a summer grilse coming free of the salt flow into the bright fresh water leaped and sent a great lacing of rainbow-touched spray into the air. They lay back together, but separated, needing no present contact or regard for one another, their eyes on the cloudless sky, and contentment possessed them. So much so that he felt hard put not to believe that it was all a dream or, perhaps nearer home, some sudden reversion to adolescent romanticism, some uninformed and immature first stirring of eroticism, and almost wished it were because it had been so long since just four legs in a bed had been all his content. And hoped, almost, that he would wake up tomorrow and find it all a dream. Felt this so much that he suddenly shivered and had the gut-wracking impulse to get to his feet and run, knowing that he had no grace in himself to live with the promised future.

Maybe Rachel sensed his mood, for at this moment she reached out and took his hand in hers. They lay watching the swallows hawking for the high-flying insects.

Going back he took the tiller and when they reached the quay Cassidy was waiting for them and Rachel fed him with the remains of their sandwiches and cheese which they had brought away from the inn. But when they moved towards her house the dog whined at the door of the car and Corbin opened it and let him in.

She made supper for them while he sat on a stool in the kitchen and kept her company. Right across the grain of the feelings they shared their talk was casual, commonplace, but far more guarded on his side than hers. She talked about her childhood and parents and then of her days at horticultural college and the jobs she had had before coming to Illaton. When he asked her a question it was answered fully as though, he felt, she had a need to exhibit herself and her past in detail. But when in turn she asked him a question and he either avoided it or answered sometimes briefly, or now and then with a broad generalization to avoid a truth he was not yet ready to tell, she put no pressure on him as though she sensed that there was all the world and time enough for him to conquer his wariness. Once or twice he was near to the edge of resentment at her show of confidence and certainty, no matter that he shared, though needed more time to demonstrate in confidence and freedom, all that absolute knowledge of themselves so suddenly to have flowered to surprise them.

When they went up to her bedroom after their meal and made love and speech was the least part of their communion he was happier because there was no impediment lingering from the past to inhibit either of them. Bodies and sensations were melded and their passion carried them free of all constraints or the risk of some revelation as yet far too soon to be made, though he knew that if the bondage to which they were both committing themselves were to be final then at some early moment he would have to shrive himself before her . . . *With mine own weakness being best acquainted, Upon thy part I can set down a story—Of faults conceal'd, wherein I am attainted.* In the dying light of the evening, the sweet rankness of the now exposed mud flats coming through the window, he knew that, had he spoken aloud, there would have been no recognition of the borrowed lines for there was no poetry in her of that kind. She was simple and uncomplicated, a lovely animal; and, too, she was straightforward and practical and perhaps wise enough even now to know him without knowing anything of him. That he wanted her, needed her to give his life true direction and meaning, he shrank from acknowledging. There was superstition enough in him, though, to force the belief that the continuing gift of herself, naked now in light sleep against his side, was—if rejected—never to be matched by anyone else. But—if accepted—where then would he be led? What was food for love was not food for living. Handling a run-down, never-to-prosper, small nursery between them? Or a struggling garden centre in some suburb with credit dwindling and their small capital slowly being eaten up . . . Oh, God, yes—and maybe children? Not even maybe, because she would want them. He would be mad to contemplate such a future. Freedom farewell.

He rolled off the bed and in the last of the dusk began to dress. She woke and watched him and after a while said, "You don't have to worry, Johnny."

Lightly, he said, "I have no worries. Only problems."

"Such as?"

"Of worthiness."

"Why bother? I love you and that means whatever you are."

"And I love you. But that is no part of my problem. All my life I've treated each day as a new adventure, a new lease of time in which to astonish myself at some doubtful and often dishonest stratagem. I never thought to find myself on the road to Damascus . . . or rather at the crossroads leading to it."

"Nothing you've done or been makes any difference."

"How can you be so damned sure?"

"I don't know, but I am. It's not a matter of knowing. It's a simple fact of being. I've been in bed before, but not with you. I've gone up the river before with someone for an outing, but not with you. And now—I've never been in bed before or up the river before with anyone but you. That's enough for me. What more do you want?"

He laughed, but it covered a new understanding in him, the awareness of the strength of her instinctive simplicity. He said, "I'd be happier if I had a certificate of worthiness and a guarantee of future good behaviour to hand over to the Registrar of Marriages. I'm a sod, you know. And you're the first one I've ever admitted it to. Don't ask me why."

"I don't have to."

"You're mad."

"For the first time in my life. I just want to be with you whichever way you see it. There's no need of a certificate to hand over to anyone. So, there's no need for me to say any more. Give Cassidy a run before you drive off or he'll probably pee all over the back seat. That's why he wouldn't come in the boat. He's embarrassed by his own incontinence. We all have something that embarrasses us. The thing is not to let it get you down."

He went to the bed and leaned over and kissed her. With her lips on his and her arms around him, he thought that if he could be transported back now to the moment of opening the Bishop's letter, knowing that she was waiting for him in Illaton, he would have thrown it into the waste-paper basket. Settled and lasting relationships were no part of his scene.

He gave Cassidy a run and then drove back to Illaton Manor. The next day he denied himself his usual routine of walking round some part of the gardens before starting work because he had no wish to meet Rachel since his irresolution was still strong.

He worked in the library bringing the Darvell papers and estate records into some rough chronological order so that eventually he could go through them in proper sequence and begin to make notes and take extracts from which to frame his final work for the Bishop. It was already clear to him that his chief problem would be less what to use than what must be rejected. The family, it was clear, from the beginning of the nineteenth century had not only from their own industry become wealthier and wealthier, but had also been smiled upon by good fortune. Envy ran gently in him at the thought of their Midas touch.

An entry in the day book of the Bishop's great-grandfather, Henry Boyd Darvell, for September 1847 ran:

It is now a little under three years since the seventh Duke of Bedford granted a mining lease of twenty-one years on his land at Gunnislake and a stock issue was made of Great Devon Consuls at one pound each.

Under the hand of God the venture has prospered and the mine now produces more copper than any other in Europe. At the time I bought one hundred one pound shares. Today those same one pound shares are worth eight hundred pounds each. After due thought I have decided to sell half my holding and with the money shall build a lady chapel in the wood clearing overlooking the river and with any surplus begin the new plantings of Deodar and Atlas cedars to the south of the wall garden. I shall hope that my good friend the Bishop of Truro will consecrate the chapel in due time and that God's hand will rest benignly on the growth of the new cedars. It is a pity that the arsenical and other wastes now leaching into the Tamar from the mining and other works have killed the salmon run for good. But for every good in this world there is always surely some evil, but I console myself by the knowledge that the eye and mind of God reaches far beyond the small handful of years which is our lot . . .

Wryly Corbin thought that to him that hath shall be given. For one hundred pounds invested Henry Darvell had picked up eighty thousand pounds in a few years, and had made good use of it. There was trouble over the lady chapel for the Bishop of Truro was opposed to the idea. Not one to be trifled with Henry Darvell built instead the mock Grecian temple as a pagan riposte. The cedars stood high now, but were approaching their end. And God, of course, had known what He was doing. Around Calstock and Gunnislake the mining and granite quarrying had all long ceased and the salmon had long ago returned to the river. An entry in the journal of the Bishop's father, John Boyd Darvell, which he had come across a little before read:

June 17th, 1911. A message from Endsleigh today that the Duke of Bedford took an eight pound salmon from his water—the first since the mining ceased. This, no doubt, a splendid occasion for him, but I cannot forbear to recollect the terrible misery that plagued this valley when the mining stopped at the turn of the century and so many good men and true with their families were forced to emigrate to foreign parts in seek of work. Out of His infinite wisdom God balances each joy with its fellow grief and for a purpose beyond all human understanding. The late-

flowering Rhodendron crassum *was in full fragrant bloom this morning . . .*

Corbin left his table and went to the window and helped himself to a glass of sherry—a mid-morning touch of serendipity, Miss Latham had said when she brought it, to clear his throat of dust. On the table lay a whole past world. But with him it was the living moment. Unexpected bitterness turned in him. Whenever he had—infrequently—bought shares they had turned up their toes and died. Envy, too, moved slowly through him. He humoured its assault as he remembered Rachel lying in the summer grasses, sleeping naked in the twilight on her bed, and there was a strong feeling in him that without cause—and certainly not from merit—something was being offered to him. She should have been like any other woman to him, an entertainment and—if the chance arose—a source of some small and mean profit. That's how he liked it to be . . . He would be out of his mind to seek anything else. God had shaped him that way. There was nothing to be done about it. And suddenly he was decided. Whatever there was going to be between them had to be for fun only, and fun could only promise a short future. She could either take it or leave it.

He went back to his work and immersed himself in it. After lunch he worked through until six o'clock oblivious of the passage of time and marking, in a detached but exciting way, the rise in him of pleasure as he began to see how he could shape the book which he had been commissioned to do. Outside, for it was one of the open days for the gardens, visitors passed by, but he was hardly aware of them. The gardens he was coming to love, but more rewarding to him at the moment were the records under his hands of their creation. The real triumph lay not in the final accomplishment—though that such gardens could ever be truly said to be finished he knew was a paradox—but in the passion over the long years of the various Darvells. That was a love affair which had survived from generation to generation.

He went back to his cottage and fixed himself a light supper and then went up to the little work room under the roof and sat blocking out a rough form for the way he was beginning to see his book could be shaped. As the dusk began to fall he went down to take Cassidy for a stroll before going to bed. But as he moved off Cassidy refused to follow him and sat by his car and whined. He would have moved on without the dog but Cassidy suddenly barked and the sound in the still, warm gloaming seemed loaded with an imperative insistence which unexpectedly moved him sharply. All his life he had believed in luck, in omens and portents. He could not have lived as he had without some substitutes for logical and rational decisions. God and or the Devil made a sign. Without making any effort to isolate from which provenance he now fancied this one came, he found himself going to the car and opening the door. Cassidy jumped in. He got in himself and began to drive down to Illaton Quay.

When he walked into her room she was sitting by the window with a lamp close to her on a small, round table working on a piece of embroidery set in a tambour frame. She looked up at him and smiled through a pair of steel-rimmed spectacles perched low on her nose. He went to her and kissed her on the forehead and said, "Surprised?"

"No. Happy, yes. But if you hadn't come it would have been all right. I should have understood."

He grinned. "Cassidy brought me."

"Perhaps he's not a dog at all. Some disguised imp . . . playing tricks with us."

"I don't care." He took the needlework frame from her and examined it. It showed, partly finished, a clump of gentians flowering against a rock.

She said, "I do about one a month and they sell them for me in the garden shop at the Manor. Help yourself to a drink, Johnny. Or if you like . . . have second thoughts. They are often the wiser ones."

"Too late." He walked to the sideboard and helped himself to a whisky. He gave her a look but she shook her head. He went back and sat on the window seat close to her and said, "I think I can make a good job of the Darvell book. There's a mass of stuff in their papers. I began to get really excited today."

"How do you write . . . in longhand?"

"Yes."

"I've got a typewriter. When I wouldn't go to University my

father made me take a business course before horticultural college. If you like I will type your stuff." She reached out and took his glass, sipped at it and then handed it back to him.

He drank, his lips on the brim of the glass where hers had rested, and he knew that she had noticed this. He said, "That would be helpful." The words were polite and banal but he knew that they were committing both of them.

CHAPTER FIVE

HELDER VERY SOON realized that if Sarah Barnes did happen to have any knowledge of John Corbin's whereabouts she would be very unlikely to help him. Not that she was unfriendly or antagonistic towards him. She was charming and easy and also slightly amused. Worthless and errant the man might be, but there was clearly some element in his nature which evoked a protective instinct in the women he courted or used. Knowing that she was a school teacher he had risen very early and driven down to Exeter on a Sunday morning and called at her flat at half-past ten.

She had shown no surprise when he had explained that he was acting for the husband of a woman with whom Corbin had been intimate and had then used this bond to move on to blackmail.

She said, "He is completely amoral where money and women are concerned. Unless a woman realizes that—and she should because the signs are there to be read—then she's in for possible trouble."

"Did that happen with you?"

"No. I have no ties, and no money to speak of. I was quite safe."

"You knew he was using your flat at times?"

"Of course."

"Bringing a woman here?"

"He never said so specifically. But he's seldom specific. But all the signs were here to read when I came back. A lipstick left behind. Her scent still in the air."

"And you didn't mind?"

"Of course not. We're not in love. I know what he is. He would have offered me the same unquestioning courtesy if the roles had been reversed and I wanted to bring a friend to his flat." She smiled. "That's assuming he ever would have anything permanent like a flat."

"Did he give you any idea of his future plans?"

"Vaguely and almost certainly untruthfully. He said he was going to Wales to hold the fort at a friend's house. But I doubt that for two reasons. I've never known him to be positive even about his immediate future. Or specifically truthful about his next place of call. When he left here he sent me flowers. A quite genuine gesture of affection—but this time also mildly revealing."

"How?"

"Well . . . from here if you were going to Wales you would have to go north up the M5 to Bristol to take the Severn Bridge. The flowers came from a shop which is to the west of the town. I would say that's where he's gone—westwards."

"Does he always act like that?"

"What? Covering his tracks? Yes, I think so. It comes naturally to him. Not necessarily because he knows he's being followed. In your case clearly not. No, it's just part of his behaviour pattern, dictated by his instinct for survival. All animals obey it even when they know there is no immediate threat to their lives. To survive you must assume always that there is a threat somewhere ahead. Disaster may not come today, but—for the Corbins—you must act as though it well could."

Helder laughed. "Is it botany you teach?"

"Yes. But the same principle applies. Deception, camouflage, a hundred seeds in a pod and only a few ever to germinate, scents, colours and nectars . . . all part of the apparatus of survival."

"I think you love him."

"Oh, no, Mr Helder. Quite wrong. Make love. But not love. He's the last man I would ever marry. I'm sorry for any woman who ever really falls in love with him. He's a recidivist. Tell me—what would your outraged husband do if you ever found Corbin for him?"

"I'm not too sure. But that's not the point. I want to find him for my own personal satisfaction. Have you any faintest idea why he might have gone west?"

"No. He might do it for the most basic of reasons. That he was travelling in the morning, for instance, and it was pleasanter to drive without having the sun in his eyes. The Devil, as you must long have learnt, looks after his own. John has no true destination. The time might come when he will have. When that happens you could find it easy to track him down." She got up and went to a small bureau by the window and coming back to him, handed him a slim gold cigarette lighter, saying, "On one of their visits she left this here. It had slipped down the back of an armchair."

"Thank you. I'll see it goes back to its owner. You could have given it to him."

"I know. But he would have pawned or sold it. I thought I'd save him from one small sin. And now I'm going to push you out. I have forty botany test papers to mark, most of them from girls who have no care for the bees and the flowers, but all of whom in time, no doubt, will know the joys and traumas of procreation." Then, as he stood up, she went on, "Yours must be a very strange life."

He smiled. "Yes, strange, often frustrating. But sometimes, and not in any professional way, very rewarding. You'd be surprised at the number of very nice people I meet."

She laughed, and said, "It's a pity about the test papers. Otherwise I might ask you to stay to lunch."

That evening, sitting in his London flat with his sister who was reading a book while he sat listening to a Chopin prelude on the radio, he said, "Did you ever get a copy of John Corbin's book?"

"Yes, I did. I'm reading it now—and enjoying it very much. And I don't understand why the man can behave as he does and yet write so well. The whole thing is a complete contradiction."

"The Medicis loved beauty, were great patrons of the arts—but they knew all about poisons and their use."

"Maybe . . . but I find it hard to reconcile your John Corbin with the one who wrote all this. Listen."

She read aloud:

Deep in the hearts of all gardeners is an abiding nostalgia for the Garden of Eden, for the perfection which Adam and Eve knew before the Fall. The world is full of their suburban and rural descendants slaving to restore Eden yet knowing in their hearts that, despite their transient rewards, the perfection they long for can never be. From that first sin sprang all others, and from that first disruption of perfect order we have inherited the challenging chaos of random fruitfulness and heart-breaking failures. It is only the indomitable optimism and pig-headedness of all good gardeners which keeps them going. Nearer we may be to God's heart in a garden, but at times our language must surprise and sadden Him. However, I have always felt that there is a special dispensation made for all those who get dirt under their nails and sudden wilt on their clematis plants. And further, it seems to me that there is some room for presuming a considerable Divine partiality to bless the work of those who have dedicated their spiritual lives to Him. Some of the loveliest gardens in the world have been the work of eminent divines and churchmen. Perhaps, though, there is no contradiction for men mostly love plants as possessions of great beauty whereas from the humblest parish priest to the highest prelate it is manifest beyond question that the creation of a garden is an act of worship. After all, most of it is done upon one's knees.

"Now," she said when she had finished reading, "does that sound like a man who seduces women and then makes them pay for the privilege?"

"No, I can't say it does. Yet we know it to be so. Well . . . well . . ." He was silent for a while, then reached out and turned off his music, and went on, "There is something I would like you to do."

"If it is embarrassing, no."

"In no way. I telephoned his publishers when I learnt about the book and asked for his address and they said that they were not at liberty to divulge it. If I wrote a letter, though, they would be glad to forward it."

"But you know his address. He lives with his Aunt Lilian."

"Not often. There's just a chance that he uses some other. After all he goes away and doesn't keep in touch with her. Doesn't—for some odd reason, as now—want her to know where he is. But he's not the kind to go without his mail. The publishers may have such an address. Must have I should say."

"So what do I say in this letter?"

"Write a fan letter. Say that you have enjoyed his book

immensely and would he be kind enough to autograph it for you. With it you send the book and the return postage. Then let's hope that out of politeness and touched vanity he'll do so, and may even enclose a letter or note which will give his address. The least we can get, anyway, will be the postmark. Now will you do that?"

"Very well." His sister smiled. "You know, I really should like an autographed copy. I really am enjoying it. It's a pity he's a rogue, of course; but at least he is very different from the types you are usually concerned with. Would you like me to read some more aloud to you?"

"My dear sister—no, thank you. I will read it for myself. Just now I prefer Chopin." Helder reached out to switch on the radio and then checked himself, and said, "Perhaps you should write under an assumed name."

His sister gave him a sharp frown. "I shall do nothing of the sort. I want a copy autographed to me, not to some imaginary Mrs Bloggs. Now, don't be tiresome and keep interrupting. I want to read."

Helder sighed.

* * * *

At mid-morning, as she often did, Miss Latham came into the library carrying a tray of coffee and biscuits.

She said, "If you are deep into something and don't want company, I'll take my coffee away and leave you in peace, Johnny."

He grinned. "If you do so you will take the sunlight out of my morning."

"Blarney, my dear boy. But nice blarney." She put the tray down on a window table and poured their coffee, saying over her shoulder, "There's some mail for you too. Oh, yes, and I heard from them this morning—the dear Bishop and his wife, my sister, are coming down tomorrow to stay for a week."

"That's nice. I'd like to have a talk with him about one or two things." He went and joined her at the window and said, "I haven't had the pleasure of meeting his wife."

"You'll like her. She's charming and beautiful. As a girl she was a dream . . . golden hair and periwinkle eyes. He adores her—and so he should." She gave him a sudden impish look and added, "And, of course, you must long have known or guessed that I lost my heart to him as well. But I was far too heavily handicapped in that contest."

"Well—if it means anything to you I can say that I lost my heart to you from the first moment I saw you."

"How nice. Do say some more."

"What? That I count the loss all gain?"

"At eleven o'clock in the morning! Does it always come so easily to you?"

"What better time for then the whole day is before one. At eleven o'clock at night there is no need for words."

Miss Latham laughed. "My goodness—don't you dare talk to Mrs Bishop like that. I begin to think that you really are a dangerous and unscrupulous rogue. But I must say it makes a change from the day's often dull routine. I adore gossip and scandal. And talking of gossip—you have already started some."

"Ah, I felt that you were steering me somewhere. Rachel?"

"Of course."

"Then set your mind at rest."

"It never was uneasy—only curious. I shall be very happy if you tell me that it is serious."

"Oh, yes, it is serious. But only time will test the lasting of that quality. In this world no more certainty can ever be offered. For lack of that—we must fall back on faith."

"You should have gone into the Church."

"I prefer glasshouses and a different worship."

"Well, it is none of my business, though I quite enjoy talking about it. And anyway, Rachel is well capable of looking after herself."

"And me, I hope. What would be the point of marriage otherwise?"

"I can see you don't intend to be serious. And perhaps I know why. To be frank would be to share some part of the thing you have between you—and the moment is too soon for that. However, I'm glad for you both, and if you cause a little gossip . . . well, I never officially listen to it."

"You wouldn't disapprove of our being lovers?"

She laughed. "My dear Johnny—what an old-fashioned idea. What two people in love do is their own business. It is only when they start having a family that they must start living responsibly and recognize that they are then part of the community and must fully or, at least, apparently conform."

"I'm sure that the Bishop would never approve of that attitude."

"No, of course not. But then he has given his life completely to Christ and to the cherishing of the Christian religion. If he came to know about it he might speak to you both and then leave you to make your own decision. On the other hand he might not say anything on the grounds that it is better for people to find for themselves the truth and wisdom which rest in the Christian ethos. Marriage is a sacrament. You cannot skip that and take the bread and wine just because you are hungry and thirsty. Dear me—how did we get to this point?"

Looking full at her, he said, "I think because you deliberately led the way there."

"I wonder?" She laughed suddenly. "Oh dear, Johnny—if you could see your face. And all because an old-fashioned spinster who would have given anything to have had what you and Rachel have makes a little plea for you to treat it reverently. Forget it, my dear boy." She got up and touched him on the shoulder and as she turned away went on, "I'll leave the tray. You haven't finished your coffee."

He sat there for a little while thinking about her, vaguely disturbed, and then brusquely dismissed her from his thoughts. As a welcome distraction he picked up the mail which she had brought for him, a letter and a small brown paper parcel which had been forwarded to him through his London club. The handwriting on the letter envelope he recognized at once as his Aunt Lily's, which surprised him because he had never told her that he used the club as a convenience address.

Her letter read:

Dear Johnny,

It does worry me when you go off like this and I get no news of you for ages. I know you will say not to fuss but I do. So you must forgive me for taking a liberty. I have known for a time that you use your club as a forwarding address (through the envelopes in your waste-paper basket) so I am sending this through them.

All I want is a word from you just now and again and I don't care whether you put an address on it or not. You might think I am angry with you, but I am not. Oh, I do wish I knew why you are like this. So, please, love, do send me a note to say you are well.

Everything is much the same here, except that a fox got one of the hens the other night—the White Leghorn that always roosted out in the orchard.

Please, love, do write.

All my love,
Aunt Lily

He put the letter down and then opened the parcel. It contained a new ccpy of his book, a sheet of brown paper and a stamped and addressed sticky label with a name and a London address on it.

The letter read:

Dear Mr Corbin,

I am sending this to you through your publishers who have promised to forward it to you.

I am sure that you must get many letters from readers who admire your work—and I certainly come in that category. I found Green Pleasures *absolutely enchanting and felt that I must tell you so. It has given me so much pleasure that I have dared now to hope you would do me the great kindness of autographing it. It would be so kind of you if you would.*

Yours very sincerely,
Constance Winters. (Mrs.)

P.S. Please do, do write another one very soon.

With a shrug of his shoulders he dropped the letter to the table and then, walking to the window, looked out across the lawns to the great blaze of colour from the rose beds, the light summer breeze just stirring the hanging canopy of a tall weeping willow while from below him came the sound of sparrows quarrelling in the wistaria growing along the house wall. Three women, he thought, all wanting something: Miss Latham, cherishing a hopeless love, wanting him to marry—well, he would in his own good time . . . dear Aunt Lily just wanting to hear from him . . . well, she would . . . and this Mrs Winters wanting him to sign a book for her . . . well, why not? He felt in a generous mood. Something was happening to him down here. At any other time and place he would have taken Rachel or her like as a bonus. At any other time he would have stuffed Aunt Lily's letter in his pocket and, with the best of intentions to write, would have soon lost and forgotten it. And at any other time he might have taken Mrs Winters' praise of his work without pleasure, writing her off cynically as a collector of signed copies which she would flog somewhere. Hedonistic with Rachel; unfilial—for she had been mother to him—with Aunt Lily, and cynical about Mrs Winters. God knew why. And perhaps God had got tired of him, but was giving him one more chance nevertheless. The lost lamb restored to the fold. A new John Corbin rising from the ashes of the dead. But not too suddenly. To slough a skin took time. To live in a Bishop's house in an odour of sanctity, to be nearer God's heart in a garden, to love and cherish, build a home and a business with Rachel . . . well, not all that could be done in a rush, but some of it could.

Elated with an unusual euphoria he went back to the library table and wrote a letter to his aunt telling her where he was and what he was doing. He then autographed the copy of *Green Pleasures* for Mrs Winters—*Delighted to do this for you—John Corbin*—and parcelled the book up to go out with the Illaton Manor post. And that evening when Rachel came in for a drink at his cottage on her way home, he said to her out of the blue, "It's not a question, you know, of *why* don't we get married—but of *when*."

She looked at him with surprise and then took a hand mirror from her bag, studied herself and touched her hair needlessly to tidy it. Then she said, "What's brought this on?"

He grinned. "Well, I finally found myself on the Damascus road—only just, mind you—so I thought I would anticipate coming events."

"Why the sudden rush?"

"I'm not rushing. It's simply a matter of when. At least I'm assuming it is."

She smiled. "You're an odd sod, aren't you? Oh, don't get me wrong. I love you and you love me. But I'm basically very conventional. Sleeping together is one thing—but getting married is a big step. Hasn't it occurred to you that I might like all the conventional preliminaries?"

"You mean like an engagement and an announcement in the *Daily Telegraph*?"

"That's what my family would like—and so, I imagine, would yours."

Cheerfully he said, "Well, I had an idea that you might be like this. And I'm delighted to be proved correct—otherwise I've had a wasted trip today."

"What trip?"

"Well, I knocked off after lunch and drove into Plymouth. Of course I could only guess at the size, but they said if it's wrong just to go in and have it altered. So, my dear Rachel, I love you dearly—and please will you marry me after a decorous engagement period?" He put into her hand a small red morocco ring box.

Rachel opened it. Inside was a platinum ring set with one small diamond which he had bought with almost the last of the money he had been paid by Mrs Barwick, telling himself that money had so many provenances that neither guilt nor conscience could ever pass with it. And that, anyway, he was a reformed man and like all penitent sinners was owed a fresh start. Meanwhile Rachel sat with the ring in her hand, and then looked up at him and burst into tears—which surprised him for he had never marked her down as an over-emotional type.

He went to her, raised her from her chair and put his arms around her and held her until the emotional spasm died in her. Then as she moved away from him she said, "You're an impossible fool. Of course I love you and of course I'll marry you. But look at me—in a dirty old pullover and khaki shirt and trousers and my hair looking like God knows what. Here, take it back." She put the ring box into his hand.

"But why?"

"Because I'm going home. And you can come down in an hour's time and have dinner with me, and I'll be looking like the real me—and then you can start all over again as though this had never happened."

"But it has happened."

"I know—and it was lovely. But I'm greedy. The next time I want it with all the proper trimmings. Is that too much to ask?"

He laughed. "Why should it be? Once more and this time with feeling. If you like we'll do it every evening for the rest of the week." He paused and then went on heavily, "You know I'm bloody serious, don't you?"

Rachel nodded and then turned and went from the cottage. He stood and listened to the sound of her driving away and then turned to take up his drink. Cassidy came into the room and dropped to the floor with a long sigh, sprawling in untidy ease.

He looked down at the dog and grinned. "Well, what did you make of that, Cassidy? What? Yes, you're quite right. Something must have happened to me today. I've been possessed. But if so, surely by a benevolent spirit since I now serve one of God's anointed."

He went upstairs whistling to bath and change.

* * * *

After Johnny had gone Rachel lay awake in her bed knowing that sleep would be long coming to her. Through the open window came the sound of the mill stream that ran through the small garden. Now and again a little owl gave a bad-tempered screech from the woods on the Illaton cliffs and was answered once by the sharp bark of a fox. The night was full of its own life and sounds, all familiar to her but now heard with a new awareness for Johnny had wakened in her a joy which had given her the feeling that she had miraculously become a new person. Everything now was fresh and unique as though she saw and heard and felt for the first time. Nonsense, of course, but it was a lovely feeling.

The ring had been too big for her, but Johnny would go to Plymouth, taking one of her dress rings for size, and have it made smaller. Johnny would this and Johnny would that, and with Johnny she would make a new world. They had had a lovely evening, had talked and planned, and laughed and made love. And they had decided that for the time being they would tell no one and that she would wear the ring only when they were alone. This was more his wish than hers but she had been touched by his reasons and respected them. Her own instinct would have been to shout it to the world immediately, but he had said—and his insistence on the proprieties had amused her—that they would take a long week-end off soon and he would drive her first to her parents in Oxfordshire to tell them, and then go on to his aunt in Sussex to give her the news. It was odd: she had marked him down as unconventional but here was this very correct streak suddenly revealed and she had agreed willingly. Well, she could keep a secret for a while as securely as anyone. And anyway, what Johnny wanted she too wanted.

They had talked too about the future and, although there had necessarily been a certain amount of vagueness over the details, their main conclusion had been that they wanted to do something together and on their own. There was complete accord between them that they wanted to be their own masters, to build and run some concern together . . . a farm, a nursery—all demanding more money than they could muster—or (as he said, 'Great oaks from little acorns grow') they could start small with a corner florist shop and go on to bigger things. Their talk had been wild, improbable, and then suddenly sober, and anyway what did it matter? They would be together with the whole world before them. For the moment that was enough. She was content with what had happened. She sighed happily and stretched herself, enjoying the slow run of ecstasy which flooded through her, hearing his voice with a clarity which matched the sensual memory of his caresses . . .

"Maybe if I make a good job of this book for the Bishop I really will start writing again. I've got lots of ideas . . ."

"What does it matter if it's hard going at first? Before the fruit there must be the flowering. You know, or if you don't you must now, that I've been a bit of an odd sod. Always found it hard to settle to anything, and sometimes been pretty fed up with myself. There's a nasty little John Corbin inside this one. A real bugger who ought to have his neck twisted——"

She had put her hand over his mouth then, and said sharply,

"That's enough. We've all got or had something . . . Now say something nice before you go . . . my love, my love . . ."

He had leaned over and kissed her and then quoted—

> *. . . What I do*
> *And what I dream include thee, as the wine*
> *Must taste of its own grapes . . .*

Gorgeous. She moved her hands comfortingly and luxuriously over her breasts and blinked at the small tears which misted her eyes.

*   *   *   *

The reaction came while he was working in the library, sorting through some papers and accounts from the early years of the nineteen hundreds when the Bishop's father had been master of Illaton Manor. He had inherited the estate in 1911 when his son, the Bishop, was still to be born and he was thirty-one years old.

He was going through a bill for the supply of books from a London antiquarian bookseller. At the bottom of the account John Boyd Darvell had written: *He grossly overcharges me, but he's a likeable rogue and looks like a smartened-up Fagin.* Going through the list—knowing that the books stood now in the glass-fronted cases in the room—he knew that overcharged then as the Bishop's father might have been the books now showed a very handsome profit. Among them were a C. Linnaeus—*Flora Lapponica* (Amsterdam, 1737) and a *Species Plantarum* (Stockholm, 1753) and a W. Turner folio—*A New Herball* (London, 1551). With the money from that little lot . . .

He sat back suddenly. Money. What in God's name had suddenly got into him? He smiled wryly. Perhaps just that. God had got to him at last. He really had been on the road to Damascus. All his life he had done things on impulse from time to time and, even while he was beginning to regret some move, he still carried on with it, pride or greed compelling him. Like the affair with Sue Barwick. The thought of blackmailing her had never been in his mind until one day reading through her letters and on the point of tearing them up he had had some imp whisper over his shoulder that he would be tearing up money; and, that thought with him, there had been no resisting the temptation. And now here he was as good as saddled for life with a wife and all that would follow. After the euphoria of yesterday there was now the reality of this morning . . . and a raining one too. Perhaps the gods wept for him. For a little while he sat there invaded with sudden misery and doubt. Then, angry with his self-doubt and pity, he got up and going to the table by the window poured himself a glass of sherry. Dear Miss Latham. How she cosseted him. Her life was barren of love fulfilled. Would she now have made any compact with the Devil to go back to some idyllic point of maidenhood and be granted a promise such as he had given Rachel? If he broke that now where would he end up? Like some shuffling old bachelor, living in one room on his memories of sweet dreams gone sour . . .

He laughed suddenly at the mental picture and the mood broke in him and shredded away like a morning mist before a suddenly risen wind.

From behind him he heard Miss Latham's voice.

"Don't tell me that the strain of your work is beginning to show? I had a brother who used to stare out of the window and suddenly laugh to himself."

Turning, smiling, glad to see her, he asked, "Did he ever give any reason?"

"Oh, yes. He would say that he was practising his laughing in case he ever needed it. He was a dear fellow but he would always look on the dark side of things. In fact, though, he had everything a man could wish for in life, a loving wife, a lovely family and a good business. So much, in fact, that he couldn't bring himself to believe his good fortune. They put him in an asylum in the end."

"You're pulling my leg."

"Of course. I never had brothers. So to make up for it I invent them. It's really quite fascinating when I can't sleep. I wipe them all out and invent a new lot . . . in the most exact detail, you know. That's the fun. One of them, a bachelor, I made Mayor of Huddersfield and he asked me to be his Lady Mayoress. I had a marvellous time for a whole week before going to sleep."

"Why Huddersfield?"

"Because I had never been there—so I was free to invent it the way I wanted. He finished up with a knighthood. I thought he'd deserved it. But he got so swollen-headed afterwards I had to finish him off with an attack of scarlet fever and invent another. I do that for myself, too, you know. It's a good way of chasing away the glooms. I just make up a life for myself. You've no idea how exciting it can be."

Touched, on an impulse, he went to her and kissed her on her cheek.

"That's nice. But why?" she asked.

"Because you are *to my thoughts as food to life, Or as sweet-season'd showers are to the ground.* I was going through a bad patch, but it's all over."

"Splendid. And I'm too nice to enquire why. I really came to give you this." She handed him a folded copy of *The Times.* "There's a letter in it from the dear Bishop who, by the way, telephoned to say that they are not coming for another two days. Apparently he wanted a visa or whatever it is you have to have to go to Poland and the Polish authorities have refused him one. He won't give up easily though." She smiled. "Sometimes I think I ought to take him in hand and re-invent him a bit. Not much, but perhaps enough to make him a little less outspoken, a little more subtle."

* * * *

A day later Helder's sister received her signed copy of *Green Pleasures* in the morning post. She handed it to Helder, opened at the autographed title page.

"Now wasn't that kind of him? But sadly no address—and really in a way I'm quite glad about it."

"Gladness and sorrow don't come into my business, as you know." He reached for the brown paper wrapping and, with difficulty, read the smudged post-mark. "Tavistock. Well he did go west to keep the sun out of his eyes."

"Why do you say that?"

"Because it was said to me."

"By whom?"

"Someone who knew him."

"Who?"

"A woman."

His sister sighed. "I'm finding this conversation a little unsatisfactory. Will you go to Tavistock?"

"I might."

"I was there once with Harold. His ship was at Plymouth and he had four days' leave. I used to sit and knit while he fished . . . dear, dear, you should have heard the naval language when he lost one. He wasn't like you, doling out words as though they were golden guineas. He was positively scabrous. It used to make me laugh so much."

"I was extremely fond of Harold, my dear."

"I know, love. And I'm very fond of you even though you do have such a love for this sordid profession of yours. I don't know whether I've said it before, but I think Mrs Barwick got everything she deserved."

"You have said it before."

"Yes, I thought I had." She was silent for a moment or two and then went on, "If you did go to Tavistock I could come with you, if you wished, and show you the places Harold and I visited."

Helder, folding up his napkin, smiled suddenly and said, "My dear, if I do go I shall certainly take you."

"Bless you."

That morning too, when Aunt Lily had cleared away her breakfast, she sat down and wrote a letter to Miss Simpson before writing to John Corbin. In it she wrote—

. . . I thought you might like to know that I have now heard from Johnny. What an unpredictable man he is. He never went to Wales at all. Apparently at the very last moment he had the offer of another job down in Cornwall at a place called Illaton Manor which belongs to some Bishop or other—Darble or Dawble—his writing can be awful at times. He wasn't very clear about what he was doing. Some kind of work in the library there, all connected with botany and the family history. Anyway, he seems to be loving it and I thought you would like to know. It really is a relief to know where he is and what he is doing.

With this I am enclosing some snapshots of this cottage and the garden, and one of our old donkeys. I'm afraid the colour isn't very good on the one of the roses. They're Super Star and have done so well. The white things in the background are our hens. I know it may not be likely but if you are ever in this part I would so like you to come and see me. I could put you up and we might hire a car and take some trips around.

But, anyway, I had to write to let you know about Johnny. He really isn't a bad boy at all. Just thoughtless at times.

The letter was to be the beginning of a more or less regular correspondence between them.

CHAPTER SIX

THEY WERE HAVING a drink together in his cottage before going up to the Manor to have dinner with the Bishop and his wife and a few of their friends. He looked marvellous, she thought, in his dinner jacket and there was a simple pride in her that he was her man . . . her husband to be.

When he had given her a drink he dropped back into a chair and picking up a newspaper asked, "Did you read the Bishop's letter? You know the Polish authorities barred him from going over there for some conference?"

"Miss Latham told me about it. But I haven't read it."

"I'll read you some. He may be a stout Christian, but he's no diplomat. He lets his pique come through a little uncharitably at times. Have I told you that you're looking bloody marvellous?"

"You have. But if you want to say so again I have no objection."

"You look so good in green. As crisp as lettuce. I feel I want to nibble you."

"You can do that, perhaps, later. What about the letter?"

"Ah, yes. Listen to this——"

He read:

The political brotherhood of Man, and an obliged worship of the State—no matter how democratically constructed—can never be an adequate substitute for religion since they lack the abiding imperative of Divine and unchanging love. All brotherhoods, such as political parties, sporting groups, social clubs and charitable groups, are by their very nature mundane, no matter their often clear worthiness.

The only true brotherhood is that which, under Christ, offers Divine grace and love to all who seek it. To grant apparent religious freedom with one hand and then to cripple it with a crushing blow from the other is a cynicism of the godless, and in some countries the common practice of those who would preserve their own political powers and elitist privileges by any means . . .

"Then there's a lot more like that. But you have to give it to him, he certainly knows how to put the knife in himself. There's some more *blah, blah*—and then he finishes up much better than he began——"

Nation, it seems, can no longer speak face to face with Nation. Before you can cross some frontiers today you must be proven first not to be carrying the love of Christ in your heart or that—to many—subversive handbook the Holy Bible in your baggage.

"I think it makes good sense."

"Maybe—but not good diplomacy. It won't get him anywhere. And I wonder how much good it will do him in the preferment stakes in the Church?"

"The Church has got to move with the times."

"That's the last thing it wants to do politically. Now and again they make a clumsy show of keeping up—like revising the beautiful and well-loved language of our forms of prayer and worship so that you stand in Church now and read from something which is no more than an illiterate's first reading primer."

Rachel laughed. "Are you going to tell him that?"

He grinned. "No. I know which side my bread is buttered. It's a curious thing how sensitive to criticism all reformers are. You'd have thought that by now, like time-hardened sinners, they would have grown skins like rhinoceroses."

"How's yours doing?"

He laughed. "Coming along nicely."

"And we'd better be going along, too, or we shall be late."

The dinner party, as John Corbin had expected, could never have been described as going like a ball of fire. The vicar and his wife were there, full of local news and a too obvious deference to the Bishop who, for the most part, sat like some benign patriarch, smiling and indulgent and listening and clearly more interested in his meal than in the fact that the Illaton church would have to have a new central-heating boiler before the coming winter. There was a wealthy neighbouring landowner and his wife who seemed obsessed by a recent cruise they had taken, designed entirely for bridge addicts. That topic being eventually exhausted, they turned to the militant behaviour of Trade Unions and the difficulty of getting good household staff. Then there was the Bishop's wife, small, with greying hair, and a faded blue-eyed prettiness from behind which Corbin could reconstruct the bird-like, blond, China-fragile beauty which had once been hers. He was sure that she suffered from headaches, and was suffering now from boredom. The Bishop, he decided, had made a mistake in not marrying her sister, Miss Latham. And Miss Latham, in a smart black silk dress with a harp-shaped gold brooch set with tiny pearls, her hair touched with a shade of blue rinse, her bright eyes and ready chatter full of life and sparkle, was enjoying herself and clearly pleasantly excited because her dear Bishop was here. For some, he thought, the dinner, and then the port and cigars and the final joining of the ladies in the drawing room for coffee, could have had its longueurs, but not for him. These were people and people for him always had the promise of some potential which he could exploit so that—a reformed character now—he still could not deny himself the exercise of old habit. The landowner's wife, in her forties he guessed, was a good-looking woman, almost buxom, with a hearty, slightly vulgar laugh. She would have been easy game for he sensed at once that her husband bored her and had few merits except that he played a good game of bridge and kept her in luxury. He would have had to brush up his bridge a bit though. Looking at Rachel, he thought, she shone out like a bright evening star. He liked the vicar's wife: one of the good women of this earth, slaving away at her husband's side, always ready with coffee and biscuits, mothering the Mother's Union, always taking the same stall at the Women's Institute annual fair, working at her tapestry covers for the church hassocks and a first-class flower-arranger. And dear Miss Latham . . . his Aunt Lily all over again . . .

When the vicar and his wife had gone and the local landowner and his, the Bishop's wife announced a headache and went to bed and, when she was gone, the Bishop said, "Well, before you two young people go, I wonder dear"—he looked at Miss Latham—"whether you would look after Rachel while I have a word in the library with John?"

He followed the Bishop up to the library in the wake of his cigar smoke. Once in the library, the Bishop said, "Now, John—tell me how things are going."

Knowing that the question would be asked him, Corbin was well prepared with his answer. He had by now gone through all the papers . . . the accounts of contractors and botanical suppliers of plants and trees and the gardening diaries which had been more or less consistently kept over the years. In addition there had been the files of the correspondence kept up by the various Darvells with other collectors and owners of great gardens and the various surveys and plans which had been drawn up as the Illaton gardens were gradually expanded. Towards the end of his account he said, and he chose his words carefully because he realized that the pride of the Bishop in his ancestors was greater than his pride in the estate and gardens, "I thought that the best way of tackling the book was to concentrate on the theme of the creation from a wilderness—the neglected old farm lands and the woods and river cliffs—of a paradise. The whole project being for each Darvell part of a continuing act of worship . . ."

"Ah, yes. A splendid approach."

"Yet of course, my lord, it would be an incomplete picture if one lost the impact of the character of the various Darvells." He smiled. "They were all men with very decided views and idiosyncrasies, and they could be very demanding masters at times. A badly turned-out horse, a job slackly done, never missed their eyes. Yet, at the same time, it's clear that they all had a great love for and sense of obligation to those who worked for them. Only the persistent sinner or idler was in the end turned away. I would like to draw a parallel between each one and the mark he made on the gardens. They all had their favourite projects . . . the water and bog gardens for one, the great trees for another . . . and your father, for instance, who clearly thought that the magnolias and camellias were without peers. But over all I would like to stress the personality of the garden because at times, as you must know, it asserted itself and would not co-operate. It developed its own personality and just refused to take kindly to some plantings however well meant."

The Bishop smiled. "Perhaps it is as well that I have left the gardens more or less as my father handed them over to me. Anyway, what you've outlined seems a good line to take. And you are happy here?"

"Very much so."

"I'm glad of that. Very glad." The Bishop moved to the great window and looked out at the dusk-shrouded garden and the clustering of moths against the small panes, drawn by the room lights, and said, almost to himself, "So much beauty and peace. It is good to come back here from time to time." Then, after a pause, he said turning, "Have you read my letter in *The Times*?"

"Yes, I have, my lord."

"And what did you think of it?"

"I agree with every word you said but . . ."

"But? You surely stopped when you reached that word, John, did you not?"

"Yes, I did."

"Why?"

"Well . . . I don't think it will do any good. The impulse to change must come from within. Not from without. With the greatest reverence I think that for a man or men to change sincerely the word must come from the heart. I happen to believe in revelation."

Unexpectedly the Bishop laughed and said, "So do I. But it is hard not to speak out boldly at times."

Below in the withdrawing room, while the Bishop and Corbin were upstairs, Rachel had on an impulse taken her engagement ring from her evening bag and slipped it on her finger and held it out to Miss Latham.

For a moment or two Miss Latham looked at the ring and then at Rachel. Then she said gently, "You know, my dear, I'm not really surprised. You ate hardly anything and your eyes were on him more than they should have been. It is Johnny, isn't it?"

"Of course. Oh, dear—I shouldn't have told. But I had to tell someone . . . No, not someone. Just you."

"Bless you. What a nice thing to say."

"Do you think the others noticed anything?"

"No, of course not."

"I hope that's so. You see we've decided to keep it a secret until we've both told our people."

"Well, I'm your people. So it's all right."

"But you won't say anything to Johnny, will you?"

"Certainly not. He's a lucky man. And you're just the kind to keep him in order. Don't you ever stand any nonsense from him. There's a little bit of wildness in him, you know. You don't mind my saying that?"

"Of course not."

Miss Latham stood up and bent down and kissed her. Turning away to hide the beginning of tears in her eyes she said, "Now put it away, and we'll have another glass of liqueur. They'll be ages talking up there yet. Oh, dear . . . what a lovely thing to have happened. I thought the evening had been so dull with the Bishop not quite himself and poor Dorothy clearly with one of her migraines coming on, and me with either bridge or combined harvesters on one side of me and the vicar sniffing away on the other with a bad cold . . . Oh, but this makes up for everything." She turned with the liqueur decanter in her hand. "The Bishop will marry you. Oh, yes, he must do that. And I'll come shopping with you in Plymouth or wherever for your trousseau. Oh, dear, I'm sorry. I'm letting myself run away. Now, I'll take a firm grip on myself and pretend it hasn't happened."

Rather shakily she filled two glasses with Grand Marnier, spilling it a little.

*   *   *   *

A week later Aunt Lily had a visit from Helder.

He said, "I'm calling on the off-chance that you might have heard from your nephew—and this, believe me, isn't an entirely professional call. It's just that I happen to know he hasn't gone to Wales."

"That's kind of you. But how do you know this?"

"Because my sister, who very much admires his book, sent a copy of it to be forwarded through his publishers for autographing. He kindly did so and sent it back to her."

"With a letter?"

Helder smiled. "No. Just the autograph. But the post-mark on the parcel was Tavistock."

"And you took the trouble to come all the way down here to tell me? That was very kind of you."

Helder looked at her in silence for a moment or two, and then smiled. There were some people whose faces gave them away, and others by the tone of their voices. He said, "You knew this already?"

"Yes, I did. I had a letter from him. He's got himself a job—the kind of job he likes."

"I'm pleased to hear it."

"Do you really mean that?"

"Why not? Whatever I may be professionally is one thing. But, I can tell that you are happy about him . . . and that makes me pleased."

"I am happy about him. I've never had such a warm letter from him in all my life. I may be imagining it—though I hope not—but he sounded as though he were . . . well, much more content with himself."

"And if I asked you to give me his address?"

"You know the answer to that. No. I disapprove entirely of what he's done, but blood is thicker than water, Mr Helder."

"Yes. Well, I respect your attitude."

Aunt Lily was silent for a while and then she said hesitantly, "You're such a nice, calm, good-hearted man. How can you bear to do the kind of work you do?"

"I've often asked myself that question and have never found a really satisfactory answer. The nearest I've come to it, I think, is that I'm timid and very ordinary. Just a sort of grey shape living a grey, humdrum life like so many people. So, to escape from all that, I mix in other and more unorthodox people's lives to add a little crude colour to my own. I sometimes wonder how it all came about, but for the life of me now I really can't remember."

"I'm sure you can but won't say."

"No, it's the truth. I just live vicariously. I found I had the knack of doing that—and you must have it in my profession to get anywhere. That's why when I talk to people I find that often I'm talking from inside them, being them, knowing them and, sometimes, suffering with them. It's happening now. So, why don't you ask me the thing that really is on your mind at the moment?"

Aunt Lily laughed. "Good Lord! What are you, psychic?"

"Sympathetic, I think, is the true word. Shall I help?"

After a moment's thought Aunt Lily shook her head. "No, I can speak for myself—and I hope you really will prove to be sympathetic. I want Johnny left alone. I want this whole business cleared up. So I'd like you to talk to Mr Barwick for me. After all, from the way I imagine him, he must perhaps be more reconciled to his wife's infidelity. Or perhaps, yes, infidelities? Maybe he's used to them. But having to live with the thought that another man has indirectly made him pay two thousand pounds for—well, you know what for . . ."

"Entertaining his wife?"

"If you like. But this is the point. I can draw two thousand pounds from Johnny's trust fund and pay it to Mr Barwick. I should, of course, tell Johnny what I was doing. Do you think he's the kind of man who would settle for that?"

"He might. It could depend on his mood at the moment. I know from even the little I've had to do with him that his nature is changeable. He wavers from time to time trying to decide whether he's been cheated financially or insulted personally. So, you can understand, I can't make any promises or even guesses on his behalf."

"But you would try. For my sake as well as Johnny's?"

Helder smiled. "For your sake, yes."

"And you'll do it soon?"

"As soon as I can."

"You're a very good and kind man."

"It's nice of you to say that. But my modesty compels me to question it."

"I know you can do it. And it must be done. I get the strong feeling that Johnny is at some turning-point in his life and I want him left undisturbed by this sordid business."

"All that? On the evidence of one letter from him?"

"More than that. Really the first letter I've ever had from him. Listen to something he wrote, because I have it by heart, and he's never used such words to me before. *I don't know what it is about this place. Perhaps the first oasis I've ever reached in the desert of my life. All I know is that here each day peace comes dropping slow and I lie awake at nights and, although no nightingales sing because it is too late in the season, the silence itself is a song. I wake each morning with a joyful hunger, eager and full of appetite for the coming day . . .*"

Driving away, Helder, so much did he feel for Aunt Lily, hoped—against his own natural scepticism—that Corbin's was really a true conversion. In his experience it was not unknown for the wolf to lie down with the lamb, but only when it was gorged to repletion. His guess was that—for whatever reason—Corbin was gorged with some euphoria and fascinated by some enchanting new image of himself.

* * * *

On the morning when the Bishop and his wife left Illaton Manor, after a very much shorter stay than they had intended, there was an answering letter to his in *The Times* from the Press Counsellor at the Polish Embassy in London. Corbin read it while he was taking his mid-morning coffee in the library. It was a restrained letter—written he felt diplomatically more in calculated surprise than genuine anger—pointing out that under the Constitution of the Republic of Poland there was complete religious freedom. The recent visit of the Pope testified to that. There was no objection to the visits of any churchmen of no matter what religion from abroad so long as they were of a pastoral nature and not politically motivated. The Bishop had been told that he could visit the country immediately so long as he recognized that this did not entitle him to meet and encourage supporters of dissident political factions—a promise he had refused to make in almost peremptory terms under the sophism that a man, no matter what his religion, was nevertheless a citizen entitled to form and uphold his own political views so long as in so doing he broke none of his country's laws. It finished:

> *The Polish Government is little concerned with whatever may be carried in the Bishop's baggage. But it is concerned with his obvious intent to give comfort to certain dissident factions in this country. All governments—his own included—are, in the same way as any*

householder, entitled to use their own judgment as to whom they invite to be their guests.

All of which, Corbin realized, would not be the end of the matter for now the regular writers of letters to *The Times* would begin to weigh in with their own views until the editor judged, for one reason or another, that enough was enough. But—and the thought now seemed a little less disloyal than it would have after his first meeting with the Bishop—this was all perhaps that the Bishop had had in his mind. Publicity for people in high places was an addictive drug. Maybe the Bishop was looking to the years ahead when, after a deliberate switch to a calmer, more diplomatic manner, the York and Canterbury stakes might be coming into the ecclesiastical calendar, and he might emerge as a fancied runner. Cynical, perhaps, but Fame was a sharp spur and the last infirmity of a no longer perhaps entirely noble mind.

On the long library table before him was a small, slim metal deed box, green in colour, and inscribed in white paint letters—*John Boyd Darvell,* the Bishop's father. Among all the library keys he had been unable to find one which fitted its lock. He had meant to ask the Bishop about it when they had talked after the dinner party but had forgotten to do so, had only remembered it again at night in bed the day before the Bishop had left but had arrived the next morning to find that the Bishop and his wife had already left after an early breakfast. He decided to bring a screwdriver up from his cottage and force the lock some time.

Suddenly bored with the prospect of working on until lunchtime, he decided to take a walk around the gardens and to look at the Grecian temple which the Bishop's grandfather had built on the cliff edge overlooking the river. In Alfred Boyd Darvell's papers that morning he had read an account of his plantings around the temple and wanted to check which of them still survived, particularly the mention of an *Aquebia quintata* placed as climber on one of the façade pillars—which he doubted had survived over the years—and, along the banks of a small stream which ran into and out of the ornamental pool at the side of the temple and then waterfalled over the cliff fall, a plantation of indigenous and other ferns . . . the large Golden

Scaled, the Broad Buckler and the Lady and Shield ferns.

When he got there it was to find no sign of the *Aquebia quintata,* only the very ancient wistaria—which he had noticed before—which had wreathed itself round one of the temple columns and half covered the domed roof. Behind the temple, on the river fall side, the little stream dell was covered with a long-established and thriving colony of ferns.

As he sat there, on the low balustraded wall, looking down the long drop of cliff to the tawny waters of the Tamar, he was joined by Cassidy who flopped into a patch of sunlight and went to sleep. A little later Miss Latham came on to the small terrace. She was wearing a shapeless straw sun hat and carried in one hand a cane collecting basket and in the other a pair of secateurs. The basket was partly full of flowers and foliage. Sitting down and sighing on the small stone seat at the back of the temple she said, as though they had long been engaged in conversation, "I'm collecting for a display vase in the hall. I wish I were good at that kind of thing. I used to enter for the floral arrangements at the local show and never even got so much as mentioned—so I gave it up. And Johnny—you shouldn't perch on that balustrade like that. It gives me vertigo just to see you there."

To humour her he went and joined her, saying, "I've got a good head for heights. Did you see the letter from the Polish people in *The Times* this morning?"

"Yes, I did. And now there'll be a lot of rubbishy correspondence from other people. I do wish the Bishop wouldn't get involved in this kind of thing. But there's no telling him."

"Never underestimate the value of publicity—good or bad."

She smiled. "Are you really cynical? Or do you do it just to tease?"

"Perhaps a bit of both. Tell me—did you ever meet his father?"

"Yes, I did. He was seventy when he died in 1950. The Bishop—though he wasn't a bishop then and, in fact, had only recently decided to take Holy Orders—was in his twenties. Why do you ask about him?"

"From the things I'm picking up in the library papers he seems to have been quite a character."

"Oh, yes, he was. He would go for days without speaking to anyone. And then, suddenly, he would be the life and soul of the party. He was like that with everything. Generous—and then suddenly terribly mean. He didn't speak to the Bishop for a year after he told him that he was going into the Church. Then suddenly again—he was all over him. Personally I think he was a little mad. But when he was sane and sociable he was great fun."

"And his wife?"

"She had a hard time, poor dear, I gather. And probably died from the strain of trying to anticipate his moods. But she absolutely adored him. She died five years after the Bishop was born. You haven't seen it yet, but in the main bedroom there's a painting of the two of them together by Augustus John. She looks absolutely ravishing. A Dresden china shepherdess. And he . . . well, without disrespect he looks like a gypsy ravisher . . . a red scarf round his neck, corduroy trousers, a little black waistcoat with mother of pearl buttons and a really rough-looking lurcher dog at his heels. He would shoot anything that moved and was good to eat. The vermin——" she grinned, "——as befitting a gentleman he left to his keepers. I'll take you up and show you the painting sometime."

"Yes, please. I'd like to see it. And now to something quite different. I'd like to take a long week-end off fairly soon. There are some things I have to attend to at home."

"My dear Johnny, you don't have to ask me. You are your own master."

"That's nice of you."

She was silent for a moment, her eyes on him, full of amusement. Then she said in an openly teasing tone, "Now, isn't that a coincidence because Rachel—again unnecessarily—asked me the same thing."

Corbin laughed. "It just proves that coincidences are far more common than we imagine."

"Oh, I'm sure they are. Particularly the nice ones."

* * * *

Harry Barwick listened without interruption while Helder outlined to him the substance of his recent meeting with Aunt

Lily. Helder had soon realized that the man's mood was now rather different from any which he had exhibited before. He was relaxed and at times the small flex of a smile touched his lips. All hurt or personal affront, Helder got the impression, had long mellowed in him. His wife's infidelity and the loss of the two thousand pounds were in the past; a nacreous layer now laid over the unpleasant memories. Except for the money, perhaps, it had all happened before, and now even the money had lost importance. Against his wealth it was nothing. But pleasure had risen in the man, he sensed, and it was a pleasure probably which he could not easily relinquish. For Barwick the whirligig of time was bringing in his revenges. The whole thing for him now had become almost the same as getting the best of a business deal. To do that was the only point of honour at stake.

When he had finished Barwick was silent for a while, rolling a gold pencil between the tips of his fingers, and then he said, "You like this Mrs Hines?"

"Yes, I do. She's a straightforward, honest soul—and genuinely distressed at her nephew's behaviour."

"But won't tell you where he is. Except that you think he's somewhere in the neighbourhood of Tavistock?"

"That's so."

"Does he deserve such loyalty?"

"Clearly not. But loyalty with some people is unconditional."

"And what would you advise me to do, Mr Helder?"

"Whatever I would advise—I think you've already made up your mind."

Without emphasis Barwick said, "You're dead right I have. Tell Mrs Hines for me that I appreciate her loyalty to her nephew and also her concern for the way my wife was treated. After that all she has to do is to send me a cheque for two thousand pounds. As there's a trust fund involved and these things take a little time, tell her I'm in no hurry. I want the cheque post-dated for three months from the day she sends it off."

"I shall be glad to do that."

"I don't think you will because I haven't finished yet. Oh, I know your sympathy for her and I respect it. But I've got no time or pity for this young bugger who played about with my wife. Hence post-dating the cheque for three months. She is to tell him that if during those three months he comes to see me then I'll hand the cheque back to him. There won't be any emotion on my side. Nor any talk—more than to say 'Good morning' and 'Goodbye' before he goes out with the cheque. If he chooses not to come in that time, then I cash the cheque and the matter is ended. How does that strike you?"

"I don't think he will come."

"Neither do I. Though I would have some feeling for him if he did. If I have to choose between rogues—then give me a brazen-faced one."

"And in the meantime, Mr Barwick, what do you wish me to do?"

"That for which I have employed you. Go on looking for him. That contract between us holds good until I either cash the cheque or he comes and collects it."

"Very good, Mr Barwick."

"You think I'm doing the wrong thing?"

"On the contrary, Mr Barwick. He's had his pleasure at your expense. You're entitled to yours at his. But from a personal point of view, of course, you must see that I would rather that Mrs Hines had not been caught between the upper and nether millstones."

Barwick shrugged his shoulders. "I agree with you. But there it is—something that is always happening to the Mrs Hineses of this world."

An unusual practice for him, Helder, as soon as he was in the street, turned into the nearest bar and ordered himself a large whisky.

When he got home he telephoned Aunt Lily and told her of Mr Barwick's decision, finishing, "I'm not making any comment on his attitude at all. You know the position now. Until the thing is resolved one way or another then I have to go on looking for your nephew."

"And you're not going to enjoy it."

"Enjoyment is an emotion which comes too seldom into my work."

"Poor Mr Helder. But don't worry too much about it. I'm

sure that Johnny will see sense. And we do have to look at the other side of things. Mr Barwick is the injured party. He's entitled to make his own conditions."

"You think Johnny will go to see him?"

"Frankly, I don't know. But at the right moment I will put it to him and let you know what he decides."

"Very well."

Going from the sitting room where the telepone was into the kitchen Helder found a note left for him by his sister.

Such a lovely day. Have cut sandwiches and gone up to the Heath to lunch beside the ponds. Salad already made up for you in the fridge. Open tin of salmon or corned beef. Have looked up two hotels in Tavistock area—names and numbers by the phone if you still want them.

* * * *

As Helder was eating his lunch, John Corbin, in the library at Illaton, had just finished his. He stood at the window looking out over the gravelled sweep and the close-cut lawns watching the summer visitors moving around. It was an open day and on such days he kept clear of the gardens. He had spent the past evening and most of the night with Rachel at Illaton Quay, going down in her car, and then walking back up through the woods at near dawn with Cassidy at his heels. They had decided that in two days' time—the coming Thursday—they would visit first her parents in Oxfordshire and on the Saturday go on to Aunt Lily in Sussex and then come back to Illaton on the following Monday. Rachel would have telephoned her parents this morning and an hour ago he had telephoned a telegram to Aunt Lily, saying—*Got a few days off. Be with you Saturday sometime. Bringing friend. Female. Love. Johnny.*

The door opened behind him and Miss Latham came in and, as he turned, she said, "The place swarms with humanity and the maid's gone off to help in the Barn buffet—so I've come for your tray. What is it about gardens that gives people such appetites? And come to that, my dear Johnny, what is it about stately homes and gardens which brings them in crowds? Some dim nostalgia for a lost Eden—and a chance to pinch a few cuttings or so? More than that sometimes. You'd never believe. Last autumn Rachel and her boys made a new rhododendron planting down by the old glebe field and three days later we'd lost two 'Pink Pearls' and a *citriniflorum*. I didn't grieve much over the P.P.s—but the *citriniflorum* hurt."

"Introduced by George Forest from Yunnan in South China, somewhere around the early nineteen hundreds, I think."

"Well, I wouldn't know. All I know is that sometimes I despair of the human race. Some of them are a thieving, magpie lot. They were probably taken away to be planted in limy soil to die quickly."

Teasingly, Corbin said, "Man—having been cast out of Eden—seeks always to create his own. That's very laudable."

"But no excuse for theft."

He grinned. "If you have the right temperament you don't need one."

She smiled. "Sometimes when you tease me I get a faint whiff of sulphur. Whose side are you on?"

"Well, being musical I go where the best tunes are."

"Ah, one of those moods. Well, that being so I'll take you to meet someone who would probably have agreed with you. I'll get the tray later."

They went out of the room, climbed the final great turn of the oak stairway which ran up from the hall, and into the master bedroom with its great run of mullioned windows and a vast four-poster bed hung with sky blue velvet canopy and curtains. On a side wall, above an eighteenth-century English lacquer commode, hung the Augustus John painting of John Boyd Darvell and his wife. The painting showed man and wife walking by the side of the reed-fringed Tamar. The woman, wearing a beribboned little bonnet, carried an open straw basket full of meadow flowers. Just behind her, shotgun in the crook of his arm, came John Darvell, a lurcher at his heels. He was bareheaded and wore a gold-buttoned black velvet jacket and baggy red canvas trousers.

"Look at them," she said. "Was there ever a more lovely, enchanting woman or a more wicked-looking rogue than he is?

It was painted after the First World War. He went right through that, you know. In the Artists' Rifles and was wounded severely twice."

"He doesn't look much like the Bishop."

"And why should he? One carries the odour and air of sanctity and this one . . . Well, look at him."

John Darvell had a lean, sunburnt face and was smiling as though he had just recalled some particularly pleasant memory of a recent wickedness. It was a Pan face. What had he been doing in the reeds by the river? Probably breaking the golden lilies afloat while he poached a neighbour's salmon. He could understand why such a man would not have taken kindly to his son deciding to become a clergyman. He asked, "Were they happy?"

"Devoted. Like two kittens in a basket. He married late. It's a lovely painting, isn't it?"

"Yes, it is. And worth a lot of money."

"I said 'lovely'. That's all there is to it. What it is worth is irrelevant."

"Am I being chided?"

"A little."

"Well, it's a common reflex of those who have not. I'd like all the money in the world to buy beautiful things. I think money is a splendid thing. If you have it a lot of virtues come easier . . . like being charitable, being kind and tolerant, creating great gardens and commissioning Augustus Johns. With it there are a hundred short cuts to grace if not to true godliness—for that you have to go and sit on a pillar in the desert, or crawl on your knees all the way to Jerusalem . . ."

Miss Latham laughed. "Oh dear! You do tease, don't you? And I like it. And so would he have done. He used to laugh like a donkey braying at anything that touched his sense of the ridiculous."

"You liked him, didn't you?"

"Of course. He was my godfather."

Back in the library and with Miss Latham gone with his lunch tray, John Corbin, because the man was still in his mind, took up the green deed box with John Boyd Darvell's name on it and without much difficulty, since he had from a boy onwards opened many a cash box with the aid of a knife and screwdriver, forced the lock.

Inside was a stout manilla foolscap envelope carrying three red wax seals on the back which had been stamped with a signet-ring device which he eventually made out as the intertwined letters JHB. The front of the envelope was inscribed in faded ink with the words: *Not to be opened until twenty-five years after my death,* followed by the signature of John Boyd Darvell. From his own research work on the family John Corbin knew that it was a considerable number of years since that date had been passed. He sat for a while holding the envelope in his hands wondering, not so much at the nature of its contents, but why the Bishop had never opened it. Probably, he decided, because he had never gone through his father's papers scrupulously and so had never found it. Well, the next time he was down he would draw his attention to it. He put the envelope back in the box and walked to the safe. As he put the box away he was thinking how nice it must be to have the money to commission a painting . . . to have the money to turn dreams into reality as the Darvells had done at Illaton.

CHAPTER SEVEN

THEY DROVE ON the Thursday to Rachel's parents in Oxfordshire and stayed two nights there before going on to visit Aunt Lily. Her parents were two very pleasant people who were clearly delighted at the engagement and gave John a warm welcome and each of them—as he had expected—at some time during his stay took a private opportunity of a talk with him about his prospects and the plans which he and Rachel had for their future. They did so, however, without any undue probing, content to follow a form they clearly felt was an expected convention. They both of them, too, were enthusiastic about his and Rachel's plans for the future . . . setting up a nursery garden together. When this arose he found himself, less from habit than a desire to please them, over-exaggerating the amount of money which was being held in trust for him. Rachel would bring more than he could but he saw no harm in narrowing the gap between their respective resources, But to ease his own conscience—and realizing too that his fanciful account of his finances might easily come to Rachel's ears—he was honest with her about it as they walked in the garden on the evening before they left.

He said, "I told a bit of a white lie about the money being held in trust for me. Upped it by a few thousand. After all I didn't want them thinking we were going to have too hard a time of it in the beginning."

Rachel smiled. "There was no need, Johnny. They started on a shoe-string."

"Then all the more need. Parents like to think that their children are starting off better than they did. It may be going to be hard, but there's no reason why they should have to fuss about it. Anyway, there's no harm in a comforting little white lie."

For a moment Rachel was silent, watching a trout rising under a willow in the stream which ran along the bottom of the garden. Then she said, "Will you make me a promise, Johnny? Never try and comfort me that way?"

"Of course. No secrets between us. We'd never get anywhere otherwise."

"And you do like them, don't you?"

"What a question. Of course I do. And I don't mind telling you that I envy you. My parents were only a hazy memory to me. Oh, I've always had Aunt Lily, and she's been marvellous. But it's not the same thing, is it?" He took her hand. "But now, glory be, I've got you. We're going to be all right. It's my business to make it so. Come hell or high water. Together we can face anything."

It was then that she almost told him, but forced herself to go on holding it back until she could be absolutely certain. There was no point in acting on what, at this stage, might so easily be a false alarm . . . upsetting all their present happiness and harmony just because she had missed a period now by three weeks. More disturbing still—and she hated herself for the thought—was that she could have no idea what his reaction would be if it did turn out that she was pregnant. It was impossible for her to guess. Intimate as they were, and her understanding of his nature filling out as each day went by, she knew that there was far from complete understanding in her of his full character. Oh, God, yes—she loved him and he loved her; and to that she must trust. He might say have the baby or lose it, might be angry or happy, might even leave her. Perhaps the thing to do was to tell him her fears now . . . *No secrets between us. We'd never get anywhere otherwise.* His words of only a moment ago. In that moment she felt herself poised, readying herself to turn to him and tell him, when he took her hand and, with a touch of old-fashioned gallantry which he used sometimes and which she loved, he kissed it and said, "With you I can face anything. I say it again and then let another say it better for me . . ."

Then still holding her hand he quoted:

Thou art my life, my love, my heart,
The very eyes of me:

And hast command of every part
To live and die for thee.

"Oh, Johnny . . ."

She put her arms around him, held him tight and kissed him until at last he gently held her from him and said, "Good Lord . . . you've got a real touch of the emotions. Come on—let's walk down to the pub and have a drink. I've arranged for your mother and father to meet us there later for lunch." Then, standing back from her, he went on, "Do you know what I miss at the moment?"

"No. What?"

"Old Cassidy. He should be around somewhere, keeping a tired, weary eye on us."

She laughed then, freely and gaily, knowing that one way or another everything would come right.

* * * *

With Aunt Lily things were different. Any talk there was of their future was vague and swamped by her immediate liking of Rachel and a recognition that perhaps this was what Johnny had always needed to happen to put him straight in life. She was not going to question anything. She was entirely content to believe that something had happened at last to Johnny which was going to change his life. For that she would pray. Only once—and that with Rachel—did she ever show even the shadow of concern for their future.

She said, with Johnny safely working in the garden, "I don't know what you've done, Rachel—but you seem to have made a different man of him. Up until now he's always been a restless, unsettled type. As though he's always been looking for something. Or perhaps——" she smiled, "——all young men are like that until they meet Miss Right. He never would settle to anything for long. I used to get very cross with him. But now I can see the change in him. And it's all due to you, dear, I'm sure. You're what he wanted. Someone to love and to look after. Oh, dear, am I sounding rather sloppy?"

"I don't think so at all, Aunt Lily. I think, in a way, I was the same. I was quite happy by myself, but not really content. Johnny was the same. And anyway, he has so many talents I think he found it hard to choose which to settle to." She laughed. "He can still surprise me. The last evening at home he sat down at the piano and began to play for us. Just like that . . . out of the blue . . . Chopin, Mozart, and then old dance tunes and songs. I'd no idea."

"That's Johnny. He always keeps something up his sleeve to surprise people with." Although she laughed, Aunt Lily made a little prayer that in the future Johnny's surprises would all be pleasant ones. So far as she was concerned she was determined to believe that, so far as unpleasant surprises were concerned, she had known the end of them from Johnny. And the last thing she would have done on their visit would have been to mar it in any way by bringing up with him any awkwardness from the past.

On the morning of their departure she sat down after they were gone and wrote a letter to Johnny. She told him of Helder and his work for Mr Barwick, and finally she explained to him the arrangement she had made through Helder with Mr Barwick, and finished:

I know—if you can't bring yourself to go and see Mr Barwick and collect the cheque—that this will be a blow to you. You will understand why I didn't tell you about this when you were here. How could I at such a time of happiness? But there it is, my dear Johnny, I have done, not only what I have a perfect right to do, but what I consider is the honourable thing to do. I should have hated the thought of you going into a new life with Rachel—even though I did not know of that at the time—with anything dishonourable hanging over you. I know that in the future you will need the money for the plans you two have together, so my advice is to put your often misplaced pride in your pocket and go to Mr Barwick. In any case I would like you to let me know your decision since I have promised to pass on your decision to Mr Helder who, by the way, knows that you are working somewhere in the Tavistock area. Just how does not matter. But he does.

Please, Johnny, be sensible. You have love and happiness now with Rachel and the prospect of a good future—so settle this thing, no matter how much it goes against the grain, by seeing Mr Barwick. It is humiliating, but what does that matter? He was humiliated once. It simply wipes the slate clean—and that you must have for the sake of your future. Please, please, be sensible about it.

Then, to cheer herself up, she poured a glass of sherry and wrote to Miss Simpson giving her the news of Johnny's coming engagement.

... and she is such a sensible thing as well as attractive, and clearly just what he needs. It was a joy to have them and to see their happiness. The announcement will be in the Daily Telegraph *some time next week. While they were here they summer pruned the wistaria at the back for me and then repaired our broken-down donkey shed and gave it a new coat of paint and Rachel has promised to send me, come the autumn, some plants from the place where they work. Oh, my dear, I am so happy about all this ...*

That evening she telephoned Helder in London after trying twice before during the day without getting a reply. This time the call was answered by him and she told him that she was sending a cheque to him for Mr Barwick and that she had let Johnny know the conditions for its return.

Helder said, "You wrote to him about it? Or told him personally?"

"I wrote to him today. As soon as I hear from him I will let you know."

"Thank you, Mrs Hines."

As he put down the telephone his sister turned to him and said, "Mrs Hines?"

"Yes, Mrs Hines."

"Why didn't you tell her that you knew exactly where he was?"

"Because I didn't think it would be of any comfort to her."

Their few days' visit to Tavistock—as he had felt it might be—had been unproductive while they had been there. But his sister had enjoyed herself going back to the places which she had known with her husband. And it was interesting too, he thought, how finely balanced were the ironies of life for on the day before they left they had decided to make a visit to the gardens at Illaton Manor but the day had turned out stormy and rain-laden so they had gone to Plymouth for lunch and spent the afternoon at a cinema—his choice, not his sister's who had wanted to go to the aquarium on the Hoe. But on the way home, from a sudden spur of sentiment, he had turned off the main road for a few miles and visited Miss Simpson. She had been glad to see him and full of talk during the course of which he had learned that she now corresponded fairly regularly with Mrs Hines and gladly informed him—in reply to an apparently casual enquiry—that John Corbin was now working at Illaton Manor, writing a family history. Thinking about it now, he smiled to himself for the rather smudgy ethics of his profession clearly demanded that he should tell Mr Barwick of his find. But since talking to Mrs Hines he had decided not to for the present for her sake. Far better that John Corbin should be given his chance and perhaps please her by going to Barwick. As to that likelihood he had doubts. It would be a matter of pull Devil pull baker and he did not wish to speculate which would win.

At this moment his sister said, "Why are you smiling in that rather silly way?"

He said, "I was just thinking how dull life would be if we always knew what was going to happen tomorrow."

"Rubbish. You were thinking nothing of the kind."

"And also how unlike me to have decided not to tell Mr Barwick for the time being that I know where John Corbin is."

"I should think not. The man's quite capable of changing his mind and go charging after Corbin."

"That's what I mean. Do you think Corbin will go to him to get the cheque back?"

His sister considered this for a moment and then said, "I don't think so. Dishonest people often set the most exaggerated store by their pride. And quite rightly so. They must have at least one thing on which they can rely. And your Mr Barwick knows that. He knows his money is safe."

* * * *

As he walked up from his cottage to the Manor with Cassidy sloping at his heels the day was like an enamelled jewel. The windless sky held a few still, high cumulus clouds, bold against the aquamarine sky. A kestrel hung over the second cut of newly laid hay in the home paddock, fixed it seemed for ever in its place. It was as though some power held the world in a long caught breath so that the eye would have fuller term than ever before to catch the enchantment of the fresh morning world. Fanciful, he thought, but it suited his mood for there was a deep happiness in him which was like a cool, still well of contentment. A toad squatted at the side of the track, fixed bow-legged, its skin green and brown serpentine and, grinning at his own fantasy, he stopped and leaned over it to see whether its bulbous eyes would be of agate or jade. All happiness, he thought, lay in the arrested morning beauty, and within him too. He was in love and loved. Yesterday he had written the first pages of his book and knew that they were good. An hour's nailbiting seeking the right move into the work and then had come the sudden, certain flow of words. Yes, today God was in His heaven all right, and all was well with the world.

Cassidy growled at the toad and he called him off. As he walked he wondered where was the old John Corbin? A nasty little bit of work. Gone forever. Now he walked, not on the road to Damascus, but along a glade of Paradise. Passing one of the gardeners hoeing a flower bed he called out, "Lovely morning, isn't it?"

The man leaned on his hoe and said, "'Tis that. We'll have a crowd today. You'll see. Throwin' paper all over the place instead of using the bins."

Well, let them throw paper, he thought. Paper today and confetti tomorrow or whenever the day came. He went into the Manor and up to the library and sat down and read what he had written the day before. It still read well, which delighted but surprised him. Usually some malevolent sprite had turned the gold to dross overnight.

At eleven o'clock Miss Latham came up with his coffee tray. She was wearing a tussore silk summer dress with a scrap of red scarf at her throat and for a moment he saw her as she must have been as a young girl, all Spring and beauty, and there was no surprise in him because he now saw all the world through new eyes. The euphoria which the glory of the morning had wakened in him, he knew, would go, giving way to abiding contentment.

Miss Latham said, "You've got a grin on your face like a cat that's been at the cream. Or am I getting my metaphors or whatever they are mixed?"

"I wouldn't know. But does it matter? Are you joining me for coffee?" He nodded at the two cups on the tray.

"I thought I would—if you can bear with me."

"Bear is not the word. Besides I want to tell you something."

"Oh, yes. What?"

"Pour the coffee first. While your hand is still steady."

Smiling Miss Latham poured the coffee and then sat down in the window seat opposite him and said, "Now tell me."

"Rachel and I are engaged. There's to be an announcement in the *Daily Telegraph* soon."

"Johnny! What lovely news." She came round to him and kissed him. "Oh, I'm so happy for you both. So that's it—you both went off together to see your people?"

"Yes." He looked at her slyly. "You really are surprised?"

"Of course."

"Rachel hasn't said a word to you before?"

"Good gracious me, no."

He smiled. "You girls stick together, don't you?"

"Would you have minded?"

"No, of course not."

"And when are you going to be married?"

"Not until I've finished my work here. After that . . . well, we're planning to start something on our own. It's all a bit up in the air at the moment."

"Oh, Johnny—I really am delighted. And so will the Bishop be. He's very fond of Rachel and has a very high regard for you. By the way there's another letter from him in *The Times* this morning. I'll send it up for you at lunchtime. Oh, Johnny, what an excitement. You and Rachel. Was your aunt pleased? Oh, of course she was."

"Oh, yes—and I got a strict lecture from her about my duties and responsibilities and so on."

"Ah, well, one's loved ones always like to get the most from this kind of occasion. Perhaps I should give you a lecture too. By the way, I've a confession to make. I came up here last night after you were gone . . . I usually do to tidy ash trays and so on . . .

and I did an awful thing. You'd left your papers out and I read the draft of your foreword to the book. Am I forgiven?"

Johnny laughed. "That depends very much on what you thought of it."

"I thought it was splendid!"

"Really?"

"Yes, really. My dear Johnny, you've got a great gift. I loved the little wicked asides. The Bishop will too. He's got a great sense of humour though he keeps it well covered mostly. I loved the bit about all the best gardeners not only having green fingers but also being light-fingered in other people's gardens . . ." She got up, leaving her coffee untouched, and turning towards the window went on, "Well, what a lovely morning. Oh, I'm so happy for you both. Some time later in the week you must both come up and have dinner with me . . . but for now I must get on with the hundred and one things." She turned to him briefly and her eyes were touched with tears. At the door she paused and said, "Oh, there's a letter for you on the tray with the newspaper."

But instead of going about her various household duties Miss Latham went to her bedroom and sat at her dressing table looking out over the garden and remembered the day, long past, when the Bishop—though no Bishop then—had told her of his engagement to her sister Dorothy. She had thought then that perhaps with time she would be reconciled . . . that inevitably some other love would come into her life. But none ever had. She was still as much in love with him as she had ever been. Completely and utterly devoted to him.

Suddenly she sniffed and wiped the tears from her eyes, telling herself not to be an old fool.

Back in the library Corbin picked up *The Times* and read the Bishop's letter with little interest, though it became clear to him that the argument was wandering far from its original base and he suspected that the Bishop was not only enjoying himself but also far from unaware of the publicity value of these exchanges. There were two other letters supporting him. One was from a Conservative Member of Parliament, and the other was from the headmaster of a public school. Against these was a very long letter from a member of the Trades Union Council deploring not only the Bishop's attitude but also his distortion of facts. And so on and so on, he thought, it will go on until the editor—probably very soon now—called time. But by then the Bishop would have clocked up a splendid mileage of publicity. And the Poles? Well, he supposed—like elephants—they would never forget.

A glance at his letter showed him that it was from Aunt Lily. He put it in his pocket to read later and turned to his work, making notes and checking references for his first chapter and trying to create in his mind the moods and thoughts which had filled that first Henry Boyd Darvell who, in the eighteen thirties, had driven out from Plymouth in his carriage to look over the neglected Illaton farmhouse and the waste of scrub and woodland on the high bluffs above the River Tamar. Walking the land he had been undismayed by the wilderness and ruin. Wherever he went he had carried with him a vision of the future. When he had bought the place and work had begun Time was no enemy to him, but the great ally in the translation of his dream to reality. That he should begin a labour of love he would never live to finish caused him no dismay. Great gardens were like great cathedrals. Their establishment consumed time and men from generation to generation in an act of worship and praise celebrating the glory of God and the miracles of His creation.

An extract from his diaries of the time read:

With Barnes, my coachman, I spent the night at the Illaton Quay inn in rough but friendly company where we dined off sea trout and a fine saddle of lamb. The next morning it was raining and the landlord lent us a couple of cobs on which we rode up the river and cliff track to the top of the bluffs, and riding my eyes saw not the untamed wilderness but the glory which would with God's grace one day crown these heights. On our way we remarked one place where a natural stream could be dammed to create a lake and a fine waterfall, and another place at the very top of the bluffs where scrub and a growth of birches—overcrowded and many of them dead—could be cleared to give a great outlook eastwards across the Tamar and the borders of Devon, a place where the first rising of the sun would illuminate with its rays the tall spires of the great pines which one day shall be growing there. A little apart from Barnes I made a silent prayer for the good Lord's blessing on the labours I intend to glorify His name. At this moment, and I dare to think, miraculously, the rain clouds cleared to the east and the morning sun came through casting light and warmth over all as though the Creator's hand had moved in blessing and approval of all I intend.

For a moment or two Corbin leaned back in his chair, touched by the simple faith of the man and wished in his heart that he could have known such certainty of devotion and belief for without it all men were diminished.

He worked until lunch-time and the maid brought him his tray. He ate without much thought to his food, watching the visitors passing along the front of the Manor, and then went back to his work. Great faith, he thought, he might not have but dedication to the work he was now doing and the prospect of his future with Rachel were comforts which, he was convinced, were already leading him resolutely into a new life. Who knew—perhaps in time the rain clouds would clear for him? Had cleared, maybe, without his knowing it.

It was six o'clock before he finished for the day and by then he had his first chapter blocked out roughly and was well pleased with himself for he sensed now that the work had begun to run. He walked back to his cottage and Cassidy joined him from the direction of the car park where he had spent most of the day being regaled with scraps from the visitors' picnic meals. Over his first drink he took Aunt Lily's letter from his pocket—forgotten until now in the run of the day's euphoria—and was about to open it when Rachel came in on her way home. He gave her a hug and a kiss and fixed her a drink.

He said, "I haven't seen you around all day."

"I was in Tavistock all the morning. We took a load of tomatoes in and then I had to hunt around for spare parts for one of the big mowers. It's been one of those days. When I got back somebody had driven off with one of the visitors' cars and we had the police out. Didn't you hear about it?"

"No. I've been locked in my cell with Henry Boyd Darvell. Why the hell don't people lock their cars properly?"

"Because they're people, I suppose."

"By the way, I've told Miss Latham about us."

"I know. She told me."

He smiled. "Did she need to be told? You can't tell me you didn't leak it some time ago. Confess."

She smiled. "What did you expect? That I could keep something like that bottled up inside me? I'd have burst. Oh, Johnny—it really is happening, isn't it?"

"Of course it is. And I'm glad you told her. Do you mind if I don't come down tonight? I've got all this Darvell stuff churning round in my head . . . I thought I'd make some more notes and then turn in early."

"No, of course not, darling. I like to see you so worked up. You're really pleased with what you've done?"

"At the moment, yes. The great test is when I read it tomorrow morning . . . No, no, I don't mean it. I know it's good. But, better than all that, is us. Oh God, isn't it marvellous! Just you and me. Everything is perfect. *Go, little book, and wish to all—Flowers in the garden, meat in the hall . . . a living river by the door, a nightingale in the sycamore . . .*" He did a little dance around her, spilled some of his drink, and collapsed laughing in a chair.

She reached out and took his hand. "You're mad, but it's a nice madness. Say something else nice to me . . ." As she spoke, though she was delighting in his good spirits and his joy in his work, she knew that deep in her there was a small core of anxiety for which she needed some temporary balm.

"What can I say to you that really comes near the truth? Well," he grinned, knowing the euphoria in him, "perhaps I can by taking a little licence . . . *More to be desired are you than gold, yea, than much fine gold: sweeter also than honey, and the honeycomb.* Dear Rachel . . ." He reached out and took her hand.

She felt the prick of tears in her eyes, and leaned forward and kissed his hand. Driving away from his cottage, she let the tears come freely . . .

Five minutes after she had gone John Corbin read his aunt's letter. His first reaction was of sheer violence. He swore and threw the glass in his hand against the far wall so that Cassidy who lay in half sleep by the door was startled, jumped to his feet and started barking but soon ceased as Corbin dropped back in his chair and gnawed at a thumbnail as he fought down his first, violent feelings.

That bloody man Barwick . . . What the hell had he got more than he deserved? He'd never been without a mistress since his marriage and didn't really care a damn for his wife except as one of many possessions. The Barwick woman had come to him to get a little of her own back—and he, this from her own lips, far from the first of similar consolations. And damn certainly not the last. All right, so he'd made her pay for his services. Why not? That was exactly what it was. A service. But worst of all—to hell with the Barwicks—Aunt Lily had been dragged into it and had agreed to this damn fool business of paying back the money. He suddenly spat, as though to get a sour taste from his mouth, and remembered the exaggeration of his finances he had made to Rachel's father. That must have given Old Nick a chuckle. Two thousand pounds gone . . . and a few minutes ago he had been up in the clouds about the book and the way things were going to be.

He got up and taking a fresh glass poured himself a large whisky and went and sat on the bench outside the front door to escape the oppression of four walls about him. A blackbird was giving a fine virtuoso performance and the air was thick with high summer scents. Well . . . one thing was certain. Much as he wanted the money he would be damned if he would go to Barwick cap in hand and ask for it. Some time—though there was no hurry about it—he would have to tell Rachel and she would understand. She wouldn't care a button about Mrs Barwick. He had never pretended to her that there hadn't been other women in his life. She'd give him hell for taking the stupid woman for money, but that wouldn't matter in the long run. He swore aloud and Cassidy came out and looked up at him as though for the first time in their relationship he had ever truly caught his interest. He laughed then at the dog's expression and felt better.

"All right, Cassidy. It's over. Storm in a teacup. He can keep the money. I'm not grovelling to anyone."

He stayed there, taking his drink slowly, while the evening sky flamed its way through a gold and red sunset and the first of the pipistrelle bats from the cottage thatch came out and began their hawking. Then, composed, he went in and wrote to Aunt Lily.

. . . and, of course, you must know that your letter was a bit of a blow to me. But not for one moment do I think you have done the wrong thing. Where I acted dishonourably you have acted honourably on my behalf. The point is, of course, that you acted for a man who no longer exists. That man would have been angry. But I can only thank you. I shall tell Rachel all about it otherwise there could be no truth in my deep feelings for her—and I know that she will understand and forgive.

But one thing you will realize I cannot do—no matter how much the money would have meant—that is to go cap in hand to Barwick who merely wants, and understandably, to humiliate me by proving that I rank my pride lower than my wish to have the money. God will judge my sins in good time, but I don't want any Barwick playing the role of King Solomon over me. So I would be grateful if you would let your Mr Helder pass that message on to him. And since this is an end to the matter I see no reason why you should keep my present address a secret. But that's up to you, my darling.

Rachel, I am sure, would send her love if she knew I were writing. She fell for you hook, line and sinker! And why not? You are right at the top of my Christmas tree.

Love, Johnny.

P.S. You say you write to Miss Simpson now and then. Give her my love.

He fried himself eggs and bacon for supper, drank half a bottle of a Côtes du Rhône and went to bed and slept heavily and dreamlessly.

*   *   *   *

Three days later Aunt Lily telephoned Mr Helder and passed on John Corbin's decision to him.

Helder asked, "Do you approve?"

"Yes, of course I do. He's repaid the money which he extorted from Mr Barwick and that's an end to the matter. What did you expect him to do?"

"Exactly what he has done, Mrs Hines."

"Well . . . there it is. I'm just thankful the whole sordid

business is over. It really can't be very nice for you to have to concern yourself with things like this. Though I suppose you get used to it."

"Oh, yes. I'm well used to it. You'd be surprised at the number of very nice people one meets . . . like you and Miss Simpson. The work has its compensations."

Aunt Lily laughed. "Really, Mr Helder, I didn't expect such gallantry from you."

"Well, I'm a little surprised myself. But it's nice to hear you laughing. Goodbye, Mrs Hines."

The next day Helder went to see Mr Barwick and told him the decision which John Corbin had made.

Barwick gave a dry laugh and said, "Well, it's no more than I expected. He just hadn't got the guts, had he?"

"I wouldn't know, Mr Barwick."

"Well, I do. He's just a rat. He's probably scheming right now some more of his dirty nonsense. All right he may have some pride—but he won't change. People don't change. They just put on a different coat."

"Possibly. I'll let you have my account in due course."

"Do that, Helder." Barwick was silent for a moment or two, smiling at Helder, and then went on, "Why don't you ask me what I'm going to do with the money? Now that I've humiliated him—send it back to his aunt, perhaps?"

"I wouldn't know, Mr Barwick. It's none of my business."

"Well, I'll tell you anyway. I shall keep it for some while. And then . . . oh, yes, and then I'll send it back to his aunt to deal with at her discretion. You say it comes from a trust fund in his favour. Well, she can do what she likes with it because then it will be hers. But this is entirely confidential between us, you understand?"

"Of course, Mr Barwick."

That evening, as Barwick fixed a drink in their flat for his wife who had just come in, he said, "By the way, you will find this hard to believe but I got your money back from that scab Corbin today."

"Corbin? Oh . . . yes, John Corbin."

"Don't tell me you've forgotten him?"

She smiled as she took her drink from him. "Let's say long

wiped him out of my mind. I don't want to think about him or know anything about him."

"Fair enough."

"Darling, all my love." She raised her glass and drank and then leaned back and relaxed in her chair, shutting her eyes against the languor in her body and seeming to feel again over her skin the kisses and caresses of the lover with whom she had spent two hours that afternoon.

CHAPTER EIGHT

DURING THE NEXT three weeks Corbin slowly concerned himself less and less with thoughts of the money which had been lost from his trust fund. After all, it would have been some time before he would have had need to call on it. Aunt Lily would only have made it available to him on his marriage and he and Rachel had agreed that they would only get married when he had finished his work at Illaton and seen whether a publisher would be interested in his book. Their plans were vague. Only time could crystallize them. They had the whole world before them and time enough. The bitterness in him eased with a comforting rapidity. So what? It was only money. The bouts of anger which he had had from time to time after getting Aunt Lily's letter grew infrequent. His book was going well and his pleasure in it bolstered his self-confidence and at the end of a day's work he could often relax into a euphoric state seeing the future ahead . . . rose pink and flushed with gold like the evening clouds at sunset over the moors to the west of Illaton. There were times when he saw the blow as an act of the gods to test his worth. Well, that suited him. He was moving into a new life. However, he had decided not to tell Rachel anything about the money. There was no point in involving her and having to go into the sordid details of his affair with Sue Barwick. All that was dead and gone—like his money.

The Bishop came down on a flying visit and—a little against his will—he let him read the foreword and the first two chapters of the book. The Bishop was delighted with it and the sincerity of his feelings was pleasingly forcible. Since he was beginning to know Corbin better, he said with a slight cocking of one of his grey, bushy eyebrows, "And, my dear John, my pleasure I assure you does not come from any kind of ancestor worship.

Did I know nothing of the Darvells the merit and charm of the work would be nevertheless a delight to me." Then with an engaging grin, he went on, "I know that you and Rachel have plans for a joint venture eventually but I hope that you will never let this talent of yours go to seed."

"No, my lord, but I doubt whether I shall ever be able to make a full living from it. Oh, perhaps by myself it might work. But when a man marries . . ."

"Yes, I understand. What do you and Rachel intend to do?"

Corbin told him, and when he had finished the Bishop said, "I think that sounds very sensible. But it will mean a lot of hard work. But you are both capable of that."

That the Bishop did not mention that it would also mean a lot of money to set themselves up did not surprise Corbin. The Bishop believed in faith and miracles. He, himself, felt that the first was easier to come by than the second—and both likely to wilt and fade unless they had the backing of money. However, in deference to the man's cloth, he said quite genuinely, "We shall manage, my lord." And then, with a smile, added, "Perhaps you might find a moment or two to put in a word for us where it will do most good? It always helps to have a friend at court."

The Bishop laughed. "My dear John—I have already done that. Now the rest is up to you."

That evening Corbin went down to Illaton Quay to have supper and stay the night with Rachel. After supper they walked down the river in the dusk with Cassidy trailing them and the river tide running in fast covering the mud and reed banks. The air was still and warm and they walked holding hands and without much talk between them. His mind now was eased from the loss of his money to Barwick. The future and their love was all between them and that was enough. The August moon was almost full and Corbin felt a contentment in him which he had never known before. His life had purpose and direction and the gift of love. Suddenly he felt a new strength and unassailability in him. He knew where he was going and what he wanted to do—and that for him was, linked with his love for Rachel, the source of a new confidence. The skin of the old John Corbin had been sloughed. He walked a new man. He laughed suddenly, breaking their silence.

Rachel said, "Why do you laugh?"

"Because there are no words to describe how I feel." He turned her to him and kissed her and held her in his arms.

Later he woke by her side knowing it was time to leave her and walk back to Illaton in the near dawn. He began to move from the bed without disturbing her sleep when she put out a hand and held his wrist and said, "I'm not asleep."

"Then you should be."

"No. I've been waiting for you to wake up."

"What on earth for?"

The only light in the room came from the moon and all he could see of her was the pale oval of her face and the dark disorder of her hair against the pillow.

She said, "I want to talk to you."

He laughed. "You go to sleep. There's nothing which can't wait until the morning."

"This can't. Oh, Johnny—it can't. I've been wanting to tell you all the evening, but I didn't want to spoil things. I meant to leave it until tomorrow. But I just can't now."

He sat then on the edge of the bed, caressing the smooth run of her bare arm, and for a while was silent, not waiting for her to go on talking, but held by a sudden coldness and sense of rising disturbance because quite positively he suddenly knew what she was going to say, and knew, too, that unless he schooled himself he could so easily kill with a word or two all that held them together. To give himself time to master his own dismay and to order the only response he could and must make to her, out of his love for her, he raised her hand and kissed it. Seeing the shine of tears in her eyes he was filled with an excess of love for her that gripped him almost physically by the throat so that when he spoke his own voice sounded strange and unexpectedly tense.

He said, "I think I know what you're going to say. If it is what I think I want you to know that it makes no difference to us. Not a bloody bit of difference. So that's that part of it over."

"Oh, Johnny!"

She came to him then and put her arms about him, her face on his shoulder. He held her until she had recovered a little and then reaching to the bedside chair took her dressing gown and draped it over her bare shoulders. Holding both her hands in his, he said, "Tell me all about it. I never asked you when we first made love . . ."

"I know. It was damned stupid of me. But everything was so marvellous—I just took a chance. There were only a few days to go and I thought it would be all right. I went on the pill the next day and kept my fingers crossed. I've missed twice since then. Two weeks ago I had a pregnancy test."

"And it was positive?"

"Yes. Oh, Johnny! I hate myself for all this. And I would understand if——"

He put his hand gently over her mouth.

"There's only one thing for you to understand. It makes no difference to us." He laughed to give her comfort. "So—we've jumped the gun like thousands of others before us. Nobody thinks anything of it these days." He leaned forward and kissed her.

She drew back from him after a moment or two and, as he handed her his handkerchief to wipe her eyes, she said, "We could have something done about it."

Angrily he said, "There's not going to be any bloody thing like that. It's ours. It's a life. Christ . . . I may be all sorts of things, but that doesn't come in my book. Or yours. Jesus—I've done some pretty awful things in my time. Yes, shabby, dirty things. And very often they've caught up with me. But not that kind of thing. It's a life we've created. It's part of us. It's come a bit soon, that's all. But there it is—we'll just have to accept it and more than that—be glad about it. All right, it'll bugger up our plans a bit, but that only makes the whole thing a bigger challenge. You're going to be my wife and there's going to be no messing about——"

With a sudden movement she took his hand and kissed it and then pressed it against her cheek, saying, "Oh God, Johnny—you don't know what it does for me to hear you speak like that. I've been worried sick for you about it all."

"Then your worries are over. Now you stay there."

As he moved to leave the room, she said, "Where are you going?"

"Where do you think? A man doesn't get news like this every day—or night—of his life. We're going to *arroser le bébé*. And you can drink to a girl and I'll drink to a boy and then we'll leave it in the good Lord's hands. We haven't got any champagne—so it's a choice between sherry or white wine. I'll bring both so you can make up your mind while I'm gone."

When he came back they both drank white wine and, although he knew the underlying disturbance in him might grow, so too he knew that nothing could alter his love for her. He lifted his glass for a second time and said to her, "Would you like something nice for a great occasion? Then you shall have it and worry no more for my love for you is as 'Continuous as the stars that shine and twinkle on the milky way . . .' "

Rachel lay back in the bed, her eyes blurred with loosely held tears, and felt her joy in him move through her like a great tide, sweeping before it all the drift and wrack of her past fears, and then suddenly she began to cry with happiness and relief.

Later, Corbin walked back to his cottage with Cassidy at his heels, taking the old bridle path which still existed that Henry Darvell had ridden on his first visit to Illaton. There was a grey light of early morning on the lake and a wet fingering of spray to touch his cheeks from its waterfall, and at the top of the bluff, as he stood on the terrace below the Grecian temple, the sun—just as it had once done for Henry Darvell—broke over the eastern horizon and gilded the crests of the tall pines which that long dead gardener had vowed to plant there. Facing the sun and looking over the river he knew for the first time in his life that everything he had said and done in Rachel's bedroom had been from the simple truth and honest emotion in him. He loved her and would protect and cherish her. There was the truth, he told himself. And truth was unalterable. Emotion, like the mist over the far fields beyond the river, was evanescent. Calmly now, his feet on earth again, he acknowledged the new truths which he would have to face. Things were not going to be easy. In fact, they were going to be damned difficult. He stood there biting at his lower lip and, knowing himself, realized that the black moments would come and a way would have to be found to overbear them. Ten minutes' pleasure shared with Rachel had changed dramatically the simple pattern of the future which he had envisaged. Quite suddenly the bee had quit the clover and the high summer of their romance was over. The hard facts of winter lay ahead . . . He laughed suddenly and shrugged the whole thing from him. The early morning was no time for planning a future.

He walked back across the dewed lawns, past the front of the Manor with its great stone urns blazing with the pink heraldic blooms of *Lilium rubellum,* and on to his cottage where he shaved and washed while his eggs and bacon cooked. He ate with appetite and from a habitude long acquired he dismissed all unpleasant thoughts from his mind. There was no point in harrowing himself with regrets. Something would turn up. Something always did . . . always had. The gods had no time for men who whined at the unexpected kinks and turns in their destinies. If a man whined they would abandon him. But for a man who turned and faced them undaunted they could often loose some unexpected charity. He was in a pot mess. Well, not for the first time in his life.

He went calmly to his work that morning and was pleased with his writing. He was still living in the time and writing of the labours of the first Darvell and growing to feel that he now knew the man for instance far better than he would ever come to know the Bishop. Nothing had ever daunted him. No disaster was so great that he ever turned away from it. That God was on his side he knew and he never whined when things went wrong. Just before Miss Latham came up to share coffee with him he wrote—

Transport was a major problem in his day and building materials and plant consignments often came up the river from Plymouth on sailing barges which were frequently at hazard from shifts of the wind and miscalculation of the tide run. Once one of the barges went aground on a mud bank with the tide falling fast. The barge heeled over as the river ran out and the cargo shifted so that on the returning tide the craft would have been flooded with salt water and the large consignment of plants ruined. Henry Darvell wrote later in his diary 'that the bargemaster was incompetent and, as I later discovered, also of an intemperate habit which on this day had been the main cause of the accident was of no immediate consequence. We brought down the plough horses from the Manor farm and also those from our good friends from the two Illaton Quay farms. Six strong young men, at some considerable risk to their persons, crossed the mud banks and swam the now narrowed main river to make them fast on the craft. Within an hour of the hawsers being secured to the barge and the horses set to strain it off the bank the craft was hauled back into the main stream, listing perilously but, by God's good grace, with all its cargo safe. There it rode until the tide returned and it could be brought to the Illaton quayside.

With something less than my usual charity I was in mind to dismiss the bargemaster, but thankfully on reflection—seeing that the man had been taught a lesson he would not forget and knowing that he had a large family and a bad word from me would bar him from finding a placing with any other employer—I spoke with the utmost severity to him and had his word that never again would he take charge of his barge in an inebriated condition.

Sadly, though perhaps predictably, the bargemaster did not long keep to his word and Darvell was eventually forced to dismiss him. If one looks now at the marble statue of Diana in the little temple overlooking the Tamar cliff it will be seen that her naked legs have a slight sunburnt flush which came from the river water which to some extent flooded the barge before it was pulled off the mud bank. Perhaps it would have been more appropriate if the goddess had been totally immersed for surely she must have been a dusky beauty.

Time and time again Darvell was faced with unexpected problems and many disappointments in the building of Illaton and the setting out of its gardens and landscapes. Never once does his diary carry a shadow of despair or disappointment. Like all great gardeners he kept his true love, not for those plants or works which flourished easily, but for those which challenged and opposed his will. When one walks in Spring through the apple orchard to the west of the Manor where the ground under the trees is a vast oriental carpet of variegated polyanthus blooms it should be remembered that hundreds of tons of unsuitable soil were cleared from the area and new, acceptable loam brought in to give the plants the conditions they needed for growth. Nature is a hard mistress and is not often constrained by man's efforts. But when She is and sees the result of his impertinence surely the corners of her mouth are touched by the crease of an approving smile?

It was at this point that Miss Latham came in with the coffee and, as she laid it down on the table in the window, she eyed him and said, "You look pleased with yourself, Master Corbin."

"And so I am, Mistress Latham. Though I can't think why."

"One should never question the source of happiness. Just thank God for it."

"I often do when I remember to remember."

"Ah, one of those moods."

She stayed and had coffee with him, but when she was gone and he returned to his work he found himself lost to the mood which had marked him earlier, and not really surprised by this because he knew that all along there had been something false in his own elation. He had put a good face on with Rachel and even deceived himself into a robust acceptance of the shift in their circumstances, but now came the reaction which he had known must come. He was in a bloody mess. Rachel with a baby to come, two bloody thousand pounds of his money gone to bloody Barwick . . . and all his future ahead unexpectedly conditioned in a manner with which he felt he was unable to cope.

He got up and walked around the room, biting his lower lip and feeling a savage thrust of anger unmanning him. Helpless, that's how he felt. Bloody helpless—and trapped. No matter his love for Rachel was true. Love by itself was no balm for the lack of pounds, shillings and pence. Nobody could live off love. Nobody could hand it over to a bank as surety for a large overdraft to start a business, to create a home and to furnish it with beds of roses and bright prospects before one every time the front door was opened. He was bloody well trapped—and now wished to God he had never come to this place. Wished more than that—wished that he could . . . maybe might eventually . . . find the selfishness to abandon all here . . . and Rachel . . . and go back to what he had once been. Why in God's name had she ever let him sleep with her and take such a risk? For all she had known their affair might have proved short-lived and no question of love ever intruded into it.

Then, with a familiar shift of mood, going from sudden gloom into sunshine, he was ashamed of himself. There had to be a way out. There just had to be some solution, and if it did not lie at hand waiting to be picked up—well, then he would have to create it. The real animal, when trapped, turned and fought. Only sheep lay helplessly on their backs and waited for death. With an uncontrollable impulse he suddenly reached out with his hand and swept a mass of papers, files and boxes to the floor.

The sudden outbreak of violence at once appalled and quieted him.

He picked up the litter from the floor and restored order to his working table. As he did so he saw the deed box in which lay John Boyd Darvell's envelope. He had meant to hand the sealed letter to the Bishop on his last visit but had forgotten to do so.

He took the envelope from the box and flexed it between both hands. There was little in it. He turned it over and saw that the gummed flap at the back had come partly unstuck. Glad of the diversion, glad to escape from his mood, he picked up a thin-bladed paper-knife which he had used now and then to separate stuck pages of Henry Darvell's diaries and worked it along the flap, opening it without damaging it. He felt no sense of violating privacy since he had been given access to all the family stuff in the safe. The thought struck him that, had the Bishop had as much interest genuinely in his family as he now had, the man would long ago have found it and opened it. Inside were two sheets of letter paper each with the printed heading of Illaton Manor and attached to them a smaller paper with a printed Harley Street, London, address at the top and the name *R. Pickford, Ph.D., M.D., F.R.C.P.*

The first two-page letter was written in very close handwriting, the ink faded somewhat, and was signed by John Boyd Darvell. Underneath his signature, and still written in his hand, was the statement: *I, the undersigned, Dorothy Jessie Gould, housekeeper at Illaton Manor, Illaton, Cornwall, although I do not know its contents, was present while this letter was written by my employer John Boyd Darvell of Illaton Manor and witness that the above is his true signature.* Then came her own signature which was also written at the bottom of the first sheet of paper. The letter, dated July 11th, 1924, and written in a small, neat and very legible hand, read—

A month ago my dearly beloved wife, Helen, presented me with a son who has been Christened Michael Boyd Darvell. In due course, if God grants him the life, he will find this letter among my papers and has my full permission to dispose of it as he chooses. He should know, too, that I have no great feeling in the matter, except that I think a family's records should deal only with the truth of those people concerned in them.

Nations distort their histories and conceal their truths. The Darvells never have. The greatest respect one can pay to one's ancestors is to welcome the truths about them, though not make those truths public at any time when harm can be done to others. Within the family no harm is done. Only another skeleton is added to those already in the cupboard.

The simple fact is that Michael Boyd Darvell is not my son. He is the child of my brother Philip Boyd Darvell who is now farming in Kenya. For many years my wife and I had wanted a child and our prayers had not been answered. Eventually we both took medical advice about this and—as the attached letter shows—the reason became evident. I was impotent. A series of tests proved that there were no sperm cells in my semen. A fact which, inter alia, explains why in the loose days before my marriage I never was called on to acknowledge a bastard. My wife however was found healthy and well capable of child bearing. We could, of course, have adopted a child, but there was a more acceptable solution at hand, and one which would not much outrage the continuation of the true Darvell line since it would still carry the Darvell blood strain. My wife consented to consort for a time with my brother Philip and he, for a substantial consideration and the promise to settle in Kenya, agreed to father the child. The birth of our child and the knowledge of his provenance has in no way altered the loving relationship between my wife and myself. In fact it has strengthened it. We have her child in which she takes joy, and my joy I take from her as I have from the first day we met and shall have until my last breath. My prayer is, my son, that you shall, too, when one day you come to read this, know no shame but only gratitude since without your mother's love for me and mine for her you would have had no existence.

And so, when at some moment in the far future you are reading this and may feel the need of comfort, just walk out into the Illaton gardens and see how a wilderness was turned into a paradise and know that you are there, living in that moment, with beauty all around you, and consider that you owe it all to two people who loved truly and nobly, and who have given you the chance to do the same.

The Harley Street specialist's letter, which was brief, was a confirmation of John Darvell's impotency.

After reading the letters Corbin sat for a long while with them before him. Outside he could hear the sounds of the visitors to the gardens. Now and again the house martins, late brooding, flashed across the window to feed their young in the nests below the eaves. Once, he was sure, John Darvell had sat in this room and written the letter, and it had been summer and other house martins had been homing to their broods after insect hawking over the gardens. Then suddenly he said aloud, "The Bishop is a bastard. God, what would he make of that if he knew?" Almost immediately he added, "And what could I make of it?"

* * * *

He had lunch that day with Miss Latham and during the course of it he said casually, "I was looking up some stuff this morning and I came across some references to the Bishop's uncle, Philip Darvell. Would you have ever met him?"

"No, never. He was long before my time here. But I know about him."

"Tell me. I'm interested in his relationship with his brother John. He was a few years younger than John, wasn't he?"

"Yes. But they were very close. Both wild as hawks, too. They were both in the First World War—John was Army and Philip in the Navy. After the war he never settled down and eventually, some time in the late twenties, he went to Kenya and, I think, started some small tea estate. But it never came to much. He had enough money of his own not to need to work."

"There's no record of a marriage."

"No. He never married, but he liked the ladies. And the bottle, too. That killed him in the end. He died in a car crash after some party in Nairobi. The Bishop told me once that while he was still at public school his father came and fetched him and they both went to Nairobi for the funeral. He didn't want to go but his father insisted on it. Said there had to be family representatives there. Are you interested in him for any particular reason?"

"No, only generally." He smiled suddenly. "Well, yes, perhaps. I was hoping that I might have come across an interesting black sheep type to liven up the botanical stuff a bit."

"Oh, dear, is it so dull?"

"Not at all. But there's nothing the public like more than a whiff of scandal now and then."

"I prefer the scent of flowers. Anyway, when you come to the records of John Darvell after his wife died you'll find enough, I think, to titillate jaded palates. He went completely wild—that's what caused all the trouble between him and the Bishop, though of course he was far from being a bishop then."

After lunch Corbin found himself restless and unable to settle to his work. In the end he went out, called up Cassidy, and took a long walk along the bluffs upriver. Slowly he began to realize what was in his mind and, although he kept turning from it, he could not put it from him. If Fate gave you an advantage, he thought, and turned up a card which could prove a high trump, you had to be a fool not to play it. But at the moment he could not see the play. But play there had to be—and one which would take him clear of the mess he was in. Don't rush it, he thought. Let it all simmer. The pot would come to the boil eventually. And, over all, there must be no chink in the armour to be worn. Into his hands John Darvell's letter had dropped from the skies like a weapon gifted miraculously by the gods. Dark, rather than bright—but nevertheless a gift from the gods who seldom took kindly to any spurning of their gifts.

He walked back through the country lanes behind Illaton, stopped at a village store, and bought provisions for an evening meal and was at the cottage before Rachel came in for her usual call on her way home.

When she arrived, he said, after kissing her, "You're eating here tonight. I'll run you down to Illaton Quay later. We've got to talk seriously but——" he grinned, "not sadly. Everything's going to be all right. I took a walk this afternoon and sorted it all out."

She sat down and took the drink he brought her and was grateful for his optimism and kindness. She said, "I've been in the glooms all the bloody day."

"No need, no need. True love must always be tried. Good Lord—we're not the first couple who have had this dropped in their laps. It's happening all the time—and in the best of families. You in the mood for facts and facing up to them?"

She smiled, recognizing the lift of spirits in him, and took hope from his manner. She said, "You tell me. I'll sit here like a good girl and listen. Just work the miracle. But before you do come and kiss me again and tell me you love me."

He laughed, went to her and kissed her, and said, "I love you and only you." Then stepping away from her and leaning in the open doorway looking at the evening sky, conscious that at the beginning, until he found his stride, he wanted his face turned from her, he went on, "But now from the romantical to the practical. There's no point in shouting the news abroad just yet, is there?"

"No."

"Then before things become obvious I suggest you make some excuse and leave here and we tell your people and Aunt Lily what is happening. I've got to stay on and finish my work here. We need the money. And when all this begins to happen we will get married. I can find another job after this one, and at a pinch we could go and live with Aunt Lily for a time. She'll be useful as a baby sitter, that's for sure. But the big point is we've got to fight tooth and nail not to give up our first dream of having a place and a business of our own. . . ."

She sat listening to him, knowing that she would do anything he said, and remembering with warmth how well he had taken her news the night before. His love for her then had been so clear and assuring. Now, which surprised her a little, he began to show a hard practical sense. They had a certain amount of money between them, but far from enough to make any joint venture into some enterprise of their own. But that did not mean they had to abandon the idea. Money could be borrowed. He had a friend he had met in his short days at University who was very rich and had long ago promised that if he ever wanted to start something on his own account he would finance him. It would be a loan, of course, and eventually they would have to pay it back.

"He's got so much he really doesn't know what to do with it. I've often gone and stayed with him. He's got a big estate in Wales. And every time he's after me to set up something he can back. There isn't any reason, either, why we should stay in this country. It's getting ragged round the edges. We should have the whole world for our oyster . . . Canada, Australia, South Africa . . ."

As he spoke he began to believe it. He had to believe it because the one element which must not touch his voice or manner was even a hint of despair. And—the irony touched him from aside—it was not the first time by any means that he had talked this way in smaller and more discreditable circumstances. But if he were gulling her now it was for the sake of their love and their future. In the past it had just been the shabby deployment of a confidence trick to line his own pockets. And, oddly, he felt now the same kind of lift in spirits and sense of invulnerability which had taken him in the past. People were puppets. You just found and then pulled the right strings. The only difference was that this time far more than a quick profit or a loan never to be repaid depended on it. He was doing something not selfishly for himself but for both of them—and he had to succeed. But before he could even start to put things in motion he had to carry her with him. Any lie he told her now or in the future would be a white one and would wither with the passing of time. Nobody had ever laid down that the foundations of true happiness rested on strict virtues. And, thank God, conscience with him was an obedient dog which lay down when ordered. He wanted her, the child, and success. The fates had tripped him in his early steps towards it. From now on it was simply a matter of keeping his eyes wider open and being nimble on his feet. The prospect, too, was not without its attractions. Conscience would make no coward of him. And now—again a recognizable element from past adventures—an excitement began to rise in him. Some people were there to be used. Not Rachel. But other people—to be used for her and his sakes.

He came back from the door and refilled their glasses, still talking and sensing the ease spreading in her as though it were a visible thing. But this time it was no over-amorous slut like the Barwick woman he was putting under a spell before he made her pay for the pleasure of four legs in a bed. The writ ran true this time. No question of love is not love which alters when it alteration finds. Alteration there was and it had made their love stronger and could prompt him to the high point of audacity and guile. By God, it could. The whole thing was just the kind of challenge he liked—though would not have asked for. But now here it was and not to be escaped, but neither to be wept over. Since John Boyd Darvell had written his letter nobody but John Corbin had set eyes on it, and there it was . . . his to profit from, and no one in the world to say him nay or at any time to come point a finger at him.

He had gentled her now, he knew, and as he finished talking he went to her, drew her from the chair and put his arms around her with comforting passion unmarked by any sense of guilt or shame for his past words or the action he meant to take in the future of which she should never know . . . must never know.

"Come on," he said. "You can help me cook dinner and afterwards I'll drive you down in your car and walk back with Cassidy."

When she stepped back from his embrace, she stood with her hands on his arms and smiled at him, and said, "Oh, Johnny . . . what a comfort you are. And please believe, please believe, I'll do anything you say. And you're right—it will all work out."

"Of course it will. And now——" he patted her on the bottom, "——get your pretty arse in the kitchen and set the steaks going."

Walking back with Cassidy that night through the warm late summer night, a light mist rising along the trough of the valley through which the mill stream ran down to Illaton Quay, he worked out in detail in his mind all that he would have to say and do, elaborating the germ of the idea which had come to him when he had roamed with Cassidy through the woods and lanes the previous afternoon. He was no stranger to small sins, but the sin he now contemplated was of a magnitude he had never attempted before. It was a good, strong, sharp salutary word *sin*. No man should attempt sin lightly—not this kind, anyway. Those of his past were trivial compared with this. Those of his past he had been able to live with easily—and so he would with this, but he would be a fool not to use every safeguard he could in its commission. As for the quantum of the sin he had no conscience, and he would have to forestall all the hazards which might uncover it—the risk of it hardening all within and petrifying his feelings . . . well, he didn't care a damn.

He came back to his cottage whistling and as he stood at his door a shooting star left a trail of fading gold across the sky which he refused to regard as any particular omen for or against his coming venture. He wanted Rachel, money and a secure future, and would have them.

Euphoria was high in him. Apart from anything else he knew that his true nature welcomed the risks to which he was setting himself.

He looked down at Cassidy and said aloud, "Well, there it is, Cassidy. Nothing venture, nothing win."

CHAPTER NINE

A FEW DAYS later Corbin wrote a letter to which he had given much thought. He wrote it on a sheet of plain quarto typing paper. He put no address or date at the top, neither did he sign it, and he wrote it wearing an old pair of wash leather gloves he possessed.

It read:

I have in my possession documentary evidence, duly witnessed and authenticated by the persons concerned, which sets out certain facts concerning the Bishop of Testerburgh whose name, of course, is far from unfamiliar to you. These facts are highly embarrassing and ones which the Bishop would never wish to be made public were he aware of them, which he is not. They could be used either privately or publicly to embarrass or constrain him, and most certainly, if known by his superiors in the Church of England, could effectively block the way to future preferments.

I am prepared to sell these documents but at the moment do not intend to go into the question of price, though it would have to be a considerable sum.

If you are interested all you have to do is to insert a notice in the Personal Columns of the Daily Telegraph *reading—Barkis is willing. This done, I would communicate with you again to settle the next steps to be taken.*

He folded it and sealed it into a cheap brown envelope, put a first-class stamp on it and left it unaddressed. He then put it into his pocket and turned to his work with a completely untroubled mind. That it was untroubled was no surprise to him. In a lesser degree he had often been here before, but on those occasions he had had only himself to consider. Now, he was carrying Rachel and their love with him and found himself even calmer. His mind was completely untroubled.

Two days later, a Saturday, and a day on which he seldom went to work at the Manor, he rose early and drove to Bristol where he addressed the envelope and posted it. He had lunch in a hotel and over it considered making a visit to Sarah Barnes on his way back through Exeter and then decided against it; not because he had any thought of briefly renewing their intimate and intermittent relationship but because now he was a cat that walked by itself and a man who was putting himself at some risk and—he had to confess—beginning to enjoy himself.

He drove back to Illaton, reaching it in the late afternoon and went down to Rachel. They had an early supper and then in the gloaming took out her boat and went up the river a little way on the top of the tide and came back with it on the turn. The calm of this windless evening was like a benison and he felt perfectly relaxed, as he had so often felt relaxed on previous occasions when he had put under weigh other less great but still reprehensible ventures. Having no true conscience, cowardice was almost alien to his nature.

Coming back to Illaton Quay in a smoky-hued dusk he looked up at the sheer cliff rise to the heights above and said to Rachel, "Do you know how Henry Boyd Darvell died?"

"Who was he? The first one here?"

"Yes. He died in 1887—on the day of Queen Victoria's Golden Jubilee. They had a great celebration at Illaton. Junketings in the garden for all the tenants and people around. Fireworks. The whole thing. And in the Manor was a big private party of all his friends. They had dinner and he rose to propose the Queen's health and he came to a part in his toast when he said, '. . . and in this fair garden of England she is the fairest flower of all. She is the rose of England, a bloom untouched, of the purest beauty, a symbol of Empire to us all, and one for whom no true Englishman would hesitate to lay down his life.' Then—*bonk!* He keeled over and died. But the thing is that as he spoke he had a glass in one hand and in the other—it was June—one of his own grown red roses. I think it was exactly the way he would have wanted it. That's the way to die. Without warning and the whole thing perfectly stage-managed."

"Is that how you would like to go?"

"Of course. With a bang, not a whimper. It was a great end. The long table was decorated entirely with bowls of roses, fifty in each for the years of the Queen's reign, and they were all the same—*Mme de la Rochelambert.* A lovely crimson, shaded with purple. There are none in the gardens now."

"I know them. They were brought on by Roberts around 1850, I think." She looked at him, smiling, a great calmness in her coming from the still evening and also from him and his acceptance of the change that was overtaking their lives. She put out a hand to him and he winked at her and kissed it.

* * * *

Three days later in London, in a room overlooking Portland Place, Aleksander Jawicki, an assistant to one of the Counsellors of the Polish Embassy, sat at his desk with John Corbin's letter lying before him. He was a large, amiable-looking man in his forties, slightly bald, his receding dark hair flecked with streaks of grey. He had seen the letter before and now it had come back to him from the Counsellor's office with a short minute attached to it which read:

It would be pleasant to think that this is not the letter of some crank, but I am prepared—if you feel so inclined—to bet you three hundred zlotys that it is. However, I think we might venture the cost of a reply in the Daily Telegraph *and see what happens. If anything does I think we should initially keep our distance. I suggest you use Formby to make the first approaches. It would be comforting to have something in hand with which to embarrass the Bishop should the occasion arise.*

What is the significance, if any, of Barkis?

Jawicki smiled at the last sentence. Then he picked up his telephone and made an internal call and gave instructions for a meeting with Formby. A nice young man, he thought, but gullible and romantic; a combination which had made him easy to recruit. It would be a long time before he ever came to realize that the carrot dangling before him would never come within his reach. When he did . . . well, they would find another Formby. Love made the world go round.

The next morning Jawicki took a taxi to Marble Arch and instructed the cabby to draw up outside Barclays Bank. Formby was waiting and got into the taxi with Jawicki who told the driver to take them around the Park.

Leaning back and lighting a cigarette, but not offering Formby one since he did not smoke, Jawicki said, "Nice to see you again. I hope you have not been inconvenienced?"

"I had to cancel two violin lessons."

"Oh, dear. Well, never mind. Just charge them up to us on your next expense account. By the way, I have a letter for you from Maria. I'll give it to you before we part."

"Oh, good. She's all right, is she?"

"Yes, I imagine so. Naturally I haven't opened the letter. But we get our own reports. And things are going well. I can tell you that. It's just a matter of time and observing the due forms."

As he spoke he smiled at Formby. He was a nice young man but in many ways a complete fool, and made more so by the fact that he was in love. He had a high, pink-and-white complexion and longish blond hair. In a dress suit and with his violin tucked up under his chin, a dreaming look in his eyes as he played more than competently as he had heard for himself, there were plenty of women who would find themselves falling in love with him to the strains of some Strauss waltz. Sometimes he found it difficult to believe that it was so easy to snare his kind in the nets of love. But it was easy. He and Maria did it often between them.

"You keep saying that. But how long?"

"I can't say exactly. But not long. In the meantime we should like you to do a very simple thing for us." Jawicki passed him a slip of paper. "We want this put in the Personal Column of the *Daily Telegraph* right away. Charge it up, of course, on your next expenses." Jawicki repressed a sigh. Always he found himself talking to Formby as though he were a child. And he was a child, of course, in many ways. So much so that he needed careful handling or he would fly off into an infantile tantrum.

"Why can't you do this kind of thing yourself? God, half the things you ask me to do seem straightforward enough."

"Well, let's say things aren't always what they seem to be. Of course, if you want to pull out altogether, you can. We've never forced you. You were given a straightforward proposition and you agreed. You do a few simple things for us and eventually Maria comes out long before she would be legally entitled to. Now—I'll get out and take a walk back across the Park and you can go on in the taxi to Fleet Street. It's a lovely morning . . . though with a touch of September not far off in the air. Smile, my dear Formby, and read your Maria's letter on your way."

"All right." Formby suddenly smiled. "Sorry. I don't mean to take it out on you. I know you're doing your best."

"I certainly am."

Jawicki walked back across the Park, enjoying the morning and until he reached his office put Formby right out of his mind. But once back in his office he wrote a minute to his Counsellor, which read:

Formby is taking care of the Barkis thing. In my opinion he has almost reached the end of his usefulness—not that it has ever amounted to much. My heart bleeds a little for him—but not enough to disturb my sleep. I would suggest that we let him run for a while to see if this Barkiss thing is any good and then, one way or the other, put his mind at rest about our beloved Maria.

As for the real Barkis. He is a character in David Copperfield—*one of the works of the great English writer, Charles Dickens. Like Formby he was in love, but I cannot remember whether his love ended happily. The real significance is that Barkiss said that when a man says that he is willing it means that he is waiting for an answer. So—we are dealing with a man of education and nice turn of wit.*

* * * *

That evening, in a small flat whose windows overlooked the not far distant great roof of Paddington Station, Formby sat in an armchair reading for far from the first time his letter from Maria. It was in pencil and written on coarse brown paper with the rubber-stamped heading of the Warsaw prison in which she was being held for political offences and where she had been now for over nine months. He had gone to Warsaw originally as a member of a small chamber orchestra sponsored by the Arts Council. The members of the ensemble had been entertained by Polish musicians and at a party given in its honour he had met

Maria and they had fallen in love. She was a teacher of art in a state school and very politically minded. A week before he was due to leave she had been arrested and he had been unable to make any contact with her and the few friends he had made there suddenly became elusive or clearly uncomfortable in his presence and not at all willing to help him by making enquiries on his behalf.

He had returned to London and four days later had had a telephone call inviting him to a meeting with Jawicki in Hyde Park. From that meeting—in which Jawicki had promised that, if he worked in a very minor way for them, they would eventually secure Maria's early release and see that she was granted permission to come to England to marry him—he had lived on hope and her letters.

The one in his hand now, written in English which she spoke perfectly—read:

Darling,

Thank you for your last letter which was a great comfort. Oh, darling, it seems so very, very long since we were together. In fact looking back I sometimes wonder whether it was all not a dream. Such brief happiness we had but so much love between us. As you know I can't say anything positive to you, but there is a rumour hopefully true that—

The next three lines had been cut clean out of the letter which then ran on—

I have been advised to plead guilty and there have been hints that a great deal of clemency will be shown. Even hints of a pardon for after all

Two more lines were cut and the letter finished—

well-treated, so there are no complaints on that score. Oh, darling, I live now on the memories of our time together and the hope that there really will be a pardon. After all the offence was not great.

Often on exercise round the yard I look up at the birds which fly free overhead and wish I were one so that I could fly to you . . .

Tears blinked in Formby's eyes as he laid the letter down and he remembered the moment when playing with the ensemble his eyes had rested on her in the small audience and so sure had he been that something had passed between them that he had sought her out at the reception given at the British Embassy afterwards. From there he had walked with her along the Aleja Roz to find a place to eat . . . and had wakened the next morning in her room to see her in a dressing gown at the bedside holding a tray of coffee, her dark hair loose over her shoulders, her eyes shining with love.

* * * *

When Miss Latham brought up his coffee Corbin noticed that she was limping. Before she could reach the window table he went to her and took the tray.

"Dear boy, thank you so much."

"Does that mean it's going to rain? It looks perfect out there." He nodded to the sun-drenched gardens.

She smiled. "I don't care what the sun does or what any barometer shows. My leg knows better. It will be raining hard before sunset."

"You're always so sure?"

"Always. You would like to make a little bet on it?"

"Good Lord—do you bet?"

"Of course I do, my dear man. But only about the weather. Anyone who bets on less than a certainty is a fool or a masochist. Shall we have five pounds on it?"

He laughed. "No, thank you."

"Very wise." She smiled. "In a way I think it was a kind of punishment. As a young woman I was an inveterate gambler . . . in a small way, of course. But then I fell off a horse, and got this leg. I accepted that as a reprimand and mended my ways."

"I don't believe you—with respect, that is."

"How polite you are. And how right you are. No, it just happened. The good Lord decided to turn me into a bad-weather prophet. I suppose one should regard it as a sign of grace to be made a prophet of anything."

As he poured coffee for her, he said, "You have been in a state of grace all your life."

"Thank you."

"And I envy you."

"Ah well—there are different ways of coming to grace. Some come soon, some come late."

"And some never."

"No, no, it is never withheld altogether. The human spirit can never be entirely devoid of it. The dear Bishop preaches a very good sermon on the subject. Grace is given of God, knowledge is bought in the market." She gave a little laugh. "Have I stumped you?"

"I think you have. But it doesn't sound biblical."

"Nor is it. Does it have to be? The dear Bishop once preached a sermon on a seaside notice which said—*The public are warned that it is dangerous to bathe from this beach.* And a very good one, too. But that was in his younger days as a parish priest. Now stop bantering around and drink your coffee before it gets cold."

They drank their coffee together and when she was gone he picked up the *Daily Telegraph* from the table where she had left it with a letter to him which the handwriting of the address showed him was from Aunt Lily. He turned to the Personal Column of the paper and saw the insertion—*Barkis is willing.*

He sat down on the window seat and dropped the paper at his side. There was little feeling in him, though he knew that would come. Outside an elderly man in khaki shirt and shorts, a heavy rucksack on his back, stood reading the Illaton guide book. A young woman went by with a child in a push cart, trailed by a small boy who carried a highly coloured plastic space-age gun, swinging it round in a rapture of imaginary slaughter, perhaps, of little green men. One of the gardeners was mowing the grass verges around the sunken garden, watched by Cassidy who was stretched out on the granite flags of the garden path. *Barkiss is willing.* Well, he had got his answer. Now, he realized, was his true moment of decision. He could drop the paper and forget it or . . . For a while he was tempted to toss a coin to decide what he would do, but only for a little while. This was no time to take chances. He had lived too long to be made a coward by conscience.

After a while he went back to the long table, took his wash leather gloves from its end drawer and put them on. Then taking a small piece of white paper, he drew on it a very good likeness of a rose and set it to one side.

On a sheet of plain quarto typing paper he wrote:

From Barkis. Thank you for your reply to my letter in the Daily Telegraph. *I shall be on the Number One platform of Exeter St. David's station at two o'clock on Sunday, September 11th and shall remain in the vicinity of the bookstall. I shall expect you to send someone to meet me there. I would prefer a man. I shall be wearing a grey flannel suit with a chalk stripe, no hat, a white shirt and a blue tie with a thin yellow stripe. Your man will approach me and say, 'Excuse me, but you're Mr. Rose, aren't you? I think this is yours.' He will then hand me the enclosed piece of paper on which I have drawn—not too badly I think—a rose. To confirm this you will insert another message in the* Daily Telegraph *which should read—"B. See you at Isca. Usual day and time. C." At this meeting I will hand over in a sealed envelope copies of the documents I hold—and a note of my terms. When you have studied them you will see that their content is the last thing that the Bishop of Testerburgh of Illaton Manor would want known publicly. If you agree to my terms, you will insert a notice in the* Daily Telegraph *reading—"B. I am more than willing. Clara." After which I will be in touch with you again.*

He sealed the letter in a plain envelope and put it in his pocket and then turned to his work, shutting from his mind all thought of the Bishop. All his life he had been able to make this complete switch from one affair to another, and had had the smooth facility to move from one John Corbin to another. So much so that in a humorous way he could at times find himself thinking that he truly was not one person, but many, and not one with any real relationship to the other.

He had finished now with the life of Henry Boyd Darvell—and finished with some regrets for he had grown to like the character of the man, to admire him and to wish that he himself could have been born into his wealth and opportunities. He was now in the process of working up his notes on Henry Boyd Darvell's son, Alfred, who had inherited the estate in 1887 and who by then had fathered a son—John, the Bishop's proxy father—who was seven years old.

Alfred Darvell had been responsible for the creation of the White Garden which lay beyond the great orchard to the south of the Manor. All the flowers and plants in this garden were white or grey. In turn and in place through the seasons there came into glory a galaxy of blooms; *Lilium regale* thrusting through grey artemisia and great bouffant banks of gypsophila, a carpet of silvery *Cineraria maritima* spread under a group of willow-leaved pears . . . white veronicas, white delphiniums and white eremuri took their place in season in the beds which were all contained within low hedges of box. And every path led towards a central point where stood a high-poised white marble angel, wings part spread, holding in one outstretched hand a laurel wreath and in the other hand a tall stem of lily blooms held close to its breast, an early Victorian work of no great distinction which somehow, through time and because of the place it held, seemed entirely appropriate. There had been a very strong, almost Puritanical religious force in Alfred Darvell which later brought conflict between himself and his son John. The contrast between their characters was something Corbin was looking forward to recording. It had come to a head when John had married for love rather than seeking a bride who would have brought a rich dowry into the family. Helen his wife had been the youngest—and prettiest—daughter of an impoverished local clergyman. Recorded in a letter John Darvell had written his father answering his objections was this—*The one thing I seek in marriage is love and companionship, and that must be found—as I have found it—where the heart and the will of God directs. It is uncommonly distressing to fancy that a man should a-wooing go prepared to overlook a squint or bad breath because the lady will come into a fortune. What comfort is that to a man in bed or to the heart when the sound of a wife's footsteps are heard on her returning? God will direct my heart. God has done so. I give thanks to God. And now, my dear Papa, no more of this. Helen is an angel, and to angels no doors can be closed. I shall be back in four days and look forward to some duck shooting on the Illaton flats. Also as a peace offering I shall bring you some plants of* onopordons *from here for your White Garden. They come from Kew and by no means deviously.*

That evening, when Rachel came in on her way home, he said as they had their drinks together, "I wrote to my friend in Wales just sounding him out and I had a reply today. He didn't really say much. After all I wasn't in any way specific. But he did say he would be in Exeter on Saturday and Sunday and suggested that we meet at his hotel. I think I shall pop up there this weekend." He grinned. "Cap in hand to go a-begging."

Rachel laughed. "That doesn't sound like you."

"No, it doesn't. But I'm quite good at playing a part when it's necessary. And——" He stopped suddenly and sat listening for a moment or two.

"What's the matter?"

"Nothing. Or rather Miss Latham. She told me this morning that we should have rain. Listen to it—it has just begun."

From outside came the fat, heavy sound of rain beginning to fall heavily.

"Oh, she always knows. Her leg is as good as a barometer. We need it too." She was silent for a moment and then went on, "You really think this friend of yours will help you?"

"I think so. But if he won't . . . well, I'll think of something else." He went and put an arm round her shoulders. "I'm not just being an optimist. If you're timid about asking you never get anything. Everything's going to be all right. Faith is the thing. Faith—and then acting on it."

When Rachel had gone he took from his pocket the letter from Aunt Lily which Miss Latham had brought up on the coffee tray with the *Daily Telegraph* and which he had not yet opened.

As the rain poured down outside and the roof gutters began to overflow and through the open door came the sudden, rich smell of wet earth and growths, he sat and read it. It was full of her usual gossip. Part of it read—

> *. . . and then on Thursday I had a most pleasant surprise. I was mucking out the donkey shed which you and Rachel repaired when a car stopped outside and a woman got out and came through the yard to me. And, guess what? It was dear Miss Simpson! I've told you, of course, that we had started to write to one another. Well, she has a sister who has friends in Kent and she had brought her in her car to drop her off to spend the afternoon with me. All in a rush and with no time to warn me. Oh, I was so pleased. And she was just as I had imagined. Such a kind, gentle person—though I don't think she really knows much about gardening. Just enjoys it.*

We had such a pleasant few hours. And she took to the donkeys! I had to drag her away into tea. She spoke after you and asked me to send her love. Her sister didn't come to pick her up until much later than she'd said so we had a lovely long time together. I gave her some carnation cuttings I'd struck and half a dozen of our eggs . . .

He finished reading the letter and sat listening to the rain. Dear Aunt Lily. What in God's name would she make of all this Bishop and the Polish Embassy business if she could know? She would never believe it. Never.

For a moment of two—and unique for him—he had dark doubts about what he was intending to do. But almost at once he pushed them from him, knowing that there was no point in giving them even brief house-room. He was going to do it. Had to do it.

On Sunday morning he drove to Exeter and posted his letter to the Embassy. Afterwards, out of a whim, he drove down from the town centre to the station, bought a platform ticket and went on to the Number One platform and stood for a while by the magazine stall. He was quite calm and fully determined to go ahead with his scheme. Absolutely determined. The Bishop of Testerburgh meant nothing to him. Rachel meant everything.

He drove back to Illaton and went down to have supper with Rachel and over their drinks told her of his meeting with his friend.

". . . I know he's a pretty easy-going type—well, he can afford to be, of course—but he did surprise me a bit. You know, I thought he'd want to go into the pros and cons and all that. But no—he just said if we came up with a good proposition he'd lend us the money and only charge a modest rate of interest. So, isn't that marvellous?"

"Oh, darling, of course it is."

"Well then—troubles are over. I said, too, that we might decide to go abroad somewhere and start. But he said that made no difference. God, how marvellous to have so much money that you can just say to someone like us 'Go ahead, my children'. Good old Morgan! He's really prepared to come up trumps."

"Morgan, is that his name?"

"Well, of course it is. I told you, didn't I?"

"No. This is the first time."

"Well, I thought I had. William Morgan. He's got about three thousand acres in Radnorshire, a lot of it just hill country. But he doesn't need to be a serious farmer—though, in some way, anything he touches just seems to turn to gold. And God knows how much he inherited from his old man. He was a building contractor. Housing estates and office blocks . . ."

He went on talking, inventing more and more detail about the Morgans because he wanted her to be comforted, to have solid hopes and bright prospects. She needed everything he could give her—and she needed it now.

Driving back in the rain with Cassidy long after midnight he faced for the first time the prospect of what he should say if nothing came of this Polish business. Well, in that case he would have to kill off dear Morgan in a hunting or car accident and look around for something else. *Deus providebit.*

* * * *

Jawicki, with Corbin's letter before him, wrote a minute to his Counsellor.

Attached to this is the latest communication from our friend Barkis. There are several points I would wish to make. His first letter was postmarked from Bristol and this one from Exeter. They are both West Country towns. The Bishop of Testerburgh is the head of the Darvell family which has long held a large estate on the Cornish side of the River Tamar. The name of the house is Illaton Manor and the gardens are open to the public two or three times a week. Bristol and Exeter are only a few hours away. It could be that we are dealing with someone who is employed there—and that someone an educated man, clearly. He might well have access to family papers and records. My feeling is that we should treat this approach on the assumption that it is genuine and go ahead with it. When he requests a Daily Telegraph *reply to see him at Isca he is using part of the old Roman name for Exeter. A man of fancy and one who likes to embroider his moves with little self-indulgent touches—but nevertheless I have the feeling that he is not one of those worthless cranks who sometimes approach us.*

I would recommend an answer since we have gone so far. We could send Formby down to meet him.

Later that day Jawicki had a minute back from his Counsellor which read—

Go ahead with Telegraph *reply and then send Formby down.*

* * * *

The day that the reply from the Embassy appeared in the *Daily Telegraph,* Miss Latham, an early riser, stood at the window of her bedroom, looking out over the grounds where the shadows of trees and shrubs were cast long by the just rising sun and saw John Corbin coming from the direction of the little Greek temple that overlooked the river. Cassidy trailed at his heels. Though there was a faint edge of disapprobation in her, she smiled to herself at the sight for it was a familiar one. She knew perfectly well that when the young man went down to stay the night with Rachel he sometimes drove down in his own car and came back in it at bare daybreak. But when he went down with Rachel in her car after work he always walked back up the woodland and shrubbery paths to the temple since this was a much shorter route than going all the way round by road.

Things were different now from her young days, and not, she felt, all for the better. But there was nothing one could do, or should try to do. Gather ye rosebuds while ye may . . . Yes, well, it all sounded very nice. Would she, she wondered, if it were possible, like to be a Rachel herself . . . to have been a Rachel? She thought not—God gave men and women their emotions and appetites not to be freely expressed and indulged without regard to decent, Christian conventions and behaviour. This world lacked discipline and true moral beliefs . . . Oh, dear, dear, she was feeling somewhat censorious. Was that envy or did it spring from true conviction, true morality? There had been a time when she had thought that dear Michael had been far more interested in her than Dorothy . . . dear stupid Dorothy with her pale blue eyes and Dresden china shepherdess prettiness. Just once, when he had been nineteen, he had kissed her and held her in his arms and that out there on the temple point and the world had spun for her. For three weeks they had been timidly close, words little used between them. She gave a dry laugh. All so proper. Just the touch of a hand now and then, but never another kiss but something in his manner which seemed to hold promise, and she had lived in a dream. Of course, she had not got Dorothy's prettiness, but—she gave a little grunt—she had been worth far more than a second look. Not this body which she dragged around now, going tap, tap, tap with her long stick when the change of weather touched up her arthritis. Had that been her who could smack a tennis ball with a strong backhander, swim like a fish and ride as well as most men? What if dear Michael had then come to her bedroom one night? Would she have been a Rachel? God knew. All she knew now was that she was sure that for a while she had been shown from him the bright edge of dawning love—and then Dorothy had come back from staying with friends and it was all over. She ought, of course, to have found it in herself to hate Dorothy—but, even though she had tried, it had been hopeless. Hate just wasn't in her nature. What a pity, she thought cynically, because hate was such a good strong emotion and it might have served her well and she could have used it to turn dear Michael . . . oh, very subtly against Dorothy. Oh, yes, he would have been susceptible for what was noble ambition in him now had then been a natural masculine vanity in his own strength, good looks, and dimly seen future.

She gave a sudden grunt of anger and disapprobation, and thought, I'm turning into a sour old woman. Bitter sweet? She grinned, as her natural good nature surfaced. A limping old lady . . . spinster, virgin still . . . sour as one of the crab apples growing wild on the cliff sides. Across the lawns lay the marks of the passing of John Corbin and Cassidy—and back at Illaton Quay Rachel lay in her bed, a woman fulfilled.

She turned away from the window. Oh dear, oh dear, she was getting into a state. But no matter—love, even though unfulfilled, was still with her. Dear Michael was in her heart for ever . . . but what a pity there had never come another man to drive him away. And what was Dorothy now? Just a shadow who followed him everywhere.

Aloud she said, "Margaret, my dear, you're getting maudlin and it doesn't suit your age. Or this moment."

For this moment was the one when each morning after rising and dressing she knelt by the window after looking out over the beauty of the gardens and said her prayers.

She got down on her knees stiffly now—there would be rain soon, she knew—and resting her head in her hands on the broad window sill began to say her morning prayer.

CHAPTER TEN

AFTER MISS LATHAM had brought Corbin his coffee that morning and, after a brief stay, had left him, he picked up the folded copy of the *Daily Telegraph* and saw the insertion made by the Embassy. For a while he was without any positive reaction and, indeed, had the sensation of being completely detached from himself. He seemed no more than some outsider observing a stranger and being privy to that stranger's thoughts and past actions. *Oh wad some Power the giftie gie us,* he thought—to see ourselves as others see us. Well, was that what was being offered to Corbin at this moment, that John Corbin who stood here with the dividing of the ways ahead of him? *It wad frae mony a blunder free us.* There he sat, this John Corbin, looking out over the gardens where a light drizzle had begun to fall and early September was weeping for the passing of Summer, this deviceful John Corbin who had gone so far and could go no farther without completely committing himself. No matter that he was a man of a happy, resourceful and optimistic nature, no matter that his present pass had sprung from the transports of love and the completely uncharacteristic disregard of consequences which had taken his Rachel in the bedroom at Illaton Quay, and no matter that the relish of risk had always salted his transgressions and enhanced his pleasure in them—this was the moment of true decision. Think it over, John Corbin. Here and now is the time when you say *Yes* or *No* to yourself. To go to Exeter or not to go to Exeter? To be or not to be? Suffer the slings and arrows? Or to take arms against a sea of troubles? Well, what arms could the poor fellow take? Except those which lay right to his hand. And no poor fellow either, perhaps. The risks were little, the reward could be great . . . And, anyway, what was the good of talking to himself when it was clear that his mind was made up? He was wasting his time—except that he had to issue the obligatory warning. Had to do it, even when he knew it would be disregarded. That was only fair.

He laughed suddenly aloud. He was talking to an unconvertible pagan. He turned and walked the length of the library, the long table untidy with the papers and documents and diaries on which he worked, the big bunch of keys hanging from the lock of the safe and over it, watching him from within the heavy gilt frame, an oil painting of Henry Boyd Darvell who had seen Illaton through the mists of a dream and had wakened to begin the long labour of turning the dream into reality. And what should he do now? The answer was already within him. Always had been. The formality of doubt only an idle courtesy. He had no care or concern for Michael Boyd Darvell but he could spare the charade of a moment's charity, the quick squeezing of a crocodile tear.

He opened the safe and took out the envelope which held John Darvell's statement and the letter from the Harley Street specialist. Pushing his work notes aside he sat at the long table and began to make copies of them. Outside the drizzle turned into a downpour. The roof gutters ran with water which overflowed and cascaded down the large windows so that the world outside became blurred and distorted. For a moment or two, but without any disturbance to his resolution, he wondered if the Heavens were weeping for him.

After he had made his copies he wrote a letter to be included in the envelope which he would hand over at Exeter station.

Enclosed are copies of the relevant documents. They speak for themselves. As copies, you must know that they are useless to you.

I am prepared to hand the originals over to you in return for the payment of thirty thousand pounds. That is my price and I am not prepared to enter into any bargaining.

When these copies are in your hands and you have considered them and are prepared to meet my terms—all you have to do is to insert the following in the Daily Telegraph. *'Barkis. The answer is Yes. Clara.' I will then be in touch with you again. If there is no insertion in the paper by the end of September then I shall regard the whole matter as closed.*

After his lunch he took the letter and its enclosures, together with the original documents, to his cottage and hid them behind the large Victorian black marble clock on the mantelpiece over the fire. Whenever he left the cottage—following Miss Latham's warning—he always locked it and made the windows secure. The cleaning he looked after himself with some occasional help from Rachel.

Now, knowing that soon he would be taking the first positive step towards getting the money he needed, he felt suddenly restless. He went back to work in the library, but found himself unable to settle to it. After a time he put on his hat and coat and walked through the rain which had fined to a light drizzle and found Rachel in one of the glasshouses where the estate raised carnations for the market. The closeness of the day had made the place heady with the scent of the blooms. Rachel was by herself and turned to him with a great basket of flowers over her arm.

He kissed her and said, "I've got to go to Plymouth to look up some Darvell documents they have in the library there. Can I get you anything?"

"No, thank you, darling. But you drive carefully. The roads will be greasy with this rain—especially down the hill into Tavistock."

"I'll be careful. Don't you worry."

He drove into Plymouth, parked his car and walked up to the Hoe. A light southerly wind was bringing the now thinning rain in across the Sound in great grey swathes. Standing under the statue of Sir Francis Drake he smiled, thinking to himself that adventuring today was not what it had been in the old sea captain's days. Today he grubbed about to fill his treasure chest from sordid little affairs with women, cheap confidence tricks, and now—he faced it quite openly—from a betrayal of trust and hospitality. But there it was. There were no Spanish treasure ships coming home from the Americas to be plundered. Only silly, amorous women wanting to match the infidelities of their husbands, or gullible spinsters to milk of their rents. The great British Empire had been created largely by men like himself... happy rogues who took risks and set no fine edge to the morality of their actions. He had been born out of his age. A good case had been made for those men of the past... maybe one could be made for him. All animals knew their predators and from fear of them learnt the tricks of survival. His role in the jungle was a necessary if not honourable one. Well, there it was. He wanted Rachel and a good life for them. If he had to come by it with a little sinning, so what? From now on he could have no time or inclination to waste on disturbing moral considerations. Survival was all.

On his way back he went down to Illaton Quay and over a drink with Rachel gave her a present he had brought from Plymouth.

She opened the little parcel to find inside a Battersea enamel patchbox with an inscription on the lid which read—*Je t'aime aujourd'hui plus qu' hier et moins que demain.*

When she had kissed and thanked him she suddenly found herself overtaken by emotion. Her eyes blurred with tears and she buried her head against his shoulder.

"What on earth's the matter, love? What are you crying for? You're all right, aren't you?" he asked anxiously.

"Of course I'm all right, you fool. I'm crying because I'm happy and because I've got you to look after me. Oh, Johnny . . . everything's going to be all right, isn't it? Everything . . . everything."

He laughed then and took out his handkerchief and wiped her tears away. "Of course it is, you donkey . . . Everything."

* * * *

Formby walked in Hyde Park with Jawicki. It was a rare event, for Jawicki usually left him in the taxi and went off on his own. But today Jawicki was experiencing one of his rare periods of compassion for the young man. He knew that the time was fast coming when they would have to get rid of him with the usual sympathetic story and a handsome cash payment to help him on his way. Unlike many they had handled he was far from ideal material . . . too temperamental and too uncertain. But then one had to take what came one's way and make the most of it. For himself he might have used him a little longer but the Counsellor had said no—and that was that. He could do the Barkiss trip to Exeter and afterwards he could be turned away.

As they walked a little to the side of Rotten Row he watched the riders and his lips curled slightly with disapproval at the state of some of the livery hacks which had been mishandled and made dispirited by a succession of clumsy-handed, unsympathetic riders. Poor beasts, they had no choice. Poor Formby. He had no choice either. It was odd how some men could let their emotions overrule their heads. But then Maria could be very convincing. And she enjoyed her work—stinting nothing.

With Formby matching his pace at his side, he said, "I'll give you an envelope in a moment. Inside there's money to cover your expenses for this trip. You just follow the instructions I've given you absolutely. You say no more and do no more than I've told you. You just collect the envelope and come back on the next train to London. I'll pick you up in a taxi at half-past ten on the Monday morning."

"Why do these things have to come at such awkward times? Now I'll have to cancel all my Monday morning lessons."

"Well, we compensate you for that."

"But I lose good-will. And sometimes I can't get in touch with people to put them off. And then they come and find me out. People don't like that. You know——" Formby halted and faced him, "——sometimes I just think you're stringing me along, that you Embassy people haven't got any real pull with the civil authorities over there at all. If Maria has got to serve her full sentence why don't you say so? I wouldn't be happy about it—but I would know where I am."

Jawicki said, "I swear to you she won't have to serve it. Not even half of it. You have my word for that. What more can I say?"

"Well . . . and what do I do if this chap doesn't turn up?"

"Give him a certain amount of time. Cars and things can break down. If he doesn't come—well, you just come back."

"Is he some poor little bastard who's working for you like I am? Having a carrot dangled in front of his nose."

"I know nothing about him. Not even his real name—which is certainly not Mr Rose—nor where he lives. You seem to forget sometimes that I often have to arrange or do things which don't make sense to me. Now at the end of the path we'll separate. I'll see you on Monday morning."

Formby sighed. "Sunday—the one day I'm free of bloody lessons and I have to go traipsing all the way down to Exeter. . . ."

Jawicki smiled. "Look on the bright side. You'll pass through some lovely country."

* * * *

It was Saturday evening. The rain had gone, leaving a breath of coldness in the evening air so that she had lit a fire of sticks and branches she had collected through the summer. They spat and flamed now in the big open fireplace where she sat on one side and Johnny on the other. He was reading to her from the *Oxford Book of English Verse*, reading sometimes the complete verses or now and again little snatches. He read well and it gave her pleasure to sit and watch him flicking the pages over to find some favourite piece. She marked now that deep concentration he had when his interest was aroused. When his mind was set on something he gave himself to it completely. And that made her happy because she knew it was a quality she would need in him, rely on from him in the future. To her—although she would never have confessed it to him now—it had its fears. Marriage and a child and leaving Illaton . . . going where? When she had asked him that once he had just said, smiling, "God will provide, and if we keep our noses clean it'll be something good."

He glanced at her now and said, "Listen to this—but don't blush."

He read:

Show me thy feet; show me thy legs, thy thighs;
Show me those fleshy principalities;
Show me that hill (where smiling love doth sit)
Having a living fountain under it.
Show me thy waist; then let me there withal,
By the ascension of thy lawn, see all.

He looked up at her, grinning mischievously.

She said, "I'm sure that's not in the *Oxford Book of Verse.*"

He laughed. "No, it isn't—but it ought to be. It's by Robert Herrick. The Oxford is too stuffy by half. What are you sewing? Baby clothes?"

"No, I'm not. It's a blouse."

"You look marvellous. Firelight suits you. Can I get you another drink? I'm going to have one."

"No, thank you. What are you so worked up about tonight?"

"Am I?" He got up and went to the drinks table by the window.

"You know you are. Is it about going to Exeter tomorrow to see Morgan?"

"Yes, I suppose it is."

"What's he doing there again so soon?"

"God knows. Chasing a woman maybe. Or perhaps he had a sudden urge to go to communion in the Cathedral."

"Be serious."

"All right. He's come down to buy cattle next week at some market. He runs a big beef herd." He came over with his drink, kissed her on the forehead, and then sat down. Picking up the book of verse, he flipped it open at random and said, "Listen—since I'm in an amorous mood—to this."

He read:

My love in her attire doth show her wit,
It doth so well become her;
For every season she hath dressings fit,
For Winter, Spring and Summer,
No beauty she doth miss
When all her robes are on:
But Beauty's self she is
When all her robes are gone.

"And who wrote that?"

"Surely you know? That well-known poet called Anonymous."

"You're impossible. And don't drink too much. You've got to drive back tonight."

"Don't worry." He put the book down and looked at her and went on in a quiet voice, "You know. It's funny how life's changed for me. I used to walk by myself. Care only for myself. Use people. Look after number one. Now all that's gone. I've got you on my hands—and I'm loving it."

"Oh, Johnny . . ."

"It's true. For you I'd do anything. Shall I put on some music and we'll dance? Or will it upset the baby?"

She laughed, loving his mood, and said, "No. You can put on an apron and go and cook the supper. Miss Latham was made a present of a salmon today. She gave me a cut."

"Dear Miss Latham. The soul of generosity, and more reliable on bad weather than any barometer. I wonder why the Bishop never married her? He made a big mistake by choosing Dorothy Mouse. All right . . . now to the salmon."

Rachel sat, full of content, listening to him moving about the small kitchen and sometimes singing snatches of song to himself. She was well used to his quick-changing moods now. There were times when he would sit brooding in a chair opposite her, lost to her, and she knew that he was thinking about his book for the Darvells. She respected his absorption and realized that some days it took him some time to come out of the past and back to her. Whatever he did he did whole-heartedly and usually full of optimism and self-confidence. His love for her she never doubted . . . though she did have other doubts. He loved her so much that he would do anything to keep her happy . . . Just now and again she had wondered whether this friend of his, Morgan, really existed, or whether he was a fiction he had invented to keep her from worrying. Real or not it made no difference. They were together and somehow—for she had now lived through her first dismay and anxiety—they would manage. If he comforted her with a fiction what did it matter? The act came from his love, and it would be just like him to drive all the way to Exeter tomorrow to meet no one and then to come back with some reassuring story . . . full of hope, full of plans and dreams. But in the end something would turn up for them and it would only have been a cruelty now to question him closely and destroy the comforting fiction he might be so elaborately creating for her reassurance.

He put his head through the kitchen door and asked, "Shall I make mayonnaise or shall we take it from the bottle?"

"From the bottle—you'll be back sooner."

"That's my girl."

He went back into the kitchen and she heard him begin to sing *Greensleeves*. She went on embroidering the yoke of her blouse and frowned a little as her fingers, rough from garden work, caught now and then in the fine silk.

That night Corbin left late and drove back to his cottage with Cassidy in the car with him. He slept soundly and woke late to a morning full of sunshine. Just before twelve he left to drive to Exeter.

That morning, too, Formby left his flat and walked to nearby Paddington Station. He had slept badly and was out of temper with himself. As he started to go down the stairs of the apartment house he heard the telephone in his flat begin to ring. For a moment or two he hesitated about going back. He had not left himself too much time to get to the station, and anyway, he thought, it was probably one of his violin pupils wanting to alter a lesson time, or something equally trivial. It certainly would not be Jawicki for he never telephoned. And anyway, if it were, he could go to hell . . . He went on down the stairs and out into the unnatural quiet of a London Sunday morning.

* * * *

That Sunday morning, too, Helder said over breakfast with his sister, "I'm driving down to Tavistock tomorrow. Would you like to come with me?"

His sister shook her head and, reaching for the coffee cup to refill it, said, "I don't think so, dear. The builder's coming to give me an estimate for redecorating the sitting room."

"Does it need redecorating?"

His sister sighed. "You know it does. We settled last week that we would have it done. Can't you go on Tuesday? Then I'd come."

"No. I want to go tomorrow and get it over."

"Get what over?"

"Mr Barwick wants me to hand back two thousand pounds to John Corbin. I'd told him where he was."

"What on earth for? The money, I mean."

"I don't know positively. I can only guess."

"Well, then, what do you guess?"

"Well, he asked me to go and see him on Friday, and the nearest he got to an explanation was that he thought he'd taught Corbin a sharp lesson—and now he could afford to be magnanimous."

"Does the man know his own mind?"

"Oh, yes—but he doesn't necessarily tell the world about it. He certainly knows his own wife, I imagine. He knows too, I guess, that Corbin was far from her first lover—and certainly not the last. Not that this means he doesn't love her. I think that he's come to the conclusion that she isn't worth two thousand pounds and that perhaps John Corbin is in some way."

"What way? He's a scalliwag. Though he writes like an angel, of course."

"Well, perhaps that's it. When I saw Barwick last he had a copy of *Green Pleasures* on his desk. Perhaps, deviously, he's decided to become a patron of the arts."

"I don't think so. I think he just likes playing at being God. Moving people about like pawns."

"Well, perhaps to some extent. But, anyway, there's some merit in being bold enough to change your mind on the strength of some new-found sentiment or conviction. I don't know. I'm just going to do what he wants."

"Do you think Corbin will take it?"

"Oh, of course he will. He may write about the birds and the bees and the flowers—but he doesn't live in cloud cuckoo land. Money is money."

"Well, his aunt will be pleased, anyway."

"If he ever tells her."

"But of course he will, won't he?"

"I doubt it. If she knew she would want him to give it to her to put back in his trust fund. That's where it came from."

"Well, I'm sorry, but I can't come. You won't mind, will you? You'll be able to have music all the way on your radio."

"So I will, but that's little compensation for lacking your company."

"What a nice thing to say—and I really do think you almost mean it."

* * * *

Driving to Exeter, knowing now that he was positively committing himself if the Embassy agreed to pay his price, Corbin was surprised to find himself remarkably calm. Before, in his other less reprehensible activities, he had always known a sharp kick of excitement in him, a surge of euphoria that was like the lift which came with drinking at that point when one knew that one had had enough and knew, too, that one would not stop. But now he was quite unmoved. The day he had driven to Susan Barwick's place to collect his two thousand pounds—God how he had needed that at the time to pay off debts and put himself in funds again!—he had had rats in his stomach. Wouldn't have been surprised to find Barwick himself waiting for him for Sue Barwick was a tricky, unreliable customer. But today he felt nothing. And preferred it that way. And why not? Give conscience or suspicion the least house-room and they would begin to take over. To start imagining now that somehow, somewhere, a tangled web was being woven for him would be not only a weakness but an absurdity. Everything was watertight since for certain the Embassy would never use any of the information he was going to provide for a long time. What would they do? Wait a few years until dear old Testerburgh was coming into line for some high preferment and then move in with some confidential leakage to somebody of importance in the Church Synod? Or perhaps never even bother with that. Wait a while and then make some direct approach to the Bishop to soften his line towards the Communist bloc? Be quite open about it with him? Push the soft pedal down or we spill the beans discreetly around. What would the Bishop do in an approach like that? Discover he was human, that his love of himself and his position was greater than his love of truth and outspoken condemnation of Communism? Then like a lot of other people, great and small, the Bishop would find good reason enough to trim his sails to the wind which threatened to blow. He wouldn't be the first churchman to find himself stumbling about on feet of clay. He was not one to light a candle to God's grace in the hour of trial. Or was he? Would he turn and say publish and be damned? No, he doubted it. Corbin smiled to himself, remembering some lines which John Boyd Darvell had written about him in his diary when the Bishop was eighteen. *Never have I ever seen anyone so awkward with his hands or, considering his lineage, so inept at things horticultural. No graft he makes or cutting he takes ever prospers. If he pulls an apple from a tree part of the branch comes away with it. He has a fine well-sounding voice but he always sings out of tune and, if there is a stone in the path, falls over it because his eyes are elsewhere. In his mind he walks with the angels and seems unaware that he is stumbling over the common ground. And now he would be for the Church and all heavenly things when here at Illaton he has all heaven around him and a great family charge which will come into his hands one day. The only hope I see for him is a managing wife who will happily and efficiently take over his common duties, though as yet he shows no signs of that amorosity which at his age and with all the comely country girls around one would have expected. Yet, for all this, I love him.*

In Exeter he parked his car in the town and walked down to the station. When he went on to the platform it was ten minutes to two. There were rather more people on the platform than he had expected. But anyway whoever was coming to meet him had enough description to pick him out. He stood abreast of the book stall and lit a cigarette and thought of Rachel back in her cottage and of their child. How good was he with children . . .? Not very with the young ones. Still, with one's own, things would be different. Fond Papa . . . he smiled to himself. Rachel would have had her lunch by now. Was probably sitting in the small garden reading the Sunday papers with the nearby mill stream chattering away to itself while overhead, high above the Illaton woods, the young buzzards from this year's hatching would be circling slowly on the air currents.

He strolled up to the end of the platform, interested to feel himself completely without any excitement. As he came back towards the book stall he saw a fair-haired man wearing a suede jacket and fawn linen trousers standing there looking around at the people on the platform. He was, he guessed, somewhat younger than himself and had a sulky, good-looking face. Their eyes met and then the man moved unhurriedly towards him.

Corbin smiled as the man came up to him and stopped. He looked him up and down, and then drew a piece of paper from his pocket and handed it to him, saying, "Excuse me, but you're Mr Rose, aren't you? I think this is yours."

Corbin took the paper on which he had drawn a rose and said, "Yes, I'm Mr Rose."

"I understand that you have something for me."

"Yes, I have. Let's walk up the platform a bit."

"As you wish."

They went together, until they were free of the other people, to the far end of the platform. As they went Corbin knew that this was the coming moment of committal, and knew no hesitation in himself.

Alone at the far end of the platform with a glimpse of the green water meadows of the river Exe away to their left, Corbin stopped. Out of curiosity, he said, "Do you know what all this is about?"

Formby shrugged his shoulders. "No. I'm just the dog's-body. I get my instructions and I follow them."

Corbin nodded and took from his pocket a brown foolscap envelope, unaddressed, and carrying along the gummed-down flap at the back four red blobs of sealing wax. He handed it over to Formby, who held it in both hands for a moment and then turned it over and studied the seals, which showed some kind of bird.

Corbin smiled and held out his hand, showing him the signet ring he wore, and said, "It's a crow. No significance. I picked it up in a junk shop years ago. So that's it then. I'l leave you here. And thank you for coming."

He turned and walked back down the platform towards the exit. Formby watched him go and then, with a shrug of his shoulders, he put the envelope in his pocket, and began to go back down the platform to cross the bridge to the platform where in a little while he would catch the London train. There was no curiosity in him about the envelope, and very little about this Mr Rose—which he guessed could be no real name. He was just a dog's-body who danced and moved as Jawicki directed. Or, the thought suddenly came to him, perhaps a donkey who was always pressing forward to try and take the carrot at the end of the stick and never would reach it. By God, he'd better! In a few moments of bitter anguish he saw Maria . . . her naked, sun-browned body lying on the bed in his hotel . . . and heard her saying, her voice husky with still passing sleep, 'One day, darling . . . I shall be with you in England. Things are easier now and it can be arranged. And if not, well, there are other ways. But I will come and we shall be together for always. But for now we must take all the happiness we can and not think of the future . . .'

* * * *

Taking a walk after Sunday afternoon tea Miss Latham came slowly down the wood path and skirted around the lily pond at the side of the cottage. She stopped for a while to admire the dragon-flies hovering over the water and saw the quick movement of a grass snake as it slid from one of the sun-warmed rock slabs at the side of the pool and swam in smooth curving esses across to the cover of the mace reeds on the far side. She knew the snake, knew that this was one of its favourite haunts for there was good feeding here on the frogs and tadpoles. A serpent in Eden. She smiled to herself at the fancy. It was too glorious an afternoon for such thoughts. And, anyway, the poor snake could not help its own nature.

As she came to the cottage she saw Johnny's car come down the green drive. He pulled up outside the cottage and got out of the car. She stood for a moment looking him up and down, smiling, and then said, "My goodness, Johnny, you do look smart."

"Best bib and tucker. I've been to see an old and wealthy friend. Never neglect wealthy friends, particularly as they get old. It's nice to be remembered in a will."

She smiled. "You're a great tease, aren't you? Or perhaps you like to give people the wrong impression? I wonder why?"

"Well, I could be telling the truth—for a change."

"I hope not."

He came up to her, put an arm round her shoulders and gave her a kiss on her cheek and said, "Why don't you come in and have some tea with me? I'll make you some toast and spread it with Gentleman's Relish."

"That would be nice. But I'm afraid I can't. Some friends of mine are calling to take me out to dinner with them. And they'll bring me back, too, which means I can tipple as much as I like because I won't have to drive. What do you call that? A serendipity?"

"I suppose you could. But I think it's a ghastly word. Well, some other time."

Walking on by herself she smiled as she saw Cassidy coming towards her. Cassidy had taken to him completely and Cassidy could be very nice in choosing friends. Dogs always knew, they said. But she was not so sure. She liked Johnny, but somewhere there was a hint of something . . . Oh, dear, what an uncharitable thought, and perhaps one that had sprung from her age and condition . . . the remorseless passing of years . . . the unfulfilment. And, yes, too, some envy of Rachel. One kiss from the dear Bishop a thousand years ago and here she was telling a little white lie about going out because suddenly the thought of his and Rachel's happiness was all too much for her. What a stupid, petty-minded woman she was.

That evening Corbin walked down to Rachel's cottage with Cassidy and had supper with her. Over their meal he told her about his meeting with Morgan in Exeter. This time, he said, Morgan had been rather more precise and businesslike. He was prepared to help them, but he thought that any positive move to finance them should be deferred until he, Johnny, had finished his work at Illaton. That was something which had to be out of the way first. If something came up now they could not take advantage of it. It was better to let the whole project of financing them rest until they could go right ahead when some suitable investment was found. They had to be free to act when they should find the thing they wanted. He talked in generalities, stressing that one thing was without doubt, and that was that Morgan would finance them. Even so, he was sanguine enough to see that, if the Embassy people turned him down, he had to have a way to shake off the mythical Morgan. Well, that was no problem. He could always die of heart failure from overdrinking or have a fall out hunting.

"What he said was sensible, of course. After all, I've got to finish this book. And, who knows, if some publisher takes it—and the Bish might do a bit of arm-twisting there—and it does well I shall have a second string for my bow, shan't I? That's always a good thing. Come on, slip something over your shoulders and we'll go for a walk along the river before it gets too dark."

He put out a hand, pulled her up to him, and then put his arms around her and kissed her. As he held her, feeling the slow, deep emotional flow of his love for her, he was for a moment or two touched with regret for the necessary deceit that he was having to practise. Still, it had to be. Love is not love which alters when it alteration finds . . . Maybe not. But bare truth, like a cold wind, could cut down a tender growth.

At the door Rachel turned and put her arms about him and said, "Oh, Johnny—what would I do without you? When you're away I get the miseries sometimes. But the moment you're back with me everything is all right again."

"Of course it's all right. And it's always going to be."

They went across the quay arm-in-arm and Cassidy followed them.

CHAPTER ELEVEN

A LITTLE AFTER nine o'clock the doorbell of Formby's flat rang. He had just finished his supper and cleared it away after getting back from Exeter and was listening to music on his radio. He switched the set off and went to the door. A man stood outside in the dim landing light.

Formby said, "Yes?"

The man smiled. "Don't you remember me? He came forward and closer under the light above the flat door. He wore a dark suit with a navy blue turtle-necked sweater under the jacket. He was tall and thin and his long face was shadowed with persistent stubble on his chin.

"No. I can't say I do."

"We only met two or three times. Stanislaw Kerblan."

"No, I don't remember."

"Oh, well, foreign names are difficult to remember. Once at a cultural cocktail party and again at a reception for your little ensemble. I've been phoning you over the week-end but there was always no reply."

"I've been away. What can I do for you?"

"I'd like to talk to you. But not out here."

"Are you from Jawicki?"

The man laughed. "No. He is the last man I am from. I think it would be polite to ask me in. I come from Warsaw and I want to talk to you about Maria."

"Maria!"

"Ah, yes." Stanislaw laughed. "The word that opens so many doors—or shuts them. I come in? I think it is better than out here. I want to help you and to tell you things about her. I come in? Yes?"

"Yes, of course." Formby stood back and let Stanislaw pass

into the room. He waved him to a chair and said, "What about Maria?"

Stanislaw sat down and said, "Perhaps you remember me now. In the light. Yes?"

"Yes, I think I do. But not very well."

"Never mind. It is about Maria that we talk, but first a little about myself, yes? Just to make you know that I am your friend."

"I'll be glad to hear anything about Maria. I still can't remember meeting you though . . ." Formby moved to his sideboard. "Would you like a drink?"

"Yes, please."

"I've only some rough red wine."

As Formby poured the wine, Stanislaw said, "No surprise you don't remember me so good. When I see you, you are all eyes for Maria. That is usual for most men, of course. She is very beautiful—and very clever. Every man fall in love with her, too. That is what makes her very useful to people like Jawicki and those with him." He took the drink Formby held out to him, sipped it and said, "Thank you."

Formby sat down, his elbows on his knees, his glass cradled in both hands, and said with a stir of resentment, "What the hell are you talking about?"

"About something which is of little importance to me because now I am away from Poland I have other more important things to do. But I liked you and enjoyed very much when you play your violin solo. Though overall, I think you agree, the ensemble is not all that so good."

"Maybe not. But you didn't come here to tell me that."

"No, of course not. But I make a little conversation to put you at ease." He raised his glass, nodded at Formby and drank.

"What have you come for?"

"First you tell me something which I know, but which I would like from your own lips. You work for Jawicki now and then? On errands and little jobs about which you understand very little. You do that—yes?"

"I could do."

Stanislaw smiled. "I know you do. I have done the same thing for his people in Poland. Though they do not make me do it because of any Maria. Something other. Not important to go into. All the time they do this. Sometimes through Maria. Sometimes other ways. They do it—you will pardon me—with little people. Not important. Use them for a while and then throw them away. With you they use Maria to . . . how you say? Enrol you?"

Angrily Formby said, "Are you trying to tell me what I think you are?"

"Most decidedly. You think she is in prison—and if you are a good boy they let her out to come and marry you in not too long time?"

"She is in prison—and I've got their promise! I get letters from her in prison—some of them cut about by the censor."

"Oh, yes. They make it all look good until they don't want you any more. I show you and tell you now something that hurts. You will forgive me. But I think only of you. Maria do this often with foreigners. It is her job. Business men from other countries, artistes who visit . . . All right. I say no more of that. I see it hurts. But you are a sensible man. These say more than I can."

Stanislaw drew from his jacket pocket an envelope and handed it over to Formby, saying, "Two are from a Polish newspaper. I take the whole page so you can see the date at the top. And one is a straight photograph which I take myself."

Formby, bereft of feeling now, took the stuff from the envelope. It contained two pages from a newspaper, and a large photograph. He spread out a folded page from a newspaper on his knees. In the centre of the page was a photograph of Maria full-faced and smiling as she presented a bouquet of flowers on the steps of some building to a tall, middle-aged man with a rugged, forceful face.

"That one," said Stanislaw, "is some American film producer who comes to arrange for some filming in my country. You see the date at the top? That makes three weeks ago. Look at the other newspaper."

Formby opened the other folded newspaper page. It showed Maria standing in the middle of a row of ice-hockey players, her arms linked with those of the bulkily clad players on either side of her.

"That," said Stanislaw, "is a visiting team from East Germany. You see, too, the date and the year. June, and this year. While all the time she is supposed to be writing to you from prison. And then the photograph. Well, no date for that. I just bring it and tell you I took it myself. I worked sometimes to make a little more money in the good restaurants and sometimes I take the photos for people dining. That, I swear to you, was no older than two weeks ago. Since then things have got bad for me and my good friends get me out. So I come to do you a good turn which is really bad turn for I show you the other side of your Maria. The man in the photograph—he is in the Polish army."

Formby sat staring at the photograph of Maria sitting at a restaurant table with a uniformed officer whose right arm was around her bare shoulder, both of them looking up and smiling into the camera.

Stanislaw finished his drink and stood up, gave a small sigh, and said, "You should in time be glad for me to bring these to you. No more work for Jawicki. They can do nothing now. Show them if you like. They drop you and forget you. We who are against them know their ways."

Formby took a deep breath, looked up at him and, in a forced voice, holding down the anguish in him, said, "You take them, please . . . just take them away. The bastards!"

Stanislaw took the papers and photograph which were held out to him. He went to the door and with his hand reaching out to open it, he said, "I am sorry because your world is broken. But believe me—from tomorrow it will begin to mend. It is the way of things."

After he had gone Formby sat where he was. Then after a while he stood up and went to his sideboard and helped himself to more wine. He stood there with the full glass in his hand and suddenly the anguish in him turned to bitter anger.

"The bitch!"

He threw the full glass from him against the far wall. The glass exploded into fragments and the red wine spread over the white plaster wall like some flower suddenly blooming. The action calmed him a little and he dropped into an armchair and said, "The bloody bitch . . . and bloody Jawicki . . ."

He put his hand into the big side pocket of his suede jacket to take out his cigarettes, his mind still seething with anger, and as he did so he felt the sealed letter which he had collected from Exeter station. He took it out, thinking how Jawicki must have despised him and laughed about him. Poor little sod. Stupid Formby with his eyes dazzled by love and his brain turned soft by it. How damned right they'd been too. Soft lights and sweet music . . . that long, sun-browned body and the dewy mistiness in her eyes after they had made love. Whore!

He dropped the envelope on the window table at his side and got up. He found another glass and poured into it the last of the red wine. He sat down again and drank it slowly, lost in his smouldering thoughts . . . Jawicki had seen the last of him . . . If only there were something he could do to get his own back, to ease a little the humiliation which had been given to him. Well, one thing was for certain. Jawicki would never get the Exeter letter. Important or not. He reached out for it and held it in his hands, tensing them, ready to pull it apart and rip the whole thing into shreds, when he suddenly dropped the letter into his lap. Perhaps this Mr Rose at Exeter was another one like himself . . . someone being strung along . . . someone, maybe, who had been lured into the same trap as himself . . . maybe even by Maria?

He worked a finger under the edge of the sealed flap and opened the envelope. He took out the contents and sat reading them. When he had finished he dropped the loose sheets into his lap and sat staring at the bloom mark of red wine on the far wall.

After a time he got up and went to the telephone on the sideboard and dialled Directory Enquiries and when a woman answered said, "I'd like the telephone number for Darvell at Illaton Manor, near Calstock in Cornwall. If it's not under Darvell it might be listed under the Bishop of Testerburgh."

A few moments later the woman gave him the number, telling him that it was listed under Michael Boyd Darvell. He looked at his watch. It was now half-past ten.

He dialled the number. It rang for quite a while and then was answered by a woman.

Formby said, "I would like to speak to the Bishop of Testerburgh, please."

The woman said, "I'm afraid he's not here. Who is this speaking, please?"

"I'd rather not give my name, but I do assure you that this is a serious call. I wanted urgently to get in touch with the Bishop of Testerburgh."

"Oh, well, that would be rather difficult. He's in Germany at the moment. Is it very important?"

"Yes, very. May I ask to whom I am speaking?"

"If you wish. I'm his sister-in-law. Latham is the name. Miss Margaret Latham. I deal with all the correspondence which comes for him here."

"You are very close to the Bishop?"

There was a slight, dry laugh. "What a curious question. Yes, of course I am. I have known him since we were quite young and I have looked after a great deal of his confidential affairs for many years."

"Well, Miss Latham, I am going out in a few moments—I am speaking from London—and shall post to you some papers which I collected today from a man in Exeter. I was to have handed them to the Polish Embassy tomorrow. But for my own reasons I have decided not to. I shall be going out in a few minutes to post them to you and will put in a letter from myself. I need say no more because when you get these papers you will make your own decision about them."

"Well, that's kind of you. But it all seems very odd, doesn't it? Are you sure you can't explain yourself more over the telephone?"

"I'm sorry but I can't."

"I see." There was a long pause at the other end of the line and then in a slightly different tone Miss Latham went on, "Are you quite sure you wouldn't like to say more? You sound as though you are in trouble . . . or very upset about something."

"That's kind of you. But I am quite all right now. A little while ago I wasn't. And, believe me, I am no crank. This is a very serious matter which concerns the Bishop personally. May I ask if you are very loyal to him?"

"Oh, dear, what a question. Of course I am. I would do anything in the world for him. But I would like to stress again—

are you in trouble and needing help because you could speak to me just as you could to the dear Bishop."

Formby said, "You sound a very nice person. And I appreciate your concern. But, no—I am not in trouble. I just don't want to see someone else get into trouble. Now . . . I've said all I can. I shall post my letter to you tonight."

"Very well."

As she spoke Formby replaced the telephone. He went to his table and began to write a letter to Miss Latham. He was quite calm now. When he had finished he put the letter with the stuff he had collected from Exeter station into a large envelope, stuck stamps on it, and addressed it to Miss Margaret Latham at Illaton Manor and then went out and posted it. The tab on the letter box told him that it would be collected at nine-thirty the next morning.

* * * *

Miss Latham, who had answered the telephone in her bedroom to which all calls were switched during the late evening and night, stood for a moment at the window in her dressing gown. She liked to sleep with her curtains drawn back, to be able to lie abed when sleep stayed obstinately from her and watch the slow wheel of the stars. What had just happened was by no means unusual. The world was full of lost souls and those in trouble and the Bishop and his household got more than their fair share of them. Still . . . this man had sounded very reasonable and composed—though that was not necessarily any proof of stability. She had met many cranks who gave the impression of sane and stable persons.

Outside the old moon was near dying. A barn owl drifted like a lost soul across the lawns. From the beds below the window rose the sweet, heady fragrance of night-scented stocks.

She took a drink of water and went back to bed. She picked up her book and went on reading, as she had read so many times in her life before—

. . . Miss Lucas perceived him from an upper window as he walked towards the house, and instantly set out to meet him accidentally in the

lane. But little had she dared to hope that so much love and eloquence awaited her there.

In as short a time as Mr. Collins' long speeches would allow, everything was settled between them to the satisfaction of both; and as they entered the house he earnestly entreated her to name the day that was to make him the happiest of men. . . .

She read on until the book dropped from her hands as she drifted into sleep. When she woke in the morning it was to find her bedside light still burning. She gave herself a good talking to for wasting electricity. Then she remembered the telephone call of the night before. How odd, and she doubted very much whether she would ever receive any letter. The world was full of strange, lonely and desperate people and the night was the time when their misery often became too much for them. She got out of her bed and picked up Jane Austen from the floor. As she passed her window on the way to the bathroom she caught a glimpse of John Corbin moving across one of the far lawns with Cassidy trailing behind him. What, she thought, would Miss Jane have made of this modern generation of young lovers?

Much later that day, around five o'clock, she went, as she often did, to the library to collect John Corbin's afternoon tea tray. Usually he was there beginning to put his papers in order before leaving. But today he had gone and the long table was untidy with his work material. At the end of the table near the safe was his pile of manuscript paper and a green folder into which he put his writing. It was an understood thing between them now that he had no objection to her reading what he wrote and sometimes discussing it with him . . . though what he really wanted, she knew, was her praise. All creative artists, she thought, were probably like that. There was a vanity in them which fed on praise. And why not? It was an innocent vanity. And her praise—sometimes punctuated with criticism—was genuine. The worst thing was to praise the bad or indifferent just in order to sustain a creator's confidence and morale. The odd thought struck her then that maybe, just maybe, if there had been a good, honest critic at hand when God had created Man his words would have been heeded and the result perhaps far better. Good Lord—she wondered what the dear Bishop would have said could he have ever known she harboured such a thought?

She picked up a sheet of Corbin's manuscript, so neatly and closely written in a small, clear hand, and read—

. . . and the idiosyncrasies of Alfred Boyd Darvell did not stop here. He was of the admirable conviction that if the Illaton garden were truly to be a paradise then it should, in addition to its flowers and plants, have also a variety of birds and animals to match the exoticism of its blooms and greeneries. To this end, with the single-mindedness which must at times have made him the despair of his family and friends, he introduced a pair of black-and-white Colobus monkeys to the gardens where in the clement weather they roamed free, and were wintered in a warmed and converted stable. They lasted six months before (and perhaps secretly to his relief for they did much damage to the garden growths) one was shot by an adjacent farmer when it was caught chasing his dairy herd and the other—now lonely no doubt for its mate—wandered off and found its way to Calstock where it got into a small rowing boat. The river, then in flood and the tide on the turn, it went down on the heavy spate just at dusk and was never seen again.

Undaunted, though he gave up monkeys, Alfred Darvell next had built a glazed-in cast-iron aviary of considerable size and stocked it with a variety of tropical and exotic birds which in the clement weather were allowed to fly free around the garden. Like a great many intelligent and able men there was a recurrent streak of stupidity in him which must have been very endearing. Mad he was not. But odd he was. Within two weeks a flock of free-flying budgerigars had been decimated by the native sparrow hawks and kestrels, grateful no doubt for this exotic addition to their habitual food; foxes, too, enjoyed for a while the epicurean delight of peacock on their bill of fare and peregrine falcons coming inland from their cliffside eyries around Plymouth Sound stooped on the flights of flying ornamental duck above the river. He wrote in his diary—'I mourn my ducks deeply, but have to confess that the stoop of peregrine from great height is a wonderful sight for it is death clothed in terrible glory falling like a bolt from heaven to destroy the innocent and I am chastised for my presumption in tampering with the natural order and placing of God's creatures.'

Even so, he kept the aviary going for a few more years and then it was left empty and neglected. Some time after his death it was dismantled in the early years of the Great War and sold as scrap for munitions. In its place now stands the tropical plant house which was built by his son after the war and where for some time—perhaps as a salute to his father—John Boyd Darvell had one section closed off in which was housed a small collection of humming birds. A severe winter and a failure of the heating system in the Great Strike of 1926 brought this filial gesture to a close. And now, of course, no falcons stoop above Illaton and their seacliff eyries are deserted. Predator had fallen victim to man.

One further aspect of Alfred Darvell's well-meaning eccentricity is of interest. Driving back from Plymouth one night in the early days of the motor car . . .

Miss Latham replaced the sheet with the others and wondered what had made John Corbin break off in mid-sentence. She went to the safe which he had left open, closed and locked it and set the ring of keys in its place on the board at its side.

Going to the window and looking out she remembered the strange telephone call of the night before. How very odd. Then, seeing Cassidy digging for a field mouse nest in a great clump of *Iris stylosa* whose bright blue blooms delighted her eyes with the coming of winter, she bawled at him like a fishwife. He turned and looked at her and then, with a low-hung, apologetic swing of his tail, he ambled off.

It was at this moment that James Helder, who had had a pleasant drive down to Tavistock, picked up the telephone in his hotel bedroom and asked the switchboard to put him through to Illaton Manor. The girl on the switchboard said, "Do you want the Manor or the Estate office. They're different numbers."

"The Estate office, please."

A few minutes later, just as Miss Latham was about to leave the library, the telephone rang.

She picked it up. "Yes?"

"Oh, Miss Latham. Is Mr Corbin there? I have a call for him."

"No, he's not here. He must have left early. I should try his cottage."

"Thank you, Miss Latham."

When the telephone in the cottage rang John Corbin was outside dead-heading the narrow bed of roses which ran down the side of the front path. He had left the library early because Rachel was coming in later to stay and have supper with him and he had decided to get some of his preliminary cooking business done . . . a young duck, now in the oven, and all the vegetables prepared and the kitchen tidied up and its table laid so that they could eat away from the sitting room to avoid carrying stuff in and out. He was in good spirits, and had been all day, because now he had done everything he could so far as the Polish Embassy was concerned. All that was left now was waiting. If they turned him down, wrote him off as a crank . . . Well, he would have to think again. Something would turn up. But, in his heart, he could not see them missing the chance. They might haggle a bit over the money, of course. Well, if he had to he would come down a little.

Stuffing the secateurs in his jacket pocket he went in and answered the telephone.

"Corbin here."

"Mr Corbin my name is Helder—though I fancy that won't mean anything to you. I'm staying at a hotel in Tavistock and I'd very much like to come and see you."

"What for? What's all this about?"

"Well, I'd rather not go into that over the telephone. But I can assure you that I shall be the bearer, shall we say, of good tidings."

For a moment or two Corbin was silent. He could not think that *they* could have acted so swiftly and got a man down here already to negotiate with him. For a moment he was tempted to ask whether this was anything to do with Barkiss and then decided not to.

He said, "Could you be a little clearer about good tidings?"

"I'd prefer not to over the telephone. My instructions are to see you personally. I will add that my visit will be altogether to your advantage, and entirely above board. In no way will you be embarrassed—the contrary, I imagine."

"I see. But I can't manage this evening. I can see you tomorrow. I'm a working man, you know. Or I presume you do. Could you get here by half-past nine?"

"Yes, I can. And thank you."
"Half-past nine. I'll be in my cottage. The people at the gate will tell you where it is."
"Thank you again, Mr Corbin."
Puzzled, Corbin went back to his roses. And then, since there was nothing he could gain from speculation, he put the call out of his mind.
A few minutes later Rachel came driving down the green ride in her car with Cassidy on the seat beside her, the dog's muzzle still muddy from digging in the iris bed.
As she got out of the car he put his arms around her, kissed her and said, "The duckling is in the oven, the wine decanted, and here, springing from her chariot, comes my love to feast my eyes with delight and so from feast to feast I go like a pollened bee happily cargoed and . . . Well, I forget the rest."
She laughed. "You mean there never was any rest. You've just made it up."
"It's a possibility. Now come and have a drink and talk to me while I make the sauce." He put his arm around her and led her into the cottage.

* * * *

The next morning at half-past nine Helder arrived at the cottage. He parked his car alongside the one already standing there and walked up to the front door outside which a rather ruffianly looking dog was sitting. The door opened before he could tug at the wrought-iron bellpull and he was facing John Corbin with no sense of this being the first time in his life that they had met for he had been shown photographs by Mrs Hines and given a description before that by Miss Simpson.
"Mr Helder, I presume," said Corbin, and, smiling, added, "Who brings good tidings and so is entitled to a warm welcome. Come in."
"Thank you, Mr Corbin."
Helder went in, amused at the light touch and the charm and knowing from experience that with this type there was never any way of deciding whether it came genuinely or designedly. He

allowed himself to be seated by the window and accepted the offer of a cup of coffee. While Corbin went to get it the dog came in and dropped flat on the floor with a thump close to his chair.

From the kitchen Corbin called, "Milk, sugar, black—how do you like it?"

"Just milk, please." As he spoke Helder looked round the room. The ash trays were still full and a woman's scarf lay across the back of a settee whose cushions had not been plumped up. There was lipstick on some of the butt ends of the cigarettes in the ash tray on the window seat.

Corbin brought in his coffee and set it on a small table at his side. He then went and sat on the settee and said, "And now, Mr Helder, what can I do for you or you for me—whichever way it is?"

Helder sipped at his coffee and then said, "I think before we come to that I should explain my position. I am a private detective. And at the moment I am working for a Mr Barwick whose name must be quite familiar to you."

"Indeed it is. How interesting. I thought all that business had been cleared up long ago. And anyway, haven't you been a long time catching up with me?"

"Which question do you want me to answer first?"

"Take your pick."

"So I will. *Seriatim* let it be. The business was, so I thought, cleared up a long time ago by your aunt—whom I have met—though she never told me your whereabouts."

"Who did?"

"A Miss Simpson who knew it from your aunt and quite innocently let it slip to me."

"Dear Miss Simpson. I was very fond of her. And now she and my aunt are very good friends and visit one another. And, yes, the business was cleared up from a small trust fund in my favour. An action which you can guess was not very pleasing to me. However, I am now happily recovered from my chagrin."

"But a just arrangement."

"To be honest, not in my eyes. A silly woman paid for her pleasure. There was nothing between us which she had not had with other men before—only they didn't see fit to charge. So what now? It seems a long way to come from London, or wherever you live, just to pick over the bare bones of a dead relationship. So why are you here?"

"Because Mr Barwick has had a change of heart."

"I would have thought that impossible. But, *mirabile dictu,* I suppose it could be, though mostly it usually happens on or near to a man's death bed. What has softened the cash register he calls his heart—and to what purpose that he should despatch you to the leafy lanes of Devon and the high moors of Cornwall?"

"It's not my place, Mr Corbin, to discuss my client's motives. In Mr Barwick's case though, I might make an exception because I think he would have no objection to your knowing. There are two reasons, of one of which I am certain and the other is a presumption based on my long years in this quite fascinating profession of mine."

Corbin laughed. "Oh, Mr Helder, I like you—so staid, but with a great sense of theatre, and so wise from the experience of a thousand human frailties. Now tell me the reasons. But let me first say—you probably have a cheque for me in your pocket. No?"

"Yes, I have. For two thousand pounds."

"What, no interest on the loan?"

Helder laughed briefly. "I'm afraid not. As for the reasons, one is only a presumption. I think he came to the conclusion that his wife wasn't worth the money—though she suits him well enough as a wife."

"Of such are happy marriages often made. And the other reason?"

"Quite a pleasing one for you, I expect, if you share the inevitable and reasonable vanity of most writers——"

"Which I do. There is no good writing done without it. Go on."

"When I was last with him and he instructed me to come down here, he had a copy of your book *Green Pleasures* on his desk."

"And he told you how much he had enjoyed it, and had thus had a change of heart about me?"

"No. He never referred to it. It was just there."

"How much better it would have been if he had said, 'The man may be a rogue and a philanderer, but he writes like a lover, a lover of all growing things and with understanding and compassion for the pride and weaknesses of those great men who have given their hearts to gardens which is to run a hazard far greater than giving your heart to a woman.' "

Helder smiled. "Perhaps there was something like that in his thoughts. Anyway he has sent back your money."

"Well, bless me. You never know about other people, do you?"

"It's a conclusion I reached long ago. Here's the cheque, Mr Corbin." Helder took the cheque from his pocket and Corbin came across the room and put out his hand for it. He was silent for a while as he looked at it.

"Well . . ." Corbin shook his head. "Some bloody funny things happen, don't they? Well, thank you very much, Mr Helder."

"Not at all. From your aunt I understand you are writing a book about this place."

"That's true." Corbin smiled. "I'll send you a copy in the fullness of time."

"That would be very kind of you. And now I must be going. Is there any message you would wish me to give to Mr Barwick?"

Corbin was silent for a moment or two and then said, "Yes. Tell him I appreciate his gesture. And also tell him that he ought to sack his gardener in Hampshire. The man is just a butchering, dragooning sergeant-major."

When Helder had driven away Corbin put the cheque in his pocket and dropped into an armchair. The thought suddenly occurred to him that if Barwick had had his change of heart weeks ago he might well not have ever even remotely considered getting into touch with the Polish Embassy . . .

* * * *

On his way to the Manor Corbin saw Rachel coming out of the Estate office. When she came up to him, he put his hands on her shoulders and kissed her.

She said, "Good Lord! In broad daylight? What's taken you?"

"You have. And what's wrong with broad daylight? We're engaged and everyone knows it. Would you have all true emotion banished to dark corners? Anyway, there's something else. I've had a bit of luck. I've just had a windfall. Some money—not a fortune, but a nice handful—which I lent to someone ages ago has just been repaid to me. I'd written it off long since. It dropped into my lap this morning."

"Not through the post surely? They're grumbling in the office because it hasn't come yet." She smiled. "Johnny—you're just making up a story. And I know why. At least I think I do. It's a lovely day and you don't want to work—and you're going to ask me to play hookey. I know that look in your eyes."

"Who said anything about the post? It was delivered personally. This chap's father just appeared out of the blue to settle his son's debt. You want more details?"

"No. Though I'm sure you could provide them."

"What trust! Just go back and ask the office. He called there to be directed to my cottage. Anyway, that's not the point. And, yes, I do want you to play hookey. I'm going to do a couple of hours' work in the library and then . . . well, why don't we clear off? Have lunch in a pub and then go on down to the sea and have a swim? Take the rest of the day off. Gather the rosebuds while we may because the summer is on its way out. What do you say?"

"Well, I suppose it's all right. Whose car shall we take?"

"Let's take yours. It's up here. Mine's at the cottage. Twelve o'clock—all right?"

"Yes. But I'll have to go back to my place to pick up my swimming stuff."

"Good Lord, how old-fashioned can you get! You won't need anything like that. We'll find a place far from the madding crowd—and Thou beside me singing in the wilderness. And I'll make it all right with dear Miss Latham when she comes with the coffee mid-morning."

He took her arm and walked with her up to the Manor and before he parted from her he nodded up the terraced entrance to the great main doors of the Manor and said, "Do you know where those doors came from?"

"No—but I've no doubt you're going to tell me."

"I am. They represent the only real mark the dear Bishop has made on this place—and I'm not sure it wasn't an act of revenge. There was a big oak up by the main entrance gates. He fell out of it as a boy and broke a leg. Just after he came into the estate it had to come down because it was dangerous. He had the doors made from some of its timber and chose the carved inscription over the top. *God never shuts one door but he opens another.* And how true that is."

"Never give up hope?"

"Right. There's always something waiting round the corner. And I'll be waiting for you. Twelve o'clock sharp."

He worked well that morning, though there were times when he leaned back in his chair and thought of Helder's visit. God, people were odd. Fancy Barwick making a gesture like that. What would have happened if he had made it much sooner? Before he had ever thought of getting in touch with the Poles? Rachel's pregnancy had come first, but it really was the loss of his two thousand that had tipped the scales. God certainly had been busy opening and shutting doors. In a way, perhaps God had sent Helder to open another. He was by no means entirely committed to the Poles. What they had and knew so far could never serve them. Before they could do anything they would have to have the original letters. Perhaps he should heed the sign and scrub this whole Polish business . . . Well, that was something he had plenty of time to consider . . . For the moment he just did not know. Leave it all to settle.

He turned to his work and went on writing, form and sentences coming smoothly to heel:

There was in John Boyd Darvell an element of gypsy raffishness which is admirably caught in the portrait of him with his wife painted by Augustus John. His wife is pure porcelain, ethereal loveliness, her feet resting so lightly on the ground that one has the impression that she could walk through meadow flowers caressing them where other mortals would crush. But following her closely comes John Darvell, a favourite lurcher at his heels, a gun under his arm and, probably, snares to be set in his large pouched pockets. He is Adam cast out of the Garden and now master in his own which he loved only slightly less than he loved his wife. He could at times be rough, and crude and draconian to those who crossed his will or served him badly. But this is a man of strange paradox. He would weep at the loss of a favourite shrub as other men weep for a lost child. Although his morals were ambivalent his courage and love of children were beyond question. With the River Tamar in a fast summer spate one year shortly after his marriage he dived from the high rocks below the Grecian temple on the river heights to rescue a gardener's boy who had slipped into the swollen stream while bird nesting higher up the Tamar. His charities to local people were always kept hidden, but they were many and substantial. It would be interesting if there were any records of his talks with Augustus John while the painting was being made. They shared much in common and it is said—

He stopped writing as Miss Latham came into the room with the morning coffee tray. As she set it down she said, "I've just been talking to Rachel. I hear you are going off jaunting?"

"A good word. Yes, we are. Is that all right?"

"Of course it is. But I should tell you that my leg says that rain is not far off."

"Oh dear . . ."

"And also so far there are no papers and no post. Apparently the mail van was in an accident coming up the hill out of Tavistock. Luckily the driver wasn't hurt. They'll be along later. By the way I read some of the stuff you wrote about Alfred Darvell, and liked it very much. You are a clever young man."

"Thank you, ma'am." He made a little bow to her.

She smiled. "I can't wait to see what you'll say about the dear Bishop."

"Don't worry. I'll find something good to say—if only to please you."

Laughing, she shook her head. "I don't know what to do about you. I only hope Rachel does."

"She'll learn. Just as John Boyd Darvell's wife learnt to handle him. She had him eating out of her hand. I can't think why there aren't more women lion-tamers." Then looking at the tray, he went on, "Aren't you taking coffee with me?"

“Not today. I have to be in Calstock at half-past eleven for a Mothers’ Union coffee morning.”

“The one Union which never goes on strike. Give them my love.”

“I’ll do that and tell them what you said. Take your macks with you. It will rain before the afternoon is out.”

CHAPTER TWELVE

THEY LAY ON a patch of sand, now slowly being eaten up by the returning tide, between two tall outcrops of rock at the foot of a steep cliff face down which they had earlier scrambled. The sun was warm on her body and its heat had almost dried out her wet panties. He lay beside her with his silk neck scarf knotted around his loins and snored gently. High above her head on the cliff face a pair of butterflies hovered over a patch of sea campion and far above the cliff crest there came the singing of a lark. Instead of having a pub lunch they had bought rolls and cheese and a cheap bottle of too-sweet Spanish wine at a village store. They had bathed and eaten and made love, and all had been perfect. There had been times when the thought of the child and their future had disturbed her . . . sometimes frightened her when she woke in the early hours and stupid fears pressed in easily upon her. But today all was bliss and the future could take care of itself. As they had come back from bathing he had taken a piece of drift-wood and drawn a heart on the soft sand and written above it—*Johnny loves Rachel*—and underneath—*Amor mundum fecit.* Sitting up now she saw that the returning tide would soon smooth all his marks away. But only the words. Not the truth in them.

Although she was—and gladly—a fool about him she knew that there were times—and she allowed herself to be convinced for her own comfort—when he lied to her. Or, at least, she suspected he did. But then she knew that a lie to him where she was concerned was no lie, only a banner flown to draw her eyes away from some fear, some dark gathering of clouds ahead. All this had only come to her slowly, but she knew it now, was glad of it, and saw it as proof of his love for her. All that talk of Morgan. He had invented that, she felt almost sure, to tide her over a bad period after she had known she was pregnant. And she was glad he had for it had done just that. She smiled to herself. One day he would come in to her with a long face and say that Morgan had been killed in a hunting accident. But very soon he would go on to replace him with some other phantom character or golden opportunity about to rise over the horizon. And why not? She understood him now and felt no need for change in him. Nobody was perfect.

She lay back and ran her hands over her sun-warmed breasts . . . dear Johnny. As she did so Cassidy came round the corner of the rock point and flopped down by her, panting, his tongue hanging out. People said dogs knew. Knew what? She didn't know. But she knew that Cassidy had taken to him, been almost his shadow.

At her side Johnny sat up suddenly, smacking his leg with his hand and said, "Bugger!"

She laughed and said, "What's the matter?"

"I've just been bitten by a horse-fly."

"Well, they've got to live."

"Oh, very funny." Then with a grin he slewed towards her, put his arms around her, and began to bite her shoulders gently. Laughing, she struggled under him and they went rolling over and over across the sand with Cassidy barking around them.

At that moment Miss Latham was sitting on the window seat in the library where she had come on her way up to her bedroom for her afternoon rest to leave a letter which had come for Johnny and from whose postmark she knew would be from his aunt in Sussex. There had also been one letter for herself with a London postmark which she had guessed at once would be from the man who had telephoned her late on Sunday night.

Shock was deep in her from reading it and she knew that she was still incapable of controlling her feelings or thinking very coherently. She breathed slowly and deeply as though there were not enough air in the room to sustain her. Then, with a sudden anger, she thought, Margaret, take hold of yourself and think straight. She got up and walked around the library, limping a little, and letting her feelings settle. Then she went back to the window seat and took up the letter with its enclosures and began to read again. The letter ran—

Dear Miss Latham,

This is what I promised you. I should explain that—under some duress which is now finished—from time to time I have worked as an outside agent of the Polish Embassy in London. They have cheated and used me and I am finished with them and they will never know I have sent all this stuff to you. This morning I was sent down by them to meet a man at Exeter station who would call himself Mr. Rose (though you can be sure that this is not his real name) and I would recognise him because he would be standing by the book stall wearing a light grey suit with a chalk stripe in it and a blue tie with thin yellow stripes. This I did and he handed me a sealed envelope—which I enclose which held also the other papers also enclosed—and I was to take all this and hand it over to the Embassy people tomorrow morning. I am sorry to be a bit rambly but I am still very much angered and upset about things, the things which I can't tell you and which have made me send all this to you. They are a rotten scabby lot and I am glad that I have kept this out of their hands and into yours for you to do what is best with them. The Mr. Rose at Exeter was fair-haired with blue eyes and spoke in an educated voice. Believe me they are a rotten lot, and believe too that I shall put right out of my mind all that I've read. Actually I shall probably go abroad. I am English and was made to do what I had to do because of a woman I was in love with, but she was a lying, traitorous bitch. I won't sign but I assure you that all this is the truth.

Calmer now, though she knew it would not last, Miss Latham took up the enclosures and read them again. There was no doubt that they were in Johnny's handwriting and—without any feeling for there was a hard numbness in her—she could read the name Barkiss and know that would be like Johnny. At the moment she kept her feelings in check. The copy of John Boyd Darvell's statement gave her no true surprise. Everything which had been arranged was exactly in his character. Neither was there any difficulty in believing that his wife, Helen, had been a willing partner in the arrangement. She had idolized him clearly and was completely his to do with and instruct as he wished. She cared nothing for the memory or the reputation of either of them. There was only one person who held her true and deep concern. He must never know anything about this . . . never. And only she could arrange that. As for Johnny . . . well, one way or another she would have to deal with him. Only one thing was clear now . . . she had less anger than contempt for him, utter contempt, and he should know it, but not before she had found the originals of the letter's enclosures and destroyed them. Thank God he had gone off for the rest of the day and left her free to act.

Suddenly she stood up and said passionately, "Judas! Judas! Oh, Johnny, Johnny, how could you be so wicked!"

Then, with tears in her eyes, she took the keys and opened the safe. Drawing up a chair because her leg was bothering her, she sat down and began to go through all its contents methodically, forcing herself not to hurry, not to overlook anything. She had to have the originals and destroy them for the Bishop's sake. No matter that the Polish Embassy would never have them. They must cease to exist.

Forcing herself to work patiently and without hurry, she went through everything in the safe without finding what she sought. She then went through all the stuff which was spread over the long library table. Again without success.

A little calmer now she sat at the table, resting her elbows on it and cupping her hands about her chin as with a bowed head she tried to think what Johnny would have done with the papers. But her mind soon turned from that problem as the enormity of Johnny's act came back strongly to her. How could any man be so base? He had come here almost as an act of charity on the dear Bishop's part and been treated as one of the family. Thirty thousand pounds . . . surely they would never have paid so much? But they would, of course. The money would be nothing to them. But to Johnny the money would be everything. He was going to be married and had big ideas, and probably little money of his own. Oh, dear God, poor Rachel. She could know nothing of this.

Suddenly, she sat upright and thought to herself . . . pull yourself together, Margaret. There's no point in sitting here thinking about Rachel or anyone else except the Bishop. You've got to find those papers first of all and then deal with Johnny. What could he have done with them? What would it be in his character to do with them? He would never carry them around with him and he would never have left them in the library here where more often than not he carelessly left the safe unlocked at night. More than likely he would have taken them down to his cottage . . .

She got up and left the room. She went down to his cottage and, since it was an open day, passed some of the visitors who often walked that way to reach the sunken garden on the slope behind the Manor.

Johnny's car was standing outside the cottage as she guessed it would be for she had seen the two of them drive off in Rachel's car with Cassidy. She tried the front door and found it locked. She went round to the back door and found that safely shut and bolted on the inside for it had no lock. All the ground floor windows were secured on their inner catches. She had a moment or two of real anger that for once in a while Johnny had been obedient. When he had first come here she had impressed upon him the need to lock and secure the cottage when he left it to guard against theft from dishonest visitors. And three or four times at least she had walked down here to find that he had left the place wide open. But not today. And there was only one key for the front door and that would now be in his pocket—and for that uniqueness she could blame herself for she had meant to have some spare keys cut to replace the lost ones. For a moment or two she contemplated smashing one of the diamond panes in a window and reaching its latch so that she could climb in . . . but the window sections were narrow and with her bad leg, aching now because of the coming change in the weather, and people passing she knew she could not do it. There was only one thing to do. Wait until he came back and face him with the whole affair and make him hand over the papers. Dear God, what an awful prospect . . .! But it would have to be done, and she would have to begin to think now what she should say and how she should act.

She turned away from the cottage to go back to the Manor. As she went the first fat drops of rain coming in from the West began to fall. By the time she reached the Manor it was raining hard and she was so wet that she went up to her bedroom to change her clothes. In the middle of changing she suddenly felt all the strength go from her body and her head begin to swim so that she was forced to sit down in the armchair by the window.

She sat there with her body shaking and, as tears began to run from her eyes, she buried her face in her hands and the odd thought came to her that perhaps she was still sleeping, that all this was a bad dream, and soon she would awake to morning sunshine and the relief of untroubled reality.

* * * *

At six o'clock that evening James Helder was back in his London flat. His sister came into the room from the kitchen and said, "Well now—that's all done and we can eat when you want to. Fish cakes in the warmer and I've made a nice trifle for you. I've only got to do the peas and they take no time. Now I'd like a glass of sherry and to hear all your adventures."

"Adventures?"

"Everything to you is an adventure, my dear. That is, people are. Tell me all about John Corbin. I don't want any of your professional business. Just about him."

Helder went to the sideboard to get her a glass of sherry and a whisky and soda for himself and said over his shoulder, "He was a very personable young man."

"Did you like him?"

"Yes, I did. With reservations. But I think he will end up . . . well, badly."

"Oh, don't say that."

"But I do."

"Why?"

"Everything in life for him is a game . . . dangerous, amusing and challenging. And he thinks he presides over it as an invulnerable Master of Ceremonies."

"My dear—he has moved you. How unusual."

"Yes, I think it is. Did you say fish cakes?"

"Yes, I did. Cod—and a terrible price it is these days. I can remember the time when as a girl in Grimsby——"

"Yes, so can I." He spoke a little brusquely.

His sister looked at him sharply, her lips pursing a little, and then she said gently, "You're very upset."

Helder smiled. "Yes, I am. I don't like waste of any kind. Particularly human waste."

"I see. Well, why don't you sit and enjoy your whisky while I take my sherry with me and tidy myself up for the evening?"

She bent and kissed him lightly on the forehead and then left the room with her sherry held carefully because he had rather overfilled it.

* * * *

On the point of leaving the Embassy at the end of his day's work Jawicki was brought a minute from his Counsellor which read:

> *Formby* et al. *I think your presumptions could well be correct—particularly as he is no longer at his flat. Paid up and gone. The truth about Maria has leaked through to others before. We can do nothing about Barkiss. If Formby did not go to Exeter he might well come back to us. We shall have to wait and see. Without the authentic material we can do nothing. I shall be seeing your friend at the reception this evening and will take up the other matter.*

Jawicki leaned back, lit a cigarette with his lighter, and then held the flame to the edge of the minute. He held the paper over his ash tray, finally dropped it, and watched the last flicker of fire die away.

* * * *

Despite the rain which had changed now from a heavy downpour to a steady drizzle Miss Latham put on her waterproof hat and coat and, stick in hand, went down to Corbin's cottage after her dinner of which she had eaten little. The grass road was slippery with rain under her gum boots and she had to walk carefully.

Corbin's car was still standing outside the cottage which was locked and lightless. The emotional turbulence which had possessed her earlier in the day had now subsided. Emotion she realized was going to be of no assistance to her. She had to keep a cool head and avoid all hastiness of action or speech. As she walked back to the Manor she heard the small cry of a wren from the rhododendron bushes complaining of the wet night.

In the Manor she took off her rain clothes and went up to the library. The thought had come to her that perhaps Johnny had hidden his letters in one of the books in the row of glass-fronted bookcases. She knew that it was too much of a task to attempt to go through them all. But she walked along the cases, looking for any volume which might be out of place. There were a few and she took them down and shook them out, but there was nothing hidden in them. Only from one of them, *The Romance of Plant Hunting* by F. Kingdon-Ward, a thick, deckled-edge sheet of notepaper fell to the ground. On it was written—*Dear John—So much enjoyed my visit with you—and the excellent game pie! I shall be happy to think that the enclosed has a place in your library. I go overland to Marseille tomorrow to catch my boat. F.K-W.*

She put the book back in its place and went and sat at the long library table. Dear John, she thought . . . who had let his brother do what he could not do for himself and that with no protest . . . no, almost certainly with loving acquiescence . . . from the wife who adored him. The varieties of human love were strange indeed. Probably hers, too, could be included among them for, denied the love she craved, she had turned from all others. There was no fathoming human nature. How could Johnny with all his talent have turned to such a base exploit? Could it be possible that there were not times when God looked down on the world and its peoples and was saddened and doubted the wisdom of His own creations?

She left the library and went to her room and began to make herself ready for bed. There would be no Jane Austen for her tonight. She set her clock alarm for half-past five, took two sleeping pills, knelt at the side of the bed and said her prayers and then settled herself under the covers and lay in the darkness waiting for oblivion to come.

* * * *

It was barely light when John Corbin got out of bed and began to dress. He pulled the curtains and looking out saw that the rain had stopped. The little stream was in a muddy spate and water dropped from the leaves of the alder growths that overhung it. Turning from the window he saw that Rachel was awake and watching him. He went to her and kissed her good-morning.

He said, "The rain's stopped, but not long ago. Everything's dripping."

"You'll have a wet walk back. Why don't you stay and come up with me in the car?"

"No. The walk will do me good. Clear the head and freshen up the whites of the eyes. And, anyway, I like walking up. You know——" he turned from her and sitting on the edge of the bed began to pull on his trousers, "——I've been wondering. Don't you think we ought to tell your people and my aunt about the baby?"

"What—right away?"

"Yes, I think so. They've got to know some time. The sooner they know the sooner they'll be over it—and I think we owe it to them. I don't know about your folk, but Aunt Lily, after the first shock, will go all gooey-eyed and start making baby clothes."

"Well, I suppose so, yes. What do we do—write or go and see them?"

"Dunno—both perhaps. Anyway, it's just a thought. Think it over." He reached back and squeezed her hand. "I'll do whatever you settle for. You know that."

"Yes, I know." She sat up a little in bed and after a moment said, "Will you do something else for me?"

He smiled at her. "What was that song? For you go through both water and fire . . . something like that. I'll do anything you ask me. Where the bloody hell are my socks."

He went down on his knees and began to search under the bed for his socks.

"Fulfil your heart's desire came into it," Rachel said. "It's an oldie. Anyway will you answer me something?"

"Try me." He went to a chair and began to pull on his socks.

"Does your friend Morgan really exist—or is that just to comfort me? No, no, hear me out. Because if it is just to comfort me then there's no need. And I wouldn't be put out either because . . . well, I would know that you had wanted to keep my spirits up."

He stood up and began to put on his neck scarf, saying, "Do you want him to exist?"

"Well, yes, of course. If he does."

"Which means he does. Morgan is a solid creation." He grinned. "All of my own. I took water and clay and shaped him and then breathed life into him and set him going on his way. God, this is a good time of day to start something like this. But Morgan lives. O.K.? He was made for you to help you get over a bad time and to give us both something to lean on for a while."

"Oh, Johnny . . . what do I do with you?

He went to her and said, "Give us a kiss first and then take it from there." He leaned down and lightly kissed her lips. Standing back, he went on, "What did you expect me to do at the time? If I'd said—which is perfectly true—not to worry we've got a little money of our own and when we find a place . . . so what? There are banks and finance houses all ready to fall over themselves to make an advance on a good business proposition—well, that would have been all away in the future. But for comfort, with a baby coming and all, you had to have something more immediate. Something positive to hang on to. So I made Morgan flesh and blood. Something right at hand to talk about. Well, he's dead now. Poor chap—*Requiescat in pace*. Dust to dust. Unless you want me to bring him back to life?"

She laughed. "Yes, I'd like that."

"And so will he."

"And those trips to Exeter? What did you do really?"

"You really are at your brightest and best in the early morning, aren't you? Well, I'll tell you what I did. I just went for a long drive around and missed you like hell all the time. Now are there any more bodies you want interred or vice versa?"

"No. Just an answer to a simple question. Do you love me?"

"Oh, yes—a simple question, but with a million answers differently shaped to say the same thing. And though the early morning finds few lovers easily attuned to song like the amorous lark, I do my best. I love you and live only for you. When I am with you no other paradise exists. And when I am away from you . . . well, as a less happier lover once said——"

He quoted:

. . . I think on thee,—and then my state,
Like to the lark at break of day arising
From sullen earth, sing hymns at heaven's gate;
For thy sweet love remember'd such wealth brings,
That then I scorn to change my state with kings.

"Oh, Johnny! How nice."

"Now you go back to sleep while I'll trudge up through the wet woods of Illaton."

He turned at the door and blew her a kiss. Downstairs Cassidy rose from the settee and jumping to the floor yawned and stretched his limbs. They went out into the rain-washed morning, crossed the footbridge at the bottom of the garden and began to walk up the steep and wooded river bluff. The sky had cleared of all cloud now and the sun would soon be rising. As he went he thought of Rachel and was glad that he had come clean about Morgan. Poor old Morgan. He smiled to himself.

Through a break in the trees he looked down at the river for a moment or two. The tide was full in and near its turn. A heron flew low over the crests of the pale green rushes on the far bank and somewhere close at hand he could hear a pack of jackdaws quarrelling. The smell of dead leaves and damp earth came pungently to him. Old Henry Boyd Darvell had come this way once on his first visit to Illaton, riding a cob. The path had been narrower then and hazardous on horseback. The man had dreamt a dream and here it was all come true long after his time. For men of vision life was too short, but that thought which he surely must have had, had not turned him aside.

Cassidy put up a hare and disappeared for a while in the shrubberies above him. Dark banks of rhododendrons, flowers gone to give place to stiff, hierarchic seed heads, overhung the path and great ferns lifted their fronds to the growing light. The smell of wet earth and damp foliage was old and ancient. A grey squirrel scolded his passing from a tall pine and, as it leaped away among the branches, shook down upon him a brief and sharp shower of water. A crow called distantly and after a while Cassidy came back, panting, his coat flattened with water and gave him a look as though to say, 'Well, it was a good try. Somebody has to show these hares.'

As he climbed higher the lip of the sun came over the horizon and suddenly fired with brilliance each wet leaf and frond and the dark side of the river below was stippled with moving points of silver where sudden catspaws of wind scuffed its surface.

When he reached the top of the climbing path he crossed the little gravelled space at the side of the Greek temple and stood by the low, balustraded wall and looked westwards and felt the growing warmth of the sun on his face. Smiling to himself, he thought, Morgan was dead and gone. Was it possible, he wondered, to deceive someone you loved and who loved you? Some undercurrent of truth ran between you. No words were needed, but truth was not to be denied or diverted.

At this moment he heard a movement behind him and turned. Miss Latham, heavily cloaked against the freshness of the morning, leaning on her stick, was coming down the shallow run of broad steps from the temple. On her head was a large, floppy red beret whose colour matched that of the short wellington boots she wore. Cassidy moved to her and she dropped a hand briefly and touched the dog's muzzle.

She stopped a little way from him, watching his face which was in shadow from the sun behind him. In the few moments before she spoke to give him good-morning she could find a certain brief sympathy for him . . . though not understanding. Here he stood, someone she admired for his talents, someone for whom she had a fondness and love. Or had had, but yet even now still left with her was a deep and affecting hope that perhaps somewhere there had been some awful mistake, some truth hidden from her which might come suddenly into the open and as the growing sun now took the low-lying mist from the far fields beyond the river, would take away all her contempt and anguish and restore to her the Johnny she had admired and held in such warm esteem. There had been other mornings when from her window she had seen him come back from Rachel and known moments of undeniable human envy for that which he and Rachel shared and which was forever lost to her. Let there, she prayed, be some horrible mistake to prove all the revelation made to her a nonsense.

Corbin gave her a smile and said, "Good morning, Miss Latham. You're up bright and early."

"I've been here some time . . . waiting for you, Johnny."

"For me—why?"

"Because I want something from you, and when I have it I want you to leave Illaton at once." She was surprised at the calmness with which she now spoke.

Corbin frowned and then, concern in his voice, said, "Are you all right, Miss Latham?"

As he shaped to make a move towards her, she said sharply, "No. Stay where you are—and listen to me. I don't want a lot of talk about this. I just want it quickly settled and then to see you go. And I would prefer all this to be done without emotion. You will understand what I'm talking about when I say that you have behaved abominably and would have betrayed those who have befriended you and trusted you and given you open and loving hospitality. I want you to hand over to me some confidential letters which belong to the Darvell family—and then to go. You understand perfectly what I'm talking about, don't you?"

"No, I don't. Are you sure you are quite well?" But as he spoke he was full of understanding, though how this moment could have come about was beyond him and—he thought with a slow mounting of raw emotion within him—until he did there was no power which could draw any admission from him.

"I am perfectly well, Johnny. And you understand me perfectly too. But I shall spell it out to you. I want a signed and witnessed statement made by John Darvell concerning the birth of his son, Michael. And also a letter from a Harley Street specialist confirming the facts in that statement. Now I wish to say no more. You will bring them to me this morning and then you will leave as soon as possible."

The magic went from the morning. Trees and foliage dripped now with cold tears. There was no warmth in the sun on his back, and . . . a picture came to him of Rachel, rising now to bath and dress, happy, carrying his child.

"I don't know what you're talking about."

Miss Latham shook her head. "That's a poor lie, Johnny. As a creative writer I would have expected better from you. And don't think because I speak calmly that I am not filled with disgust for you. Pure disgust. There is only one person my heart aches for and that is Rachel."

Corbin was silent. He turned away from Miss Latham his eyes dazzled for a moment or two by the sun which was now full above the horizon. Something had gone bloody wrong and he had no idea how. But that meant nothing at this minute. He accepted now that there was no evading the truth, but that did not mean there was nothing left to salvage from the wreck of his plans for the future. He held down the bitter anger and confusion which were slowly possessing him and forced himself to say calmly, "I don't know how all this has come about, and I don't really care. There's only one thing I care about and that is Rachel. All right, I'll give you what you want—but only on certain conditions."

"You will give me what I want and go."

Her calmness and inflexibility suddenly angered him and made him reckless. The whole thing was a bloody mess, but there could be something to salvage . . . had to be.

Quite calmly, he said, "Oh, no. Not me. All right, you've got me in a corner. But you've got to take my terms."

"No, Johnny, you make no terms with me. I am sorry for you, truly sorry. But I can find no charity for you."

Corbin swung round and now frustration and anger were full in him and the only instinct which he could follow was a desire to wound another to ease his own wound.

He said, shouting almost, "Rachel's going to have a child, my child. Rachel's never going to know a thing about all this—and that means I don't leave Illaton until I've done my work here. Oh, don't worry about any embarrassment. I won't. My skin's thick. I'll work in the cottage. You won't see much of me. But I stay. And when I've done what I came for you can have the letters back. But Rachel's never going to know a damn thing about it. Not a thing. The day I leave you shall have the letters. It's either that—or I go and take them with me. And then for the rest of your life you'll know I have them and might use them against your dear Bishop."

Miss Latham came closer to him and shook her head. She had no sympathy for him, but she recognized the genuineness of his feelings for Rachel. But they counted for little because she saw his character now, plain, and saw clearly that there was no trusting him, no hope that he would ever change, not even with the love of Rachel to influence him. He was what he was, and Rachel would only live as his wife to know misery and sadness because he would never change.

Quite calmly she said, "You may love Rachel and she love you—but love is not enough, Johnny. Not enough. You cannot stay here. I will not tolerate it. For Rachel I will do all I can—except withhold the truth from her if she asks for it. You will give me the letters today and go. What you say to Rachel is your business—and your unhappiness—since you and only you created this situation. I shall expect you to bring them to me this morning."

It was then that Corbin broke free from all restraint, let anger, frustration and savage bitterness possess him completely and knew only one wild desire, to hurt, to savage and to debase this limping, frustrated old spinster who, in some and now bloody unimportant way, had learned all about his plans and had destroyed everything for him.

With a pitying smile on his face, he said, "How much you must be enjoying this. It's balm, isn't it, to your arid old life? How many times have you slept alone at Illaton and known that your sister a room away lay in the Bishop's arms? Not that I see him as any great lover. How many times have you quietly wept as the bitter ache of your chastity kept you from sleep? How many times have you watched me come up here through the woods from Rachel—oh, yes, I've seen you at your bedroom window—and imagined to yourself the hours of love I'd given Rachel in her bed——"

"Johnny—stop it!"

"Why the hell should I stop? Yes, I'd have sold your dear Bishop for a handful of silver. That's me. That's the way your precious God created me. And don't think I don't enjoy being me. But what have you enjoyed? Tagging around at the Bishop's coat tails. Nursing a hopeless love and rejecting all others. And for what? Some little trifle he tossed to you in the past? A kiss at a dance . . . a quick fumble in the greenhouse when he was young and God had yet to call him? You deliberately and stupidly destroyed yourself. And now, at last, you have the rare pleasure of destroying someone else. Well, do what you bloody well like about me. But you never get those letters back. Never." He broke off, suddenly smiled, and then in a calm voice he went on, "Unless, of course, you would like to buy them from me? Now there, my dear Miss Latham, is a very reasonable proposition. You have plenty of money and, since we were, until a few minutes ago, good friends, I'll drop the price a little for you. Revive that friendship for a moment and keep the sunshine in my life. You shall have what you want for twenty thousand pounds and, like the now migrating swallows of dear Illaton, I will wing my way to another clime. Also, to sweeten the bargain, I take back all my hasty words, do revile them and recant them. For twenty thousand pounds you can keep your dear Bishop on his throne. The money must be in cash, of course, for I would not trust your cheque. Do this, and God will surely reward you."

Miss Latham, shaking with anger, sick from his words, suddenly stepped forward and raised her stick to him, shouting, "You are all evil! Evil! Evil!"

Corbin laughed and stepped back, avoiding the would-be blow easily. As he did so, however, the back of his thighs caught the low terrace wall and his feet slipped on the wet loose gravel. He fell backwards over the wall on to the sharp grassy slope below, the whole of his body bearing down on his right arm so that he distinctly heard the crack of the bone going.

From the terrace Miss Latham watched him in horror. He slid and rolled down the wet bank, crashed into a sloping bed of ferns and then fell twenty feet down the rocks below. For a moment or two he clung with his left hand to a young, self-sown birch sapling, but his hanging weight pulled its roots free from the rain-soaked soil and he rolled helplessly to the edge of the steep rock face. His body limp, his limbs those of a twisted marionette, he went over the side of the sheer fall to the river.

*   *   *   *

They found his body on the mud flats off Illaton Quay at low tide. For the first time in her life, and for the sake of others, Miss Latham told a deliberately calculated lie. She said that she had met him, as she had, on his way up from the woods and they had talked on the terrace where he had been sporting with Cassidy, teasing the dog to jump up to a stick he held out of reach and an over-vigorous jump from the dog had made him step back, catching his thighs against the wall and so causing him to fall. No one doubted her.

They carried the body to his cottage, and took the key from his pocket and unlocked the front door. Miss Latham brought Rachel to the Manor and made her stay there until after the inquest and the funeral. After the funeral Miss Latham went through the cottage on her own and found the letters she sought in their original envelope behind the old-fashioned black marble clock on the fireplace. She burned them in the cottage grate.

That evening, late, before going to bed she looked into the room where Rachel slept heavily from the sleeping pills she had taken. She had already made up her mind to change her will in favour of Rachel and the child.

She closed the door gently and went down to the library where all Johnny's work and papers still lay on the table. Picking up a loose page of his manuscript she began to read it, and she seemed to hear his voice, light and teasing. . . .

. . . and as with human beings so it is with plants. They may all belong to their well-defined families or species but no two are ever truly alike, be it only a centimetre of difference in height between tulips all raised under the same conditions. Or between two brothers. The infinite and often aggravating difference is no surprise. The man in the centre of a crowd has less freedom of movement than any on the outside. In a flower bed, those in the centre have the wind tempered by the blooms which surround them. God is no parade ground sergeant, has no heart for regimentation. Alfred Boyd Darvell once said in an address to an Horticultural Society—'While it is natural for most gardeners to plan and shape their gardens it must be understood that they can expect no ally in the form of the Almighty for He long ago so planned and devised a garden and found His work of no avail. No doubt He wept over His failure as gardening men weep over theirs. Plants like humans are

unpredictable, no matter how well we treat them. Be humble over your successes and be humbled by your failures. If all were perfection in this world life would be dull indeed.' It was good sound advice—except there was never known a man to rage and rant so much when some favourite shrub or plant refused to respond to his care. But then paradox is the one abiding element of all mankind.

* * * *

Aunt Lily sat late at night in her cottage, with a glass of brandy at her side, writing a letter to Miss Simpson.

. . . and I must thank you dear for the great support and comfort you gave me. I really do not know how I could have borne it without you, and so kind of you to come all that way. Bless you, and bless you.

And now two things I must say to you—though I did give my word not to mention one of them. But it is no good. I must tell someone and now you are like family. Rachel, dear, poor Rachel, is going to have a baby. There now I have told you . . .

She went on writing and of her hopes that it would be a boy. Taking a sip of her brandy she continued:

And now for something which may surprise you but I hope and pray you will carefully consider it and agree. We are both alone, both living in our little lonely cottages and, since we have become such good friends, it all does seem too stupid for us to be so. I wondered, since I have plenty of room here, whether you would care to come and live with me and we could share things since we both get on so well? And, too, you could sell your cottage and so have a nice sum in hand for . . . well, all sorts of things you can't have or do now. Now, don't make up your mind right away. Just think about it. But, of course, I shall pray that it may be possible.

She went on writing at length, only breaking off once to refill her glass, and then finished the letter after her signature with a P.S.

Oh, I nearly forgot. I had a most sympathetic letter from that nice Mr. Helder and his sister about Johnny. They had seen the announcement in the D.T. Such a nice man. But doesn't it seem an odd kind of work for him to do? But there—you never know about people, do you?